ABOUT THE AUTHOR

Jessica N. Watkins was born April 1st in Chicago, Illinois. She obtained a Bachelor of Arts with Focus in Psychology from DePaul University and Master of Applied Professional Studies with focus in Business Administration from the like institution. Working in Hospital Administration for the majority of her career, Watkins has also been an author of fiction literature since the young age of nine. Eventually, she used writing as an outlet during her freshmen year of high school, after giving birth to her son. At the age of thirty-two, Watkins' chronicles have matured into steamy, humorous, and gritty tales of urban and women's fiction.

Jessica's debut novel *Jane Doe* spiraled into an engrossing, drama filled, and highly entertaining series. In August 2013, she signed to SBR publications, which ignited her writing career with the *Secrets of a Side Bitch* series.

In 2014, Jessica began to give other inspiring authors the opportunity to become published by launching Jessica Watkins Presents.

Jessica N. Watkins is available for talks, workshops, and book signings. For bookings, please send a request to authorjwatkins@gmail.com.

Instagram: @authorjwatkins
Facebook: missauthor

Twitter: @authorjwatkins
Snapchat: @authorjwatkins
Website: www.LitByJess.com
Amazon: www.Amazon.com/author/authorjwatkins

❀ Created with Vellum

SUBSCRIBE

Don't miss these Urban Romance releases from Jessica Watkins Presents! To receive a text message when they go live on Amazon, using your phone, text the keyword "Jessica" to (872) 282-0790! To receive an email, click here: shorturl.at/nrE39

SUBMISSIONS

Jessica Watkins Presents is the home of many well-known, best-selling authors in Urban Romance, Interracial Romance, and Paranormal Romance. We provide editing services, promotion and marketing, one-on-one consulting with a renowned, national best-selling author, assistance in branding, and more, FREE of charge to you, the author.

We are currently accepting submissions for the following genres: Urban Romance, Interracial Romance, and Paranormal Romance. If you are interested in becoming a published author and have a FINISHED manuscript, please send the synopsis, genre, and the first three chapters in a PDF or Word file to jwp.submissions@gmail.com. Complete manuscripts must be at least 45,000 words.

SYNOPSIS

Heavy is the head that wears the crown.

LAST TIME IN...
PROPERTY OF A RICH NIGGA

JAH DISCIPLE

Moe was intent on putting it on me.

"It's cold as fuck in here," I fussed as I climbed into bed.

Faye looked at me oddly as she undressed.

"What?" I asked as she walked over to my dresser.

Then I realized that she was actually walking over to the thermostat that was next to it. "It's seventy-two degrees in here."

I groaned. "It's freezing."

Faye sighed as she turned toward me. "You're getting the flu or something."

"I don't get sick."

But as I pulled the covers over me, I could feel the aches in my body.

"Maybe I am," I confessed with a groan.

Faye chuckled as she climbed into my bed in a lace bra and panties. "I knew you were sick when you wanted to leave the party early."

"I think that had more to do with Moe than feeling fucked up."

Faye sympathetically watched me as I relaxed amongst the pillows. Yet, my phone started to ring.

"Fuck," I barked.

"Ignore it," Faye suggested with empathy.

"I can't."

"If it's an emergency, let your brothers handle it."

"Shauka got more shit to deal with right now. And do you really think I should let Messiah handle anything alone?"

Faye nodded once sharply. "Touche." Then she got comfortable under the covers, facing me. "I can't believe Sariah forgave Shauka just like that."

"I don't think she really forgives that nigga," I said as I grabbed my phone off the nightstand. "I think she just doesn't want to have to tell all of her friends and family that the wedding is off."

I had hoped that whoever was calling would hang up by the time I finished my sentence, but they had yet to get the hint. Looking at the Caller Id, I sat up.

"What's wrong?" Faye asked.

"It's Sherell." I answered quickly, "Hello?"

"Hey, Jah. Katrina wants to talk to you."

"Okay," I replied, nervous as to why Shauka's ex-detective dip wanted to holla at me.

"Hey, Jah. Sorry to bother you, but I know that Shauka is getting married tomorrow. So, I didn't want to bother him."

"What's going on?" I asked Sherell.

"Moe's stupid ass got into an accident. It was all kinds of crack and shit in the car. He is high as a kite, trying to give information about Miguel's murder. Luckily, I was the homicide detective on duty. I've been keeping him in the interrogation room so that no one else hears him. But I gotta get him the fuck outta here before the wrong person hears what he has to say. Can you meet me?"

"I'm on my way."

Katrina had sent me her location. So, twenty minutes later, I was speeding down the street of a block that was littered with abandoned homes on the Southside.

I spotted her unmarked car. I parked and hopped out of my G Wagon. I stalked around my ride, completely numb to the freezing temps that had layered the city in the midnight hours.

Moe was apparently confused as she pulled him out of the backseat in cuffs. His head was covered with the hoodie of a dark sweater that had been thrown over his shoulder.

We met between her trunk and my hood.

"Where you taking me?" I heard him ask her nervously. "Ain't I under arrest?"

"You wish you were, stupid motherfucka," I seethed, causing his eyes to dart toward me.

Fear washed over him as Katrina lurched him toward me. He stumbled over the curb. But I caught him.

"I told the investigating officer that he had information on a body, and that he was taking me to the location."

"Thank you, Katrina," I muttered.

She locked stern eyes on me. "I don't want this coming back to bite me in the ass."

"I got you," I insisted as I gripped Moe's elbow.

She nodded and tossed me something. Catching it, I saw that it was keys to the cuffs. She then hurried back to her car. Moe was trembling in my grasp.

"Aye, why she didn't take these cuffs off me?" he asked.

"So, she wouldn't look suspicious letting you out of there."

"So-so-so why don't you take 'em off," he fretfully stuttered.

My jaws were tight with rage as I drug him toward the nearest abandoned building.

"Wh-where we goin', Jah?"

Taking long, steady strides, I looked around the block to ensure that no one saw us. However, there were few homes on the block that were occupied. The block had been abandoned by families and was only littered with hypes and the homeless.

"I told your stupid ass to stay out of Chicago," I gritted.

"I just wanted to see my wife. And she played me. I've lost her for good. She don't want me no more."

Approaching the house, I drug Moe up the deteriorating wooden steps. "So, your weak ass go get high and get in an accident?"

"I'm sorry, bruh. I'm so sorry."

"You was willing to turn me and my brothers in over a few bags of rock?"

"I was just talking shit. I was gonna give them some bullshit information just so they could let me out."

"So, you can go get high."

I peered into the windows to ensure that no hypes or homeless people were inside. Satisfied that it was empty, I tried the door. It opened easily. A stench of piss and funk hit me, causing my eyes to burn. I coughed as I drug Moe inside.

"Wh-what we doin' here, Jah?"

Scowling, I unlocked the cuffs. I then threw Moe onto the littered wooden floor. His body hit the floor with a loud thud and a cloud of dust.

I stuffed the cuffs and keys into my pocket and then retrieved my gun from my waistband.

I was too tired to give a fuck this time. Moe had drained all of the empathy from me that I had. I was operating on autopilot.

"Wh-what you about to do?" Moe said with fear causing his words to tremble.

"Buck was right," I told him. "I should have listened. I should have given you over to Saudi a long time ago."

"Saudi is dead now. S-s-s-so I'll go out of the country. I'll dip, bro. I-I-I-I swear—"

His pleads lodged in his throat as I aimed my pistol at his head. He was too high to fight or run. All he could do was stare at me with wild, ballooned eyes.

As I pulled the trigger, I told him genuinely, "I love you, bro."

The blow of gun firing was deafening. I flinched as the bullet crashed into the space between his eyes and blew out the back of his head.

YAZMEEN HILL

I had been in tears all night. Shauka had called while at his Bachelor party and let me know that Sariah knew everything. His calls were coupled with Sariah's, who I was too embarrassed to talk to. I was relieved that Sariah had forgiven him and still wanted to marry him, but I knew that that was only the beginning of a lot more drama.

I couldn't sleep. So, when my doorbell rang at eight in the morning, I was wide awake.

I moped toward the door, figuring that it was Amazon with yet another package. Me and Shauka had been doing so much shopping for the baby and the shower that was two weeks away. So, I opened the door and was met with a beautiful sight.

Shauka was wrapped in a champagne tux. His hair was pulled up into a smooth, neat bun. He was always a beautiful creature. But the regal attire made him stunning.

I blinked slowly, unable to find words to express how good he looked. It was a daunting moment, because I envisioned him dressed like this at the alter waiting on me.

I had tried to push back my feelings since he had chosen Sariah. As long as I had him in my life and he supported our child, I wanted to be good with that. But looking at him dressed to commit to another woman for the rest of his life, I couldn't stunt anymore.

I was still in love with him.

"You okay?"

I scoffed with a laugh. "You came over here to see if I was okay. You could have called for that."

"I needed to see for myself."

I chuckled lightly, shaking my head at his persistence. I then stepped away from the doorway, allowing him in.

"Aren't you supposed to be at the church soon?" I asked.

"Yeah, but I had to come to check on my baby."

I wished that he was talking about me, but he was talking about the baby, who he reached out for. As he rubbed my stomach, he told me, "I'm so sorry that it took me so long to tell her." Then he chuckled. "I still never told her, I guess."

"How is she?"

His shoulders sank as we stood near the front door. "She keeps insisting that she forgives me. But I'm sure the shit's gonna really come out once the wedding is over."

"Well, she's still marrying you, so she must truly forgive you."

"That easily, though?" he asked, shaking his head. "That shit don't seem right."

"Don't question the blessing, Shauka."

Pouting, his eyes rested on me. "Guess that means you won't be there."

"Hell no," I spat. "That girl doesn't want to see me ever again. I'm sure the only reason that she hasn't shown up here is that she is trying to enjoy her wedding day as much as she can."

Shauka pouted. "I need you to be there."

I hated seeing him consumed with so much stress and guilt. I wrapped my arms around him. He immediately fell into the embrace. Our bodies meshed together. I could feel his heart beating wildly.

I rubbed his back lovingly. "Everything is going to be okay."

His body weight suddenly became heavy, as if for a second, he was putting all of his burdens on me. There was an energy in our embrace as if it was powering him. It was weaving our souls in a way that was a forever bond.

Tears came to my eyes. I was broken that he was marrying another woman, but I was so appreciative that he would be in my life forever.

I didn't want to make his stay lengthier with my tears, so I forced them back. I then reluctantly released him. "C'mon. You have to go get married. You can't be late on top of all this other bullshit."

I laughed, but he didn't. His expression was blank as his eyes swallowed me.

I giggled nervously under his intense glare. "What?"

Then he swallowed hard. "Nothing." He turned his eyes away and reached for the front door. "You're right. I gotta go."

I had encouraged his exit, but I watched it with reluctance. I was full of emotions, watching the love of my life leave to marry the love of his. But I never wanted to be the woman that broke the next woman's heart. So, I let him go.

JAH DISCIPLE

"You're one lucky motherfucka, bro."

Shauka grunted in response to Messiah as we all rode in the back of the stretch Bentley. The stress was all over his expression. His elbow rested in the window seal as he aimlessly stared out of the window, clutching a glass of Glen Levit.

"How?" he spat in response.

"You got two women that love the fuck out of you, unconditionally. I know you're in love with Yaz, but you got her. She may not want you, but you got her anyway, at least for the next eighteen years. Sariah forgave you. You got to keep your loyal, beautiful woman. Nigga, you a king."

"It don't feel like it," Shauka grumbled.

I hated that my brother was experiencing this anxiety on what was supposed to be such a special day. But it was hard for me to give him the pep talk that I had practiced because I was consumed with the sight of watching my best friend, my brother, die by my hands. I had been forced to leave him in that abandoned building in the cold until his body was found.

Luckily, he had made it so that I had no other choice. So, thankfully, the guilt wasn't as heavy. But the residue of the shame of watching him take his last breath with his eyes anchored on me full of disbelief was still forcing its way to the forefront of what was supposed to have been a great day.

Messiah looked between me and Shauka's perturbed mugs, irritated that we were bringing down the joy of the day. When he and Shauka had met me at the estate an hour ago, I told them what happened. Messiah was in full support of how I had handled it. Shauka was too, but he understood the dread that I was feeling since he had grown up with Moe as well.

Finally, we were pulling up to the Lyte House, where the wedding would be. A photographer and videographer was already standing out front, waiting for everyone to arrive. Sariah and the bridal party had arrived hours ago because they were getting their hair and makeup done on sight.

After the limo came to a stop, the driver climbed out and rushed to open our door. I waited for Shauka to get out first. Then Messiah and I climbed out.

As the camera flashed in our faces, I noticed a group of Mexican men standing at the entrance of the space. I tapped Messiah, and when I got his attention, I angled my head their way. His brows furrowed as we put our guards up. No matter the event, we still carried. So, as we approached the entrance, Messiah and I both reached back, placing our hands on our pieces, remaining on "go."

"Gentlemen, we've been waiting for you," one of them spoke.

That caught Shauka's attention. His eyes washed over their attire. They clearly weren't wedding guests since they were casually dressed.

Shauka looked at the videographer and photographer and angled his head toward the inside. They rushed in without question.

"Who the fuck are you?" I spit as me and my brother revealed our pieces, aiming them at their heads.

These motherfuckas didn't flinch.

He slowly grinned while extending his hand. "My name is Gabriel Castro, cousin of Angel Castro, who is the leader of the Castro cartel."

Me and my brothers shared inquisitive glances while tightening the grips on our pieces.

"Please," he said raising his hands. "We come in peace."

We slowly lowered our weapons as I said, "What you want?"

"We understand that you were the biggest distributor for Saudi, who is now resting in peace. Angel is wondering if he can meet with you to discuss continuing your operation with the Castro cartel as your distributor."

Hearing that, we returned our guns to our waistbands.

"My brother is getting married today," I told them. "We ain't got time for this right now."

"We know." Then Gabriel looked at Shauka. "Congratulations."

Shauka merely nodded.

"Since this is a busy day, we just came by to see if you were interested so that we can set up a meeting."

I chuckled at his pleasantries. He knew that we were aware that we didn't have a choice. When the cartel wanted you to sell drugs for them, you fucking sold drugs for them.

FAYE SINGER

♫ For you I give a lifetime of stability
Anything you want of me
Nothing is impossible
For you there are no words or ways to show my love
Or all the thoughts I'm thinking of ♫

"Damn, he sounds just like Kenny Lattimore."

"Don't he?" Chloe gushed as Tory nodded.

Chloe, Tory, and I admired the soloist that was belting a beautiful rendition of For You. He had been performing exquisite covers of all of the typical Black wedding songs.

"Y'all see my boo up there looking *fione*," Tory bragged as she gushed at Messiah.

The wedding party was already in position, waiting for the bride along with us. To anyone else, Shauka looked stoic and ready. But I imagined that he was full of emotions. Jah had shared with me Shauka's feelings for Yaz. The mess of it all was entertaining, but it was sad to watch him marry the woman that didn't truly have his heart.

"He don't look better than my boo," I gushed, staring at Jah. He was a beautiful man in that tux. I was anticipating fucking it off of him as soon as the reception was over. Yet, I feared that he would be too tired because whatever he had come down with was getting worse. He barely had the strength to get up that morning. It was possible that the burden of killing his best friend had been what weighed him down. But even as I watched him stand in the best man's position, I could see that the life had left his eyes. Something more was wrong than the stress of his line of work.

Sucking her teeth, Chloe rolled her eyes. "Can both of you lucky bitches shut the fuck up?"

As we laughed, Tory added, "Girl, believe me, these niggas come with a lot of ugly problems."

I laughed, shaking my head. I had dodged the tension by staying in the ceremony space with Chloe that day. But I could just imagine how intense things were for Sariah and Shauka as they prepared to walk down the aisle.

"*Awwww*! She looks adorable." I followed Chloe's smile to a little girl that was standing in the opened double doors holding a basket of flower pedals.

As she began to march with an uncomfortable smile, a notification sounded. Embarrassed, I quickly scooped my phone from my lap and unlocked it to put it on silence. As I did, I noticed that the notification was from a DM on Instagram. I hardly ever got them so to be nosy, I opened it. The message was from a page without a profile picture and the image that had been sent to me was of a newborn baby. I figured that the message was spam but the words "Tell your nigga" got my attention. So, I read the message: *This is Mia. Tell your nigga that he left this in me when he fucked me at the club that night.*

I gasped, looking at Chloe.

She noticed the animus dancing in my eyes immediately. "What's wrong?"

Before I could respond, a commotion erupted in the lobby so loud that it drowned out the soloist.

"Where is she?" a man bellowed, causing the attendees to gasp. "Where the fuck is Sariah?"

We all began to angle our heads so that we could see outside of the double doors. But I couldn't see past the guests that were seated behind me. Immediately, Shauka and his party were on high alert as muffled arguing could be heard in the lobby.

"I just want to see her!"

Shauka took off down the aisle. Jah and Messiah followed. Najia stepped out of her position in the line of bridesmaids and followed her brothers.

"Excuse me." Like Bonnie, Tory pushed me and Chloe aside so that she could get out of the aisle. She tailed Najia as she held up her train so that she could keep up with her brothers.

"Bitch, go," Chloe insisted.

Snapping into reality, I followed, feeling my stomach turn. I was delusional as I followed behind Najia. Everything was happening in slow motion.

He fucked her? Did he really get her pregnant?

Mia had always ensured that she had the last laugh. I recalled the last time that she and I had words, and Jah had checked her. Soon after that, Jah and I didn't speak for months. My knees were weak at the possibility that he would have lashed out in anger and done the improbable.

"Get the fuck off me!" a deep roar snapped me out of my misery.

As I trailed Tory into the lobby, I saw Heavy, Tank, and another member of their team surrounding a tall, slender man who was visibly upset.

The Disciple brothers immediately joined their security team. Just then, Sariah inched into the lobby, beautifully made up, holding up the train of her gown with the help of her mother. Her brow was furrowed with confusion of what was going on.

"Sariah!" the unruly man called for her, and she immediately recoiled in embarrassment. Her face instantly painted with hues of red as she looked around the lobby at our inquisitive and judgmental eyes.

"Fuck is you doing calling my girl, nigga?" Shauka barked.

I held my breath, watching the altercation with wide eyes as the guy looked Shauka up and down slowly with a disrespectful sneer. "Bitch, that's my –"

Shauka had cut off his slur with a blow to the eye that sent him flying back into the glass doors. They shattered, causing screams of terror and concern to escape the throats of the women that were surrounding them.

Shauka lurched toward the guy as he lay in a pool of shards of glass, trying to recover. Shauka began to stomp him out before he could.

"Police! Put your hands up!"

Suddenly, officers were storming into the lobby. I wasn't surprised that they had arrived so quickly since we were in such an affluent neighborhood. Yet, a female detective led the pack. The officers immediately surrounded Shauka and the man. The detective approached Messiah.

"*Noooo!*" a curdling scream left Tory's throat as the detective grabbed hold of Messiah's wrist and put it behind his back.

Shockingly, Messiah didn't fight. He just gave a stoic look to his brothers and then Tory.

"Messiah Disciple," the detective said, taking his other wrist into her hand. As she placed cuffs on his wrists, she said, "You are arrested for the murder of Kendric Spears aka Kidd."

PROPERTY OF A RICH NIGGA 3
THE FINALE

PROPERTY OF A RICH NIGGA 3

The Finale

JESSICA N. WATKINS

Jessica Watkins Presents

CHAPTER 1

JAH DISCIPLE

"Y**ou're** under arrest for the murder of Kendric Spears, a.k.a. Kidd."

My heart plummeted to the gray tile under my Gucci loafers. Anguish layered the eyes of our friends and family occupying the lobby. Detective Freemont's hands seemed to be moving in a slow, agonizing motion as she closed the cuffs. The sound of the lock securing shut around his wrists was deafening.

"No!"

Hearing the terror in my sister's voice caused my eyes to immediately find her. She was pushing past those in her path with the intent to get to Messiah.

"You have the right to remain silent," the detective stated, reading Messiah his rights. "Anything you say can and will be used against you in a court of law..."

Greg caught Najia before she could reach Messiah. With one arm, he stopped her approach, holding her back. Yet, she continued to fight against his grasp to get to Messiah as the detective led him out.

"I'm calling our lawyer right now, bro!" I called out to him.

Messiah's head turned back. His stoic irises peered beyond the detective toward me. He simply nodded and allowed her to continue leading him out of the lobby as she finished reciting his Miranda rights. "You have the right to speak to an attorney and to have an attorney present during any questioning..."

Her voice faded as they exited. Tory's whimpering was excruciating. The lobby was mayhem. Most of the wedding attendees were now crowded around us, trying to see what had unfolded. Yet, it was hard for me to even digest all of the melee, so I was sure that others were confused as well.

A remorseful stare painted my dark skin as I peered out of the exit to watch the detective open the back door of a black SUV and put Messiah inside. I hated that he was alone. Then I realized that Buck must have been following close behind, since he was standing at the SUV talking to Messiah through the closed door with his face close to the glass.

Tory was inconsolable as Faye and Chloe tried to calm her down and assist her weak knees in keeping her standing. The burdens on my shoulders were now physically unbearable. I felt my chest caving in. I blinked slowly, trying to wrap my head around Messiah's arrest as the chaos in the lobby unfolded in the background.

"Let him go! He didn't do anything!" Sariah's tearful shriek got my attention.

Her mother was holding her back as she tried to get to the two officers refraining an infuriated Shauka as he glared at the dude that was still lying amongst the shattered glass. Two other officers stood over him as one radioed for an ambulance.

"Please let him go!" Sariah shouted.

Shauka's fiery orbs darted toward her. "Who the fuck is he, Sariah?" His chest rapidly rose and fell as spittle flew from lips that were tight with rage and embarrassment.

Shame painting her eyes was her only silent response.

"Huh?!" he barked. He tried to take a step forward, but the officers held him back. "Who the fuck is he?!"

"Nobody!" she exclaimed tearfully.

Yet, we all knew better. I had recognized the look in the man's eyes the moment we entered the lobby.

"Son, what happened here?" I heard one of the officers ask the guy.

"I'm cool," Shauka assured the police.

"That motherfucka attacked me!" He winced as he tried to sit up.

"Be still, son," the officer told him. "The ambulance is on the way. Who attacked you?"

"Nobody," Queen told him as she stepped forward from the sea of onlookers. "He fell trying to get to her." She then pointed at Sariah, who recoiled into the tightest ball.

"Yeah, he fell into the glass when security was trying to keep him from interrupting the wedding," Hattie added.

Murmurs around us backed up the story.

"That nigga attacked me!" he insisted.

"What's your name?" the officer asked.

"Tristen Brown."

"Your *ex*?!" Shauka barked as his enraged pupils shot daggers at Sariah. "This is your fucking ex, Sariah," he asked.

"I ain't no ex! I'm her *right-now*, nigga," Tristen strained through discomfort. "Tell him, Sariah."

His coaxing hadn't gotten to Shauka. Though he had heard every word, Shauka's focus was on Sariah. The two officers who had sandwiched him in had let him go, but they stayed close by.

Then paramedics filed in with a stretcher. Everyone looked on as they took Tristen's vitals. Within minutes, he was on the stretcher. An officer who appeared to be in charge of the scene stood in a huddle with the officers who had attended to Tristen. Relief washed over me when he began to shrug and shake his head. He then looked at the two who were blanketing Shauka. As the paramedics carried Tristen out, he waved them over.

"You know you're mime, Sariah!" Tristen barked as he met the

3

sunlight. "You know you don't love that nigga! It's all about the money! You want his pockets, but you love me!"

Gasps erupted in a domino effect around us.

I looked back for Faye and got her attention. With a wave, I summoned her over. She left Tory and Chloe and rushed toward me with worry etched on her brow. I fished my phone out of my pocket, unlocked it, and went to my contacts. When I found our attorney's number, I clicked it and handed the phone to her. "Call this number and tell him that Messiah was arrested."

"Okay," her voice shuddered as she took the phone. She then hurried out of the lobby toward an empty hallway.

"Let's go," the lead officer told the rest of them.

As they began to file out, Sariah was the only one who looked at their exit in regret.

"Everybody else can follow the officers up outta here," Heavy told the crowd of attendees.

"No!" Sariah shrieked. "Shauka! Baby! He was just trying to stop me from marrying you—"

"Shut the fuck up, Sariah!" Shauka grimaced angrily.

Pouting with tears, she begged, "Baby, please don't do this. Can we talk in private?"

"Fuck no, we can't talk in private!" Shauka spat with flared nostrils. "That nigga embarrassed me publicly, so say that shit in front of everybody."

"Baby, please." Her head lowered as she began to sob in trembling hands.

"Yeah, everybody can get the fuck out." I had never heard Shauka sound so feeble. "There isn't going to be a wedding today."

SHAUKA DISCIPLE

Heaving, I glared at Sariah as I waited for everyone to leave. The feelings bellowing chaotically through me only felt unfamiliar because it had been so long since I had experienced this type of disappointment. I had only felt this grief and embarrassment when I was starving on the streets alongside Jah and Moe as shorties.

"Y'all heard the man!" Tank bellowed. "Ride out!"

My eyes never peeled away from Sariah. But she couldn't look at me. She was weeping so uncontrollably that her mother could hardly sustain her.

"If you ain't immediate family, you should not be in this lobby within the next ten seconds," Heavy barked. "If you are, me and my team will physically put you out this bitch."

I cringed as I realized that the attendees had been so nosy that this mayhem was most likely unfolding on social media on a few live streams.

Attendees began to slowly inch toward the exit. Many gave Sariah and me sympathetic glances. Some of Sariah's family and friends tried to console her, but Heavy forced them out.

"We down to five seconds!" he shouted.

Finally, the only people in the lobby were me, the security team, our crew, Sariah, her mother, Buck, Queen, Najia, Chloe, Jah, and Tory.

Heavy signaled for the security team to step outside. Our crew folded.

I felt a presence close behind me. Glancing back, I saw Jah, Queen, and Najia giving Sariah the same scolding glares that matched mine.

"Talk!" I roared so loud that it made her and her mother, Alicia, jump out of their skin.

In response, Sariah only whimpered louder.

I was unsure who was crying harder, her or Tory, who was still being consoled by Chloe. Faye rushed into the lobby toward Jah. She handed him back his phone and then returned to her position beside Chloe and Tory.

"Say something!" I demanded.

Her continuous, pathetic sobbing made my rage boil over. "Bitch—"

"*Shauka*," her mother warned.

Ignoring her warning, I stalked toward Sariah so fast that no one was able to stop me. I tried to grab her by the forearms, but Alicia jumped between us.

"Nigga, I wish you would," she gritted.

"And if he fucking does?" Queen asked threateningly. "Don't get beat the fuck up."

Alicia inhaled sharply as her face flushed with shock and then fear.

"You need to be telling her ass to open her fucking mouth and explain this shit," Najia spat.

Finally, Sariah's tear-drenched eyes peered up at me. "Can we please talk about this in private?"

My jaws tightened as my hands went to my mouth in a tight, praying position. "Sariah, I swear to gawd if you don't explain this shit."

"Shauka, please—"

Her pleas were met with my back as I turned away from her and stalked toward the exit.

"Okay! Okay!" she yelped, causing me to spin around. "He's been reaching out to me. I didn't want to tell you because he was a non-factor, baby. He's been trying to get me back, but I've just been ignoring him."

"Why didn't you tell me?"

"Because he doesn't matter!" she exclaimed with a frustrated heel stomp.

"That's bullshit!"

"Shauka, I swear it's the truth."

"Is this why you were so cool with Yaz having my baby?"

Alicia gasped as her concerned stare ping-ponged between Sariah and me repeatedly.

"I'm not cool with it!" Sariah cried. "I'm hurt! But I want you more than anything. More than the heartbreak of you cheating on me and deceiving me all of this time, I still want you!"

Her dark chocolate orbs watched me with such sincerity. I wanted to believe her because I didn't want to have been this foolish. My survival in the streets was dependent solely upon my wisdom. I was supposed to have been smart enough to identify an adversary, to be wise enough to know when I was being manipulated. To realize that I had been sleeping with an opp for years would crush me.

Yet, beyond hesitance and wonder, I felt relief.

I began to nod slowly. "We'll see." I then made an about-face and marched toward the exit.

"No, Shauka, wait!" she begged.

I turned my head, looking for Najia, who was right behind me. "Don't let that bitch follow me, sis," I told her.

She nodded and halted, giving everyone else room to follow me out of the hall.

The bite of the February weather brought me out of my befuddled trance. I stopped at the curb with Jah standing next to me. "We gotta go check on Messiah."

Sariah's potential deception was minuscule in comparison to my brother being arrested for Kidd's murder. As I looked up at Jah for answers and his wisdom, I caught Buck hesitantly lurking behind us. I knew that he wanted to console me and ask about Messiah's arrest, but he was still too damn ornery to be in a certain proximity of Jah. I let him out of his misery by giving him a sharp nod. He returned and walked away toward Queen. I knew that I would be hearing from him later.

Then I leaned into Jah, saying, "We were careful. What evidence would they have to arrest him?"

Jah shrugged, staring helplessly into the busy street. Many of the wedding attendees were still lingering on the block of the hall, having casual conversations as if complete mayhem hadn't just unfolded during a wedding that I had spent over six-figures on, which had gone to waste.

"There is no way they can have evidence," I said.

"There isn't," Jah agreed. "But we can't go up to the station, giving them a reason to implicate us. Besides, he's been arrested, not taken in for questioning. There's nothing we can do but wait to see if he'll be given bail. Faye called the attorney. She's on her way to the station. She'll fill us in as soon as she can."

I scoffed, fuming.

"Aye, I know it'll be hard, but try not to worry about Messiah and just get yourself together," Jah told me.

A wry chuckle left my tightly pursed lips.

"I know, bro," Jah agreed with my silent confusion and helplessness. "What you wanna do? How you wanna play this?"

YAZMEEN HILL

"Ahhh!" Immediately, I tossed my phone on my lap, throwing my hands over my mouth as my eyes ballooned widely.

"What?!" Angela jumped up from the couch, staring at me as she stood in a ready position. "Your water broke?!"

Her dramatics had forced me to laugh beyond my shock. "No, bitch. I am nowhere near my due date."

She sighed as relief washed over her. "Then what the hell are you screaming for?"

"*Giiiirl...*" I picked up my phone again to look at the video to make sure I had seen it correctly.

"*What?*" Angela urged as she plopped down on the couch, this time closer to me.

"Look," I told her, handing her the phone.

My eyes were bucked to their capacity, strained with pure awe as we watched the video on my Facebook feed. Since I had been to a few gatherings with Shauka and Sariah, a few of her cousins had added me as a friend on Facebook. One of her younger cousins, who was still in high school, had posted a video of a disturbance at the wedding. It had been hard to hear exactly what had happened in the midst of all the shouting and crying, but Shauka's voice had been clear at the end when he'd announced that there wasn't going to be a wedding. Then the video ended.

"*Oooooh* my *God*!!!" Angela screeched as she threw her weight onto the back of the couch. "*Biiiitch!*"

I continued to blink owlishly. "I wonder what happened."

"Who gives a fuck," Angela sassed as she handed me back the phone.

"Angela," I warned.

"Girl," she said, waving nonchalantly. "Why are you concerned? You've been sitting in here eating your emotions since he walked out of here this morning."

I pouted as I glanced at the multiple empty cartons of food scattered on the floor. I had called Angela the moment that Shauka left a few hours ago. I needed consolation now that it was so evident to me that I was still in love with him while he was marrying Sariah. We had been eating whatever I craved and watching ratchet reality TV to soothe my depression ever since.

"What if it was because of my baby?" I loved Shauka completely and without limits, so much so that I had been selfless with that love. I had allowed him to pursue whatever relationship made him happy. I loved him so much that I didn't want him to endure any unhappiness because of me.

"So, what if it is?" Angela shrugged.

"He'll hate me because it will be my fault that he lost the woman he loves."

Angela kissed her teeth. "That nigga loves *you*."

He did. I was sure of it. But his love for me was obviously only deep enough for him to be my best friend. "Not if he was about to marry her."

Shauka loved me like family. He wasn't in love with me. Otherwise, he would have chosen me. And I was okay with that. I had him in a way that no other woman ever could. Soul mates weren't always intimately connected. Soul mates were friends too that lasted longer than any lover would.

Scowling, Angela sat back, shaking her head.

"What?" I asked reluctantly.

"I'm sicka yo' ass," she jeered.

My pout deepened. "I am sick of me too."

CHAPTER 2
SHAUKA DISCIPLE

"May I help you?"

"I'm looking for my cousin, Tristen Brown."

The older woman gave me a scrutinizing look over her red-framed glasses. Her wrinkled, small eyes grazed over me and Jah, at our tuxedos in particular. "Are you family? We can only let family in the back."

Frustrated, I sucked my teeth. Yet, Jah reached into his pocket and pulled out a wad of cash. After looking around, he peeled off a few bills, which caused the woman's eyes to widen.

Anchoring his eyes on her, Jah raised his brow with a smirk. She then looked around discreetly as well. Seeing that no one was watching, she nodded her head. He inconspicuously slid the folded bills toward her. She caught them with her long, pointy nails and slid them under her keyboard.

She then looked at the monitor in front of her as she stroked a few keys. "He's in room 116."

I walked off without a word with Jah on my heels. I burst through the double doors. Following the signs on the walls in the triage area, I found the room number.

"I'll wait out here, bro," Jah told me. "But please don't kill that nigga in this hospital. We already gotta get Messiah out of jail."

"I ain't never killing a nigga over pussy we shared."

Even my presence at that hospital felt like a bitch-ass move, but there was no way I would trust that Sariah's words were the whole truth. I wanted to know exactly what was going on so that my next move could be made with no reservations.

I slid the glass door open. Tristen slowly peered up. His head was bandaged. His eye had already begun to swell and was purple from my fist crashing into it.

When he recognized me, he immediately gasped in fear and started to fumble as he reached for the nurse's call button.

"Chill out," I demanded, leaning against the wall near the door. "I ain't here to hurt you, but if you push that button, I *will* kill yo' ass. And I'm sure, since you know my girl, you know about me."

He grimaced and then reluctantly relaxed. "What you want?"

"I wanna know what's your relationship with Sariah."

"I already told you," he seethed with irritation.

My jaws tightened. I stuffed my hands inside my pants pockets as if that would soothe me. But, at best, it would keep me from caving this nigga's face in. "Well, since I don't know you and I was supposed to know her all this time, I'm gonna need more than your word."

Tristen shrugged his shoulder and then went into his pocket. He took out his phone, wiped through a few screens, and pressed a few keys before tossing it toward the foot of the bed. "See for yourself."

I was inwardly cringing. I felt like such a bitch for doing any of this. The altercation at the wedding had been reason enough for me to walk away from Sariah and never look back. She wasn't the woman who owned my heart anyway. This was the perfect excuse to walk away and to be able to enjoy my child without feeling guilty.

Yet, if I was done with Sariah over this, I wanted facts that she couldn't dispute. There had never been a time that Sariah had made me wonder about her loyalty, sincerity, or genuine love for me. If

Tristen was telling the truth, she had been a master manipulator all of this time.

I held on tightly to my stoic expression as I strolled the two feet toward the bed and snatched up the phone. Tristen remained silent. His eyes were on everything in the room except me as mine landed on a text-message thread between him and Sariah. It was her number, it was her words, and it was the way that she talked. The thread went back for over a year. She'd been fucking him behind my back. She'd been giving this bum-ass nigga money to pay his bills. She had made it clear that he had her heart, but since he couldn't afford it, she was choosing me.

The more I scrolled up, the more messages were revealed, giving me all the information I needed. He had kept every message they'd shared, every voice note they had sent each other. She had been fucking this nigga ever since she'd claimed to be mine.

My eyes darted toward him when I read the messages that detailed her pregnancy and not knowing whether it was his or mine. She made mention of it not being the first time that she had had an abortion. I immediately had to wrestle with the urge to hurl the phone across the room. I wasn't heartbroken. I didn't love her enough to garner that type of emotional reaction. Oddly, I related to her. Yaz had my heart, but she didn't want it, so I had chosen Sariah.

I just felt played and like an idiot.

I tossed the phone on the foot of the bed and made an about-face on the Balenciaga Chelsea's on my feet.

As I strolled out, I prayed that Tristen was a smart enough man to remain silent while I did so. Luckily, he was. As soon as I slid the door open, Jah spun around with questions pop-locking in his eyes. But as he took in my defeated expression, his shoulders sank in disappointment.

MESSIAH DISCIPLE

After hours of waiting in the interrogation room, I finally heard the doorknob turn. The nuts and bolts of the old metal door squeaked noisily as it slowly opened.

I sneered when I saw the determined, blue eyes of Detective Freemont. Immediately, I tore my eyes away. My expression was indifferent as I focused on the grooves in the wood of the old table that I was shackled to. I imagined that others had carved these lines, drawings, and profanities into the tabletop as they'd waited for hours for their miserable fate as I currently was.

"My client isn't saying a word."

Hearing her voice, my eyes darted toward the doorway, where Detective Freemont stood with the doorknob still in her hand. Julia Weisberg, the Disciple family attorney, appeared with her hand stopping the door from closing. I was relieved to see her, but I couldn't find the desire to smile. Neither of my brothers nor I had ever been charged with any major crimes. Most of our offenses had been petty when we were much younger and had gotten caught robbing houses and stealing cars. Back then, we had been so young that we had only received slaps on the wrists for those misdemeanors. Julia had been the attorney for our father and Buck for years, but we'd never had to use her outside of some crew members that had gotten locked up. Now, she was about to have to put in some real work.

She marched confidently into the room on tall heels. She placed her briefcase down next to the empty chair adjacent to me. "What is he being charged with?" Julia pulled out the chair and sat down, staring up at Detective Freemont with challenging, green eyes.

Detective Freemont scoffed with a haunting smile as she closed the door of the interrogation room. She stuffed her hands into the pockets of her dark blue slacks and approached the table.

"First-degree murder."

Fuck! I had assumed that would be the charge whenever I was arraigned, but it was crippling to hear it out loud.

"*But,*" she pressed. "We can reduce that charge and give him a lot less time if he'll save us all a lot of time and money by confessing."

"He's not saying a word," Julia insisted.

Detective Freemont turned her attention to me. "Messiah—"

"Don't talk to him," Julia interjected. "Talk to *me.*"

Detective Freemont's brow slowly rose as she unwillingly gave her attention to Julia. "We have a witness."

My brow wrinkled as my shock caused my eyes to narrow curiously.

She again gave me a taunting smile when she saw that she finally had my attention. "We have an informant that is willing to testify that they have first-hand knowledge of the murder."

The fine hairs on the back of my neck stood. I knew that no one in the crew had knowledge that we killed Kidd. They could not have even assumed that we had because no one knew that he was going to snitch. The only other person outside of me and my brothers who knew that we had killed Kidd was Tory. I imagined that Jah would have told Moe in confidence, but he was dead. And even though he had been offering information before his death, had he snitched, my other two brothers would have been locked up with me.

I was secure in the fact that she was bluffing, so I tore my eyes away from her and put my focus back on the word "bitch" that was etched into the table.

"He doesn't have anything to say," Julia pressed. "Now, please give me and my client some privacy."

I could feel the detective's eyes on me, but I continued tracing the letters on the table with my eyes. Finally, her footsteps could be heard going toward the door before the squeaks echoed in the silent room again.

Once the door closed, Julia turned toward me. "Is there anyone who could have witnessed that murder or have any information about it?"

Finally, I was able to take my eyes off the nearly illegible sketch of profanity. "No."

"Are you sure?"

I thought of Tory. But even though I knew that she had attempted to snitch, that, now, she never would. "Yeah, I'm sure," I answered confidently.

Relief flooded her eyes. "Then you have nothing to worry about. You've never been charged with a crime as an adult, so there shouldn't be a problem convincing the judge to grant you bail tomorrow."

I nodded slowly.

"We're going to fight this. Just hang in there." As she reached down for her briefcase, she asked, "Is there anything that you want me to tell your brothers?"

"Just let them know that I'm okay."

She pressed her thin lips into a tight line. She then nodded and squeezed my shoulder soothingly before standing and leaving me alone to wallow in worry and anxiety. I had always known that this day could come. Being in the streets caused a constant fear of imprisonment or death. I had always been more worried about death, but now, facing this charge, I understood that potentially being locked up for the rest of my life felt a lot like dying.

THE DAY PRIOR...

DETECTIVE FREEMONT

The day before Messiah's arrest, I was patrolling the neighborhood of a suspect in a different murder case. As a homicide detective in one of the most dangerous cities in America, I was extremely busy. Currently, I had over twenty unsolved murders on my desk. Most of them went unsolved because of the ridiculous snitching code that so many people in these communities lived by and feared. As time passed, the murders became more ridiculous and unnecessary. The current suspect that I was pursuing was only thirteen and was a known carjacker. The week prior, he had been caught on camera carjacking a woman who was leaving out of a Harold's Chicken location. She had willingly given him the keys to her Benz. Yet, he still shot her in the heart before jumping into the driver's seat and leaving her to bleed out on the cold pavement of the parking lot.

As I slowly cruised through Englewood, I kept my eyes sharp for the suspect. While doing so, I recognized Moe. Since I had been deep into the investigation of Kidd's murder, I had become quite familiar with the members of the Disciple crew. During my investigation, I'd learned that Kidd was actively working with narcotics detectives to snitch on the Disciple brothers. It was obvious that they had been behind Kidd's murder. However, lips were sealed tightly. I was sure that Tory had been close to telling me back in May, but for whatever reason, she had changed her mind. I was even more intent on solving the case after learning that one of the Disciple brothers was now dating Tory.

I brought my cruiser to an even slower crawl as I watched Moe teeter down the block. He was jumpy, wide-eyed, and anxious. To learn more about this crew, I had been asking around the narcotics department to get any intel on them. Unfortunately, they were flying very low under the radar. The only time that their names were even mentioned was when Kidd and Moe had been arrested, and they had offered information. However, nothing had ever been uncovered from that information because of how carefully the Disciple operation was run. However, because of his many arrests recently, it was known that Moe was now addicted to heroin and was a leak in their tightly run ship.

I watched as Moe hurriedly spoke to a few guys who were standing on porches. I was sure that he was looking for drugs. I kept an undetectable distance as he made a transaction that was intended to be discreet. But considering his urgency when he put his hands in his pocket and walked away, I knew that he had just made a purchase.

I waited until he was near the corner before I jumped out. I pulled over and hopped out. There was no way for me to be discreet because I was a white woman with a blonde ponytail in one of the most notoriously dangerous ghettos in this city. No sooner than I caught Moe's attention, he froze. He looked toward a car that was chaotically parked in front of mine.

"Don't do it," I warned as I pushed back the lapel of my coat to reach for my weapon.

Moe gritted and remained still. I stalked toward him and grabbed him by the collar of his hoodie.

"C'mon. I didn't do shit!" he insisted as I dragged him toward the nearest fence.

It was a cold day in February, so the streets were only occupied by a few people who dared to battle the winter. The few guys hanging out in the neighborhood began to inch back into the homes that they stood in front of.

"Get off me!" Moe fussed. "I didn't do shit!"

"I'll be the judge of that."

I began to search his pockets. It didn't take long before my hand touched something that felt familiar. I pulled it out, smiling at the rocks that I was holding.

When he saw them in my hand, he immediately crumbled. "P-please? I'll do anything you want. Just don't throw my shit away. I need that shit." The amount of need in his eyes was sickening. "Please don't arrest me," he begged.

Holding the baggy up in the air, I asked him, "What do you know about Kidd's murder?"

Dread covered him. The color left his thin face.

Through clenched teeth, I threatened, "Tell me what you know, or I'll book your raggedy ass. You will be locked up for so long that you'll be completely clean by the time you get out."

Though he remained silent, he ogled the rocks with unwavering desire.

"Was it the Disciple brothers?" I pressed.

He grimaced as his eyes lowered to the ground.

"You can get a lot of time for these rocks, especially since you have other pending cases."

"Shit," he gripped.

"Tell me what I need to know, Moe," I pressed softly. "Just tell me what I need to know, and I'll give you back these rocks so you can go get your fix."

He grimaced as he looked up at the sky.

"Was it Jah?"

"No," he quickly insisted.

"Then who was it?"

"You promise to give me back my rocks and let me go?"

"I promise. I just need a lead."

He scoffed, fighting with his morals and addiction. "It was... it was Messiah."

"Just Messiah?" I pressed.

"Yeah. He's fucking Kidd's girl now."

"You're willing to testify to that?"

He sucked his teeth and blew out breath that was so rank that I got sick to my stomach. "C'mon now. You said all you needed was a lead."

"A lead that will get me an arrest warrant and hold up in court."

"Fuck!" he barked with his eyes on his high.

So, I closed them into my palm and lowered my hand toward my pocket.

"Okay!" he conceded, barely breathing. "Okay! I'll give you a statement, testify, whatever you need me to do."

"This isn't enough."

My eyes rolled to the ceiling of my boss' office. "What do you mean this isn't enough?"

Staring at him, my eyes stung from the potent cigar stench that resonated off of him. Captain Martin often stepped out of the station to partake in his habit of smoking cigars. The bitterly intense stench followed him into the station and permanently lingered in his office.

Captain Martin laughed. "He's a junky."

"Who works closely with the suspect," I insisted as I inched toward his desk. "He has close connections to the Disciple family."

Captain Martin sat back, causing his large belly to pop out from behind the desk. He shook his head insistently. "Still, it's not hard evidence."

"He gave me a statement." Moe and I had sat in my car for thirty minutes as I took his statement and then let him go. He had given me a number to contact him so that he could testify if there was a trial, but I knew that I would never be able to find him. I just hoped that with the arrest and evidence presented to Messiah, he would confess.

Captain Martin insisted, "He's not a good witness."

I grabbed the chair in front of his desk. My grip was tight on it to keep me from punching the desk out of frustration. "Just call the judge and ask him to sign the warrant, please? I'll get Messiah to confess." He was still contemplating, so I decided to press. "All I need is a warrant. Once he's arrested, I'll secure stronger evidence and make sure that Moe is a better witness."

He scoffed and shook his head slowly. Yet, he picked up his phone. "Fine. It's your funeral if this doesn't work out."

PRESENT DAY...

TORY CLARK

I hadn't shed these many tears when Kidd died. It had only been a few hours without Messiah, and I was already in shambles. I knew that it was because I had been with Kidd out of history and obligation. But Messiah wasn't even dead, yet I already felt the suffocating effects of his absence.

"It's going to be okay."

I cringed at my mother's words and pushed away from her. I balled up in the corner of the couch, burying my face into a throw pillow as I continued to sob.

"You need to eat," my mother suggested carefully.

"I'm not hungry," I cried.

"Tory—"

"Mama, please!"

"I'm just trying to help you," she said with a comforting tone. "I don't understand. You weren't this broken when Kidd died."

My head popped up, and my tearful eyes darted behind me toward her. "Kidd didn't love me nearly as much as Messiah does. I know you have something against him because he was in the streets like Kidd, but he loves me more than anybody on this earth! No matter what he did in the streets, he loves me. He adores me and my kids. He takes care of us! I cannot lose him! I can't, Ma, especially when it's my fault!"

"Your fault?" my mother questioned with a wrinkled brow. "How the hell is it your fault?"

I hesitated. In my anxiety, I wanted to tell my mother everything. Yet, I knew it would only push her back into the distance that we had before Kidd was killed. Now that we were mending our relationship, I remembered why I needed her. Having her there with me that day was so comforting. And if I was going to potentially lose Messiah to prison, I would definitely need her.

"It's my fault that he got arrested," I explained. "Kidd worked for Messiah before he was killed. Messiah pursued me after Kidd's death, and the detective is linking him to Kidd's murder because of it."

My mother's eyes lowered with sympathy as she put a comforting hand on my leg. But there was nothing that would comfort me if I lost Messiah.

CHAPTER 3

FAYE SINGER

I hadn't slept all night. Between the constant obsession over Mia's baby and Jah's coughing, I hadn't been able to get more than an hour of sleep.

"Jah, I think you should lie back down."

He was barely standing. Both of his hands were placed on the dresser as he used them to hold his body weight upright. When he'd woken up that morning, he could hardly sit up. The coughing had gotten worse. It looked as if it hurt him each time that he did.

"I gotta be there for my brother," he insisted.

"Shauka and Najia are going to be there."

"I need to be there too."

I cringed, hearing the weakness in his voice.

Staring at his wide back, I regretfully watched as he attempted to find himself something to wear in his drawers. My eyes widened when he seemed to lose his footing. When he stumbled, I jumped out of the bed and darted toward him. I wrapped my arms around his waist to hold him up and pushed all of my weight against him to help hold him up.

"*Fuuuck*," he groaned. "I feel like shit."

"That's why you need to *lie down*." My voice was strained as I struggled to hold him up.

Suddenly, he shuddered. "It's freezing."

"Then get back in the bed under the covers."

My eyes bounced around wildly, looking for a place closer than the bed for him to land on because I was losing the battle with keeping him upright.

"Oh, my Lord!" I suddenly heard Hattie yelp.

My eyes looked helplessly toward the doorway as Hattie rushed in. She dropped a basket of clothes as she ran toward us. She then began to help me assist Jah back into the bed.

"I'm okay," he persisted, although it obviously wasn't true.

"Boy, get your butt back in this bed," Hattie fussed.

"Messiah's bond hearing is this morning," he reminded us as if we could forget.

"And Shauka can take care of it," I added.

"I gotta be there," Jah argued. He even attempted to push back as Hattie and I put him in the bed, but he was too weak to.

That concerned me. Jah was a large man with immeasurable strength. But now, he was so weak with no energy.

"You ain't goin' nowhere," Hattie urged just as a round of violent coughs erupted from Jah's throat.

Hattie scoffed, shaking her head. "Talkin' about goin' somewhere. Yeah right. Let me go fix you some tea."

"I ain't never felt this sick," Jah groaned as he laid back.

"You probably have the flu," I suggested. Putting the covers back over him, I could feel his large frame trembling. "You're still cold?" I asked.

He nodded. So, I went into his closet, where I knew more blankets were. I quickly got one and rushed back to the bed. As I covered him with it, Jah stared at me.

"What's wrong with you?" he asked.

"What you mean?"

"You've been quiet since the wedding."

"There is a lot going on."

"That's the only reason why you look so stressed?"

"Yeah. I'm just... I'm worried about you."

I wanted nothing more than to confront Jah. But he was already dealing with so much. Despite being sick, I could see the distress in his eyes over Messiah's arrest. Shauka and Jah had been insisting that there was no way that there could be any evidence that would allow the charges to stick against Messiah. They were also convinced that he had been arrested on bullshit charges since they hadn't been arrested along with him. However, the judicial system had never been fair, especially to Black men. Many of them had been found guilty with little to no evidence, whether they were guilty or not. So, there was a lingering fear amongst us all that Messiah wouldn't beat the charges.

I would only cause more chaos if I approached Jah with Mia's allegations. I was hurt, but I wasn't prepared to lose him again over what could have very well been another one of her ploys to get under my skin.

He continued eyeing me suspiciously, so I insisted, "I'm fine—"

Another round of viscous coughs interrupted me. His face balled up from the pain. He groaned once they subsided and curled up under the covers.

As my cell began to ring, Hattie came into the room carrying a food tray. I rushed over to my side of the bed to stop the loud ringtone from disturbing Jah.

Chloe was calling. I knew that she was worried after everything that had happened at the wedding, so I rushed out of the room to answer.

"Hello?" I was still sure to be quiet because Shauka was in his room. He had spent the night inside, not saying a word after he and Jah had gotten there after leaving the hospital. I had only heard movement in there once it was time for them to get ready for the hearing.

"Hey, girl,"

"Hey," I sighed as I sat on the top step of the staircase.

"You okay?"

"I'm all right. Jah isn't feeling well."

"I saw that, even before all that shit happened at the wedding yesterday. He looked so tired."

"He has the flu or something."

"They let Messiah out on bond?"

"His court case is this morning. So, we'll see. Jah can't make it. He's too sick."

Chloe sighed. "Damn." Then she asked, "How are you doing?"

"I'm okay. Just dealing with all of this."

"Nah, G. Something else is wrong with you. I could see it at the wedding. Your mood changed all of a sudden before that guy showed up."

I gritted as the reminder washed over me and made my heart race.

"What's going on, girl?" Chloe pushed.

I stood from the stair, slipped into the bathroom nearby, and closed the door.

"Girl," I groaned as I sat on the edge of the tub. "I got a message from Mia right before all that shit went down at the wedding."

"Mia?! What did she say?!"

"She sent a picture of a newborn and said, 'tell your nigga that he left this in me when he fucked me at the club that night.'"

Chloe's gasp was so loud that it made me cringe. "That bitch!"

Waves of nausea swam through my guts, causing me to bend over and rest my elbows on my knees.

"Don't trip on that," Chloe said. "She could be lying. If she was pregnant with Jah's baby, she wouldn't have held on to that information all of this time."

"Exactly. So, why say something now?"

"Because she's a bitch," Chloe growled. "She's been fucking with you since high school. Did the baby look like Jah?"

I shrugged as if she could see him. "It was a newborn. It looked like skin and eyes."

"I wouldn't say anything. Don't give that bitch the satisfaction of ruining what you just got back."

Over my spiraling thoughts, I heard the doorbell ring. I wondered who it could be since not many people randomly showed up at the estate.

"But I told him never to fuck her. What if he did?"

"Some shit ain't worth losing your man over, and Mia is definitely one of them. Don't give that bitch the satisfaction—"

Suddenly, loud screaming got my attention.

I jumped to my feet as I hurriedly told Chloe, "Let me call you back."

SHAUKA DISCIPLE

As soon as I heard the blaring scream, I ran out of my room. Because it was muffled, I could tell that the screams were coming from downstairs. I darted through the hallway and toward the staircase. Looking over the banister into the foyer, I saw Najia raining down punches on Sariah in the doorway.

"Shit!" I flew down the stairs, jumping down the last four. The sweet aroma of French toast invaded my nostrils as I bolted toward Najia and Sariah. Greg's head popped out of the entryway of the kitchen.

"Aye!" he shouted, stepping out. But I put out a hand to stop his approach.

Before splitting them up, I halted, letting Najia land a few more punches. I watched with jealousy as Najia landed blow after blow. Sariah was cowering under her, screaming as she attempted to loosen Najia's grip on her hair. But there was no use in her trying to defend herself. Najia was murdering that ass.

"What is going on?!" Hattie's frantic shouting came from upstairs as she leaned over the banister with wide, worried eyes as she stood next to Faye. When she noticed who and what it was, she gasped. "Lord."

Out of respect for Hattie, I darted toward the wrestling match unfolding. I gripped Najia's shoulder and tore her off of Sariah.

"Ah'ight, sis. You got her."

"Stupid bitch!" she spit. She glared at Sariah as I held her from behind in a bear hug. "You can let me go. I'm good, bro."

She was still heaving angrily, but I knew that I could let her go. Sariah was only part of the cause of Najia's rage. She was mostly upset because her other half was gone. She had been broken since Messiah's arrest.

"Go finish getting dressed so we can head to the courthouse," I urged my sister.

She was still glaring at Sariah with flared nostrils. Sariah was slowly standing, grunting from pain that was already brewing from her ass whooping.

Finally, Najia tore her weary eyes away from Sariah and stomped into her room. I looked up the stairs to see Faye and Hattie still peering down. Even Jah was weakly leaning in the doorway of his room, trying to see what was going on.

"Shauka, can I talk to you, please?" Sariah whimpered.

Blood trickled from her nose. The pin-up that she'd had styled for the wedding was now completely disheveled. Her bottom lip was beginning to swell.

Faye, Hattie, and Jah slowly inched back into Jah's bedroom. However, I knew that their prying ears wouldn't be too far away.

I spoke to her through gritted teeth and with reluctant effort. "Like I told you last night, I don't have shit to say to you."

Sariah had been blowing my phone up all night. I had answered only once, telling her that I didn't have anything to say to her. Lucky for her, I wasn't hurt. My heart had always been elsewhere. I simply felt stupid. I no longer trusted my own judgment.

I had grown so tired of her calling and sending me text messages that I'd eventually blocked her.

"I wasn't fucking with him," she lied, trying to convince me.

My neck rolled, her constant lying making my rage boil over. With flared nostrils, I forced my eyes on her. "Don't stand here and lie in my face."

Her pleading eyes began to water. "Shauka—"

"I'm not even gonna act like I was the perfect man to you. But I never allowed any of those hoes to embarrass you. I made clear to them who you were to me, so they knew to never disrespect you by ever showing their faces."

Her eyes bucked at my confessions. She swallowed hard, holding the doorknob to help her fearful limbs keep her standing.

"I'm glad all of this happened." I was so stern that her brow wrinkled with confusion. "My heart wasn't even in this—"

She gasped so loud that the inhale echoed around the foyer.

"Just bounce, Sariah."

"So, it's over?" she cried. "That's it?"

I laughed psychotically. "Sariah, leave before I let my sister come finish what she started."

"Shauka—"

"Get the fuck out!" I barked, causing her to jump out of her pale skin.

Fear covered her tears. Yet, she left out of the house, though reluctantly, closing the door behind her.

The click of the door securing shut felt like shutting out the years I'd spent with Sariah. They had been erased. The deception made it feel as if it was all a lie and never truly existed.

I swallowed the confusion and embarrassment. I buried it in the back of my mind because there were heavier crosses to bear that day.

"Shauka?"

As I inched toward the stairs to finish getting ready, I heard Hattie calling my name softly. I looked up to see her approaching the stairs.

She descended them as I began to climb. "Jah wants to talk to you."

I nodded as we crossed paths. I then jogged up the stairs and into Jah's room. When I walked in, I noticed that Faye wasn't in the room. But I heard the shower in Jah's master bathroom running as steam flowed from underneath the door.

"You... You good?"

My brow furrowed when I noticed that he was wheezing. That was shocking. Jah's asthma hadn't acted up since we were kids. We'd all figured he had outgrown that.

"Your asthma is acting up?"

"I guess." He then shrugged as if it were nothing. "You good?"

I shrugged as well as I sat at the foot of his bed. "I ain't got time to worry about that shit. I got other shit to do."

"You ain't gotta..." Coughing stole his words. He winced as if it hurt. Then he groaned and lay back with his eyes closed, having to recover from a simple coughing spell. Then he finally opened his eyes again; eyes that were usually confident and hard were now weak and tired. "You ain't gotta front for me. You know that I know firsthand how that...how that shit feels."

I cringed with each word that was hard to get out because of his wheezing. He had deteriorated overnight. The day before, I could see that he was weary. But now, he was clearly suffering. "Let's talk about this when you feel better, bro. I gotta get to the courthouse anyway."

I checked the time on my phone.

"I need to be there," Jah said with a weak groan.

I laughed. "Nigga, you can't even sit up. Chill. I got this. I'll be back... with our brother."

TORY CLARK

"*Shiiiit*," I groaned lowly as I marched down the sidewalk.

"What's wrong?" Najia quizzed, walking along next to me.

I tore my eyes away from Seretta and Monique, who were angrily stalking toward me.

"Kidd's mother and sister are coming this way," I quickly explained.

I figured that no sooner than Kidd's family was told who had killed him, I would get some backlash since it was no secret that I had been dating Messiah. But as they angrily pushed past others on the sidewalk to get to me, it looked like there was way more than resentment in their eyes.

As they approached, I pretended not to see them. I had never been one that was scared of confrontation, but presently, my focus was on Messiah getting out of jail. Not whatever insults and accusations they were ready to spew at me.

"So, did you set my son up?!" Seretta immediately started to lash out as Najia and I walked by. "I knew it was too much of a coincidence that you weren't hurt that night!"

I had long since been monitoring my anger. So, I ignored them, grasping for self-control as Najia and I kept walking.

"You hear my mother talking to you, bitch!" Monique spat.

Their voices were so close that I knew that they were on my heels. Others on the sidewalk looked on, brows furrowed with curiosity. Others even stopped their journey to look on.

"You wanted him dead so bad that you let your side nigga kill him?!" Monique spewed.

Blowing a frustrated breath, I spun around. "Look!" I snapped. The fury in my eyes was so violent that it caused Seretta and Monique to stop in their tracks. "I didn't have shit to do with his murder! Me and Messiah started dating *after* Kidd was killed."

"You're a lying ass bitch!" Monique seethed. "I know you had something to do with it! And I'm telling the police so that they can get my niece and nephew the fuck away from you."

No sooner than she brought up my kids, I forgot about managing my anger. I lunged toward her in full attack mode.

"Y'all don't give a damn about my kids!" I growled as I tried to grab Monique.

However, Najia was behind me, holding me back. "Chill," I could hear her insisting. "Calm down, Tory."

"Those are going to be my kids when I'm done!" Monique shouted, fueling my rage.

"You don't even care about my kids! You haven't bothered to see them since Kidd was killed! You don't even call to see about them!" Then I anchored my intolerable orbs on Seretta. "You've never even offered to help me with them! Do you know what size clothes they wear?! Do you even know what their favorite foods are?!"

"Tory, please calm down before the police come," Najia begged.

"Stupid bitches!" I exploded. "Get the fuck out of my face before I'm the one that needs to get bonded out next!"

Seretta eyed me with disgust as she grabbed her daughter's hand. "Come on," she told Monique. "We can take care of this later. Let's go."

I shot them both daggers as she drug Monique toward the courthouse. Monique turned back, glaring at me as long as she could before she was forced to look forward.

A frustrated sigh left my throat as Najia finally released me.

"You should have known that they would be upset if you're dating the man who is being charged with Kidd's murder," Najia told me.

"I know. I just lost it when she mentioned my kids. Neither of them has been in Honor or Hope's life since Kidd's murder. Monique watched them once. I know it's because they don't like me. But why take that out on my kids? They shouldn't have had to lose a grandmother and auntie when they had already lost their father." My voice started to crack, so I stopped talking, pressing my lips into a thin line.

Najia watched me sympathetically as I gathered myself.

"C'mon," I said, forcing back the tears. "Let's go get Messiah out of this motherfucker."

MESSIAH DISCIPLE

"Bail is denied." I cringed, closing my eyes as the judge banged her gavel. "Next case."

I instantly heard Tory burst into tears.

Above my heart beating thunderously, I also heard my sister spit, "What the fuck?!"

I turned to give her a supportive glance. As our eyes met, her shoulders sank, and tears came to her eyes. Then I blew Tory a kiss that only made her weep harder.

"This some bullshit!" Najia spit angrily.

Queen lay a hand on her knee, trying to soothe her. The judge began to bang her gavel repeatedly. I felt hands on my shoulders, which caused me to reluctantly take my eyes off my sister. Two bailiffs were standing over me, ready to escort me back to holding.

As they brought me to my feet, Julia stood as well. She began to follow as they escorted me through the courtroom to the door where holding was. I looked back to catch glimpses of Tory and my family. Shauka was furious. Buck's eyes seemed to have aged since the day I'd been arrested. My sister and Tory were in tears as Queen comforted them.

I had been shocked to see that Jah wasn't there. But, before the bail hearing started, Julia had told me that he was too sick to come. Yet, he had been ensuring that she was on top of things with one text message after another.

Once in holding, the bailiffs sat me down on a bench with other prisoners that were waiting to be bussed back to jail.

"Messiah, I'm so sorry," Julia said once the bailiffs walked away.

"What the fuck was that?" I asked. "You said that you were sure that I would get bail. I've never been convicted of a crime. I've never even been arrested before."

Julia drew her lips into a reluctant tight line. "Like the prosecution said, you may not have ever been in trouble before, but you have suspected gang ties. Considering that and the informant's statement, you're a flight risk."

"Shit," I groaned.

"Are you sure that this informant is bullshit?" she asked with a raised brow.

"I'm positive," I assured. "You don't know who it is?"

She shook her head, causing her blonde bob to sway. "Now that your bail hearing is over and a court date has been set, I can request a copy of all the evidence they have against you. But it's possible that they will hide the identity of the informant to protect him or her. I will just have a copy of the statement."

I nodded slowly, unable to wrap my head around any of this.

Julia opened her mouth to speak but was interrupted by heavy footsteps close behind her. We both peered behind her. She immediately rolled her eyes when she saw the prosecutor for my case approaching with a haughty smirk that traveled to his portly cheeks.

"What is it, Brian?" Julia huffed.

"Just came to offer your client a deal." He smiled as his beady eyes bounced between me and Julia. "Considering his clean record, we're offering ten years. Otherwise, he'll face the max and a deep dive into his family's organization."

Though my expression remained stoic, I began to unravel on the inside. I was to blame for all of this. Had I never pursued Tory, Detective Freemont wouldn't have so easily associated me with Kidd's murder. No matter what Tory was about to tell her, once she saw me, it was easy for her to put the puzzle pieces together. A trial would put my entire family and organization under a microscope, threatening not only our livelihood but the freedom of my brothers and the rest of our crew.

I stared straight ahead, feeling Julia's eyes on me.

"You have until the next court date to consider it," Brian said before strolling away.

Once he was out of earshot, I asked her, "That's true, right? If there is a trial, they will start to investigate my connection to Kidd, his attempt to snitch, and our organization?"

Julia nodded reluctantly. "Quite possibly."

"And though this is a murder case, that investigation will definitely be handed over to narcotics," I added regretfully.

"Most likely."

"Fuck," I groaned.

Julia laid a hand on my shoulder and squeezed it softly. "Don't worry. Let's see what evidence they have against you before we start to panic. I'll be in touch. Try to stay positive."

I nodded as she walked away. I then rested my head back on the concrete wall behind me and stared up at the ceiling in disbelief. This would have made more sense had my brothers been locked up with me. I felt like I had been set up. I didn't fear jail. Being locked up last night was like being at a big-ass kickback. I knew most of the niggas in there. The ones that I didn't know had heard of me. I was a king inside, just as I was in the streets. I had the same respect. The only fear I had was putting my family through losing me, especially my sister. Life had separated me and Najia from our birth parents and brothers since we were only six weeks old. But Najia and I had always had each other.

Tory's cries echoed in my head all night while sleep avoided me. I knew that she had stolen my heart when I couldn't shake her after knowing what she had attempted to tell that detective. But the threat of being locked away from her for the rest of my life was putting fear in my heart that could only be love and infatuation.

I had always been reckless with no responsibilities. And as soon as I figured out how to be a man, a threat was thrown into my path to take my life away. But, for some reason, this felt like the undeniable force that was going to push me to truly man up.

CHAPTER 4

NAJIA DISCIPLE

My eyes felt as if they were bleeding. But the liquid streaming down my milky cheeks were merely tears of pain and grief. I had never mourned my parents. I couldn't miss what I'd never had. I merely wished that I had known them and longed for a connection to them.

But this... this *had* to be what grief felt like.

"Here."

Reluctantly, I opened my eyes to see Nardo standing next to his bed. A plate with steam floating from the food piled on it blocked the vision of his handsome face.

I sucked my teeth and buried my face back into the pillow. "I don't want it."

I had been inconsolable since Messiah's bail hearing earlier that day. The tears hadn't stopped. I felt like I'd lost my better half. I had never felt grief like this. I had only come to Nardo's house because I had been blowing him off since the wedding. But I had known that I wouldn't be great company.

"You haven't eaten all day."

I actually hadn't eaten much at all since the wedding before

Messiah was arrested. I had lied to Nardo, telling him that I had eaten the night of when I was really locked in my room, unable to imagine my brother being locked up for the next twenty-five years.

"Najia, you need to—"

"Please don't make me," I mumbled through tears.

I felt his density weigh down the space of the bed on the other side of me. Then his hand went to my back and began to rub it lovingly.

"You think you should call your therapist and get an appointment with her?"

I hadn't been back to therapy since attempting to commit suicide. Since therapy hadn't stopped me from trying to kill myself, I assumed that it was a waste of time. My therapist had been a great help, but it just wasn't enough.

"No," I mumbled.

"You know I got you, right?"

I kissed my teeth, finally giving him my tear-soaked orbs. "I don't know that."

"Why don't you?"

"Because we just started fucking around," I reminded him.

He shrugged his shoulder. "And?"

The genuineness in his disposition made me uneasy. The tears stopped flowing. I was only used to my brother having my back. No other man had owned that responsibility unconditionally. Miguel's supportive presence in my life was always blanketed with manipulation and perversion. Shauka and Jah's protection and support was always there. I knew that I could count on them with whatever in this world that I needed or wanted. But the intimacy in that connection had yet to develop because I had been separated from them for so long.

Suddenly, I felt uncomfortable. I shifted, turning over on my back and sitting up.

"What's wrong?" Nardo asked.

"Nothing," I mumbled.

His left, dark, bushy brow rose. "You don't believe me?"

My shoulder shrugged weakly. "It's hard to believe."

"Why? I fucks with you. That isn't obvious?"

His certainty made me uncomfortable. Balls of anxiety piled up in my throat, making breathing difficult.

"It's obvious that you're *fucking me*. We're having fun."

That bushy brow rose higher. "That's what this is to you?"

"That's not all that it is to you?"

He tried to discreetly take that deep breath, but I peeped it. Then those obscure, feline eyes bore into me with a scolding look that only a nigga that cares about you would give.

"I told you that because of your brothers, I would never keep fucking you unless I had real intentions."

Nardo mentioning my brothers was still a sore subject for me. Messiah insisted on keeping Nardo at a distance. Before he was arrested, he was still pushing Shauka and Jah to cut ties with him. Thankfully, Jah and Shauka were more appreciative of the fact that he had been there for me when I tried to commit suicide. But Messiah had been the one to tell me that because Shauka and Jah had yet to have a conversation with me about my suicide attempt. I knew that it was coming eventually. They had just been busy with the wedding.

"So, what does that mean?" I asked nervously.

Suddenly, I felt out of place. There were minimal positions that I was accustomed to being in with a man. I knew how to fuck them. I knew how to tolerate them. I knew how to act as if I wasn't hurt by them. But I did not know how to deal with a man looking at me with the affirmation that was in Nardo's eyes.

It was suffocating.

It was intimidating.

He even grabbed my hand. His strong, large hand held it so softly. His thumb traced my palm as his alluring spheres bore into mine.

I tried so hard to avoid those caring eyes.

"It means that—"

Thank God my phone rang. I lunged toward it, eager for something to interrupt this conversation.

"Urgh!" Disappointingly, it was a call that I wasn't going to answer. I silenced it and then tossed the phone onto the bed next to me.

"Is that Karen again?"

It was her second time calling since I'd arrived at Nardo's house. She had even sent a text message asking that we talk because she wanted to explain what happened at Starbucks. But I was convinced that she was just trying to probe me for information about Miguel's disappearance.

"Yes," I sighed, rolling my eyes with irritation.

"You should talk to her."

A frown replaced tears that had started to dry. "Why would I do that? She's just trying to find out what happened to Miguel."

"But she said she wanted to explain herself. It sounds like it was more to it. She's your mother. She knows how close you and Messiah are. She has to know that you would never snitch on your brothers, especially Messiah. I know she asked you about it that night. But that could have been natural. She might have wanted—"

"Why are you defending her?" I spit with a frown.

He placed a hand on my thigh. It was supposed to comfort my sudden irritation. "Because I know how much you miss her. I'm just looking out for you, baby."

His words only deepened my frustration, though.

I climbed out of bed.

"Where you goin'?" he questioned.

"I... I have to go."

"Thought you were spending the night with me."

Flustered, I started looking around for my pants and shoes. I had peeled off my pants to climb into bed to cry comfortably. Now, I no longer felt like this was a safe space.

"I'm not going to be much company tonight," I explained as I pulled my leggings up.

Finally, I found my Christian Dior snow boots. As I slipped into them, I saw the blunder on Nardo's face.

Sympathizing with his dismay, I softened my words as I grabbed my coat off of the foot of his bed. "I'm sorry. I just... I need to be alone. I'll call you later. I promise."

He nodded with a straight face. The emotion that he was once feeling had vanished.

Oddly, it made me feel better.

I still hurried out of the bedroom, however. I felt as if I was taking flight. I wondered why, until I was at the front door, opening it, and hurrying out after locking the bottom lock.

The cold, biting air hit me.

And I could breathe.

I inhaled deeply, feeling so much relief.

I hurried down the porch steps. Rushing toward my car, my phone began to ring in my hand.

I groaned and reluctantly looked at it. It wasn't Karen this time. It was Jah.

"Hey, brother," I answered.

"Hey."

I cringed as I popped the locks. Sickness had overcome Jah so quickly. Suddenly, he was congested and could barely breathe.

"You sound terrible."

"I know. I was just checking on you."

I laughed dryly. "I should be checking on you."

"I'm... I'm good."

"You can barely talk. You don't have an inhaler?"

"I haven't needed one since I was a shorty."

My chuckle was sarcastic. "Well, you need one now. You need to go to the doctor."

"I'm good. I'mma—" Ferocious coughing cut off his breathy words. I cringed, hearing the croupiness of each hack. As I backed out of

Nardo's driveway, the coughing finally subsided. Jah took a deep breath and then had the nerve to repeat, "I'm good."

A sarcastic giggle left my dry lips. I hadn't moisturized an inch of my body since Messiah's arrest. "No, you're not. I'm on my way home."

"Ah'ight."

I hung up, hating the relief that I felt now that I wasn't in Nardo's presence. I had been enjoying the dick and his attention. But the seriousness in his affection tonight had suddenly given me the need to flee.

YAZMEEN HILL

I had suspected that I wouldn't hear from Shauka after the wedding. But for different reasons other than the drama that had ended up unfolding.

Though I had seen that the wedding hadn't taken place, I still had no idea why. I had cyber stalked everyone since. But the only evidence that I had seen was a Facebook status by Najia that had shockingly said #FreeSiah".

That was earlier this afternoon. Since, I had been blowing Shauka's phone up with no answer. So, when my doorbell rang that evening, I was expecting another package from Amazon. Shauka had financed the baby shower that was only a week away. I had hired a party decorator and caterer. But, since my registry was with Amazon, those that couldn't make the shower, mostly my friends from school and work that now lived out of town, had been sending gifts non-stop.

Yet, when I opened the door, a weary, red-faced Shauka was standing there weakly. I had been looking into those eyes for years, and this was the first time that I couldn't recognize them.

His broken disposition made me stutter. "H-hey."

"Hey," he grumbled as I made way for him to come in.

So, he really didn't get married.

Though I had seen the video and heard what Shauka had said, I wondered had he gotten married anyway since I hadn't heard from him. But since he was at my place, that meant he wasn't on his honeymoon.

But if Messiah got locked up, he would have canceled the honeymoon.

I watched Shauka intently as he moped to the couch and plopped down. I slowly waddled over to him. Now that I was nearing my ninth month, I was feeling every bit of being pregnant. I had read in the many pregnancy groups on Facebook that carrying the first baby was easy for most, with minimal side effects. But finally, my feet were swelling. My face had filled out, and my cravings had become intolerable.

This day had been the first of my maternity leave. I had literally spent the entire day ordering food from Uber Eats.

Shauka remained silent as I sat down beside him. As soon as I was comfortable, his head went to my lap. He laid his face directly against my belly with his eyes closed and wrapped his arm around me.

Sighing, I reached for his ponytail and unwrapped the rubber band that held it. Once his curls were freely flowing, I buried my fingers in them, finding his scalp.

"What's going on? Why aren't you on your honeymoon?"

His eyes remained closed, but they squeezed together tighter as if the question hurt.

"I didn't get married."

My heart exploded. My intestines wildly tied into a tight knot. *So, he really didn't get married.*

"What the hell? Why not? How are you so calm?" I looked down at him, blinking owlishly at the way he calmly laid on my lap, eyes remaining closed, rubbing my belly slowly as if it were somehow giving him peace.

"Sariah was cheating on me the whole time."

I took advantage of his eyes being closed. I allowed my jaw to drop cartoonishly. "Excuse me?! I know you fucking lying!"

I loved this man. My heart beat for him. But my love was unconditional enough to realize Sariah's perfection. She was so good that I could not argue why he couldn't see me. Her light had shined so brightly that it had blinded him.

Shauka chuckled deeply at my surprise, but his eyes remained closed. "That bitch was cheating the whole time. The nigga showed up at the wedding, acting a fool."

"What?!" I jumped up. He had to brace himself on the edge of the couch to keep from falling off.

"Wait a minute," I said breathlessly as I began to pace. "He showed up at the wedding?"

He stared off into space as if he were still in disbelief. "Yeah."

"How do you know he wasn't lying?"

"The ambulance—"

"*Ambulance*?!" I snapped.

Shauka laughed at my dramatic response. "I pushed that nigga through a glass door. So, when the police came—"

"Police?!" I shouted.

Still chuckling, he asked, "You gonna let me tell you the story?"

I dramatically took a deep breath and stood still with my arms folded over my stomach.

Shauka pushed himself upright and rested back on the couch. His former ponytail was now a curly fro, causing curls to fall into his face.

"I was standing at the altar waiting for her to come down the aisle, and all of a sudden, some commotion started in the lobby. It was so loud that it got everybody's attention. It kept going. We could all hear some man asking for Sariah. It was obvious to me that Heavy and the team weren't rectifying the situation fast enough. So, I went out there. And, of course, everybody followed me. I walk up, and Heavy and the team are holding this dude back because he's trying to get past them. Sariah comes into the lobby thinking she's about to walk down the aisle, and then this nigga starts calling for her." The way my eyes bulged made Shauka laugh again. "I asked him why he was confronting my girl. He called me a bitch, so I put that nigga through the glass door."

I gasped. "No!"

"Yep. I started stomping the nigga out." The recollections caused him to sigh, and his sadness deepened. "Police came out of nowhere. I assumed someone had called the police but figured they had come way too fast. I was right. A detective went straight for Messiah and arrested him."

My mouth fell open. This was way more mayhem than I could have ever assumed. "What the fuck? For what?!"

"They arrested him for Kidd's murder."

I inched toward the couch, shock blanketing my expression. I slowly sat down beside him. Then I realized something. "Wait! They didn't arrest you and Jah?"

"No."

Confusion made my brow wrinkle.

"They took him out, but I couldn't even focus on him being arrested because the nigga I had stomped out tells the police his name, and I realized he's Sariah's ex. But he says he ain't no ex. He's her 'right-now'—"

"Oh...my...God."

"The ambulance came for Tristen. The police left. I told everybody that they could go with them because it wasn't going to be a wedding. Sariah kept swearing that he was lying and that he just wanted to be with her, but I didn't believe it."

"What if she was telling the truth?" I probed.

"I went to the hospital to be sure."

My mouth fell agape once again. "*Ooooh.*"

"He opened up their text-message chat and let me scroll through it. That shit told me everything. She's *been* fucking him and taking care of him. She's even had a few abortions because she wasn't sure if she was pregnant by him or me."

I dramatically fell back against the couch. "You have *got* to be kidding me."

"I swear to God."

My eyes washed over the way Shauka was still calmly sitting there. "You seem okay with it, though. How are you so okay?"

He locked eyes with me. He remained silent for so long that I froze.

Then he cleared his throat and pulled his eyes away. "I got other things to focus on. I can't focus on her deceiving ass when my brother is in jail."

TWO DAYS LATER...

FAYE SINGER

"What's this?"

Jah eyeballed the box in my hand suspiciously as I stood on his side of the bed.

"A COVID test," I answered and then began to open the box.

Yesterday, Jah developed a fever. Though the pandemic was over, COVID was still very present. So, while at Walgreens getting more soup and meds for Jah, I decided to get a COVID test.

Hattie nodded with satisfaction as she sat on the small couch in Jah's room, folding some clothes. Since he'd gotten sick, she had been by his side, with me on the other.

Jah shook his head, pulling the covers under his chin. "Man, I don't have COVID."

I scoffed as I peeled off my coat.

Jah had only gotten sicker. Though the heat was on in the house, Shauka had purchased a space heater and placed it directly next to Jah's side of the bed. That, along with two blankets, hadn't been enough to stop his chills.

"How do you know that you don't have it?" I probed.

"Because I don't."

"Were you vaccinated?" I asked him with a raised brow.

He frowned. "Hell nah."

I groaned. "Oh, God." Then I unfolded the instructions and started to read them.

"I tried to get him to get the vaccine since he has asthma, but he wouldn't listen to me," Hattie explained with a regretful sneer.

"I don't know what's in that shit," he said, scowling.

"Take the test, Jah," Hattie ordered.

"I have the flu," he insisted weakly.

The rattling in his words made me cringe. But at least he hadn't unfolded in another round of vehement coughs amidst this conversation.

"You also have a fever that is sky high," Hattie rebutted. "And you said you couldn't taste your soup this morning."

I pushed the small tube against his lips. "Spit in this, Jah."

I wanted to be gentler and less forward, but my mind was still consumed with thoughts of him fucking that spiteful bitch. But I wasn't so heartless to have that discussion with him when he could barely breathe. So, I was fighting with being a caring girlfriend and a bitter one.

"I pray you don't have it," Hattie said as he spit into the tube.

"Are you vaccinated, Hattie?" I asked.

Hattie scoffed with a hard nod. "At my age, I wasn't about to play with that shit. Najia and Greg are too. If he has it, we'll have to tell everyone that he was in contact with in the last few days."

I cringed. "Shit." Then I squeezed the tip of the tube so that his sample could fall into the tester.

Hattie laughed. "I know. Feels like making that call to tell a motherfucka you might have given them an STD." Hattie cracked up at her comparison, and so did I. No sooner than Jah attempted to laugh, another violent round of coughs erupted.

A WEEK LATER...

CHAPTER 5

NAJIA DISCIPLE

The last week had been traumatizing. Though Jah's first COVID test had come back positive, he'd refused to believe that he had it. So, Faye had purchased two more tests that had come back positive as well. Finally, he believed it. Luckily, Karen had forced our household to get vaccinated as soon as one was made available. Faye, Hattie, and Greg had been vaccinated as well. Luckily, Shauka hadn't caught it. We had contacted everyone who had been in close proximity to Jah during the days that he would have been contagious. Only two people had reported back that they were positive. However, thankfully, their symptoms were non-existent.

Ever since testing positive, Jah's health had declined drastically. His fever was resilient. He had begun to vomit three days ago, leaving him severely dehydrated because he had no desire to eat or drink anything. This morning when I went into his room, I could hear each breath he managed to take because his wheezing was so bad.

It was haunting to see a man who was always strong and a leader be dissolved down to a weak and feeble pile of sickness that was clambering to breathe. It was terrifying to watch. Because of his asthma and severe symptoms, we had all been on pins and needles for the past week, praying that he wouldn't get so bad that he'd have to be admitted to the hospital.

With Jah's severe sickness and Messiah being locked up, many of us weren't in the mood for Yaz's baby shower that day. It didn't feel right that Messiah and Jah wouldn't be there. Yaz had even offered to cancel it. But Shauka had insisted that she get this experience.

And a beautiful, enchanting experience it was.

As I walked into the event space, I was taken aback by the grand, alluring floral center pieces that decorated the tables that sat six and were draped with gold linen. The theme was gender-neutral. So, the colors were earth-tone and nature shades, mostly cream, tan, and gold. A balloon arch lined the Step and Repeat that was designed with the words "Oh Baby!" Next to it was a brown teddy bear that was at least five feet tall. In the front of the space was a large bamboo chair centered in an even more grandiose balloon arch of the same neutral colors. Sheer balloons with douses of gold glitter covered the ceiling.

I had gotten there early on purpose. The deejay and caterer were still setting up. I looked around for Yaz since Shauka had told me that she was getting dressed at the venue. I hadn't had a chance to speak to her about who her baby's father really was since so much chaos had happened after the bachelor party. But I was sure that Shauka had told her that I knew the truth because she hadn't reached out since.

Finally, I recognized Angela behind the makeshift bar, using a large spoon to stir a concoction that was in a beverage dispenser. I had met Angela one time when Yaz and I were hanging out.

"Hey, Najia! You're early," she said, realizing that I was walking toward her.

"I know. I need to talk to Yaz. Where is she?"

"She's in that office next to the front door. The MUA just finished her makeup."

"Okay. Thanks."

Angela grinned like a sneaky Cheshire cat. "Want a drink?"

"Hell yeah." I could feel the temporary ease of stress as I

approached the bar. I had been in my head all week. Jah and Messiah were my main concerns. But coupled with them was Nardo. I couldn't shake the anxiety that had surfaced the day of Messiah's bond hearing. The devotion that his eyes had promised me was suddenly so suffocating that I had dodged his requests to hang out all week. I was regretful that I would see him at the baby shower later because I knew that I couldn't tell him that I was running from a feeling that I wasn't familiar with, and it scared the hell out of me.

"What's this?" I asked as she handed me the chardonnay glass.

Her lips contoured into a devilish grin. "Rum punch... with a whole lot of *punch*."

Giggling, I sipped the libation. Immediately, it burned the hell out of my throat. But the hint of orange and pineapple juice soothed it.

My eyes met Angela's inquisitive ones. Smiling, I answered her silent question. "It's good."

She grinned once more. "Cool."

"I'm surprised Shauka didn't contract a bar service."

"He did. They aren't here yet. A lot of our co-workers like my rum punch, so Yaz asked that I make it."

"Oh. Well, let me go find her so I can holler at her before people start to get here."

"'Kay."

I tipped out of the room on the five-inch heels of my thigh-high boots. I had paired them with straight-legged light denim jeans and a cropped sweater. It was mild that day, the weather being in the high forties. So, I was able to get away with going without a coat. After taking the bus to school in snowstorms and freezing rain for years, forty-nine degrees felt like spring to Chicago residents.

Finding the office, I knocked and slowly opened the door without waiting for permission. I poked my head in before my feet followed. Yaz was standing in front of a full-length mirror that was nailed to a wall next to a desk. A long-sleeved mermaid dress molded her curves. She had already shown me a picture of the gown that had been custom-made by a designer that she followed on Instagram. The dress was off the shoulder and made of a sheer golden material with gold rhinestone appliqués strategically placed that cover her private parts.

As soon as her sharp eyes peered through her deep, Aaliyah-bang and landed on me through the mirror, she recoiled.

"Mmm humph," I mumbled as I closed the door.

She spun around and rushed toward me. "I am so sorry for lying to you."

Folding my arms, I leaned against the wall next to the door. "Why didn't you tell me?"

"Why didn't you tell me or your brothers about your suicide attempt?"

I groaned. "I knew Shauka would tell you. I was scared to tell them. I was ashamed. And anyway, that's not the same."

"Yes, it is. It's exactly the same. I was scared and ashamed too."

"Why would you be ashamed of being pregnant by my brother?"

"Because we are just friends, and he had a girlfriend."

"Well, you don't have to worry about that bitch anymore," I said with a deep, enraged roll of my eyes. I was still seething over how that heffa had embarrassed and played my brother. Dragging her in the doorway of the estate hadn't been enough to calm my rage, but it would have to do since Sariah had gone MIA since.

Closing the space between us, Yaz gently grabbed my hand. "I'm sorry."

"I know that you're Shauka's best friend, but we were getting close—"

"I know—"

"So, it hurt that you would lie, but it's been too much going on for me to even focus on it."

Yaz sighed, lowering her eyes. "I know. How is Jah?"

"Getting worse."

"Fuck." She shook her head as the same fear danced in her eyes that we all had for Jah. "And I know you are sick about Messiah."

I leaned my head back on the wall, staring up at the ceiling. "That's an understatement."

Sympathy put a deep pout on Yaz's perfectly made-up face. Her long, fluffy, mink lashes batted slowly as her reluctant gaze took in mine, which was full of angst and despair. Then she wrapped her arms around me. It had been so long since I had been hugged with this much comfort that I lost myself in the embrace. Oncoming tears stung my eyes as I felt her hand soothingly traveling up and down my back.

"It's all going to be okay," she insisted in a promising tone.

I wanted to believe her words. Jah and Messiah were strong. They were soldiers. Yet, with such a grim outlook, it was hard to have faith in a bright future.

TORY CLARK

The guilt and longing in my heart had only multiplied as the week had gone by. The only reason that I had managed to crawl out of bed to attend the baby shower was because I felt Messiah's presence whenever I was with the Disciple family.

All of the Disciples had been sure to promise me that they didn't blame me for his arrest. Jah and Shauka had been eyewitnesses to Messiah's relentless pursuit of me. However, I couldn't help but feel as if Detective Freemont had only been able to put two and two together because of his relationship with me. But it was clear to everyone that the evidence that secured the warrant to arrest Messiah had to be made-up since Jah and Shauka hadn't been arrested as well. That only put more frenzy in our hearts, especially mine. Many people were wasting away behind bars because of a resilient detective and bogus evidence.

I was determined to have Messiah's back, however. His arrest was even more proof of his loyalty to me. He could have killed me when he found out that I had attempted to snitch. Yet, he hadn't done that. He'd remained by my side, loving me, and adoring my kids. So, when he called during the baby shower, I rushed to answer.

"I'll be right back," I told Faye.

She nodded, angst filling her sad eyes. She was so worried about Jah that she could barely enjoy the shower. For most of it, she had sat quietly drinking and calling Hattie every thirty minutes to check on Jah.

I hurried out of my seat between Faye and Najia and rushed out of the room with my phone in hand, blaring its piercing ringtone. The 1-800 number calling had been imprinted in my brain the moment that Messiah had called from jail the first time.

Once in the lobby, I answered quickly. I then entered the necessary prompts to accept the collect call.

"Hey, baby," I greeted eagerly.

"What's up?"

Surprisingly, Messiah had been maintaining. Unlike me, he was completely together. He was safe inside. He was surrounded by people who he'd grown up with when he would sneak to hang out with Jah and Shauka while still living with his adoptive parents. Those who he didn't know personally knew his reputation quite well. He had rank, protection, and respect in holding. So, though being inside was nothing like being in the comforts of the estate, he felt at ease.

"Shit," he said. "'Sup with you? You at the shower?"

"Yeah."

"How is it?"

"It's..." I sighed sadly. "I don't know. I'm just here."

"I told you to stop worrying so much about me."

"I can't help it. I miss you."

"I miss you too."

"I can't help but feel like all of this is my fault."

"I already told you that it's not. It's actually on me. She would have never even considered me a suspect if I hadn't been at your house so soon after the murder. Of course, she would put two and two together."

I sucked my teeth. "But she put two and two together and got five instead of four."

"That's how I know the evidence she has is bullshit. But that doesn't make things any better. That's why—"

"That's why what?"

"I'm thinking about taking the deal the DA offered."

"What?!" I snapped softly. "Are you crazy?!"

"Hear me out."

"No!" I spit. "You have to fight this shit. Don't give up already!"

"I'm not giving up. But trials can take a year, even more. I'm not willing to have my family under a microscope, jeopardizing everything for a case that I have a big chance of losing."

My heart began to beat wildly, causing my breaths to shorten. "They don't have any evidence, so where are you getting this idea that there is a big chance of you losing the case?"

"I'm a Black man in America that has a judicial system that has never been fair to us. On top of that, although I have never been arrested, it's on paper that Kidd was about to set my organization up. Why risk spending the rest of my life in here when I can do the time and keep the radar off of my crew and my brothers? Besides, this is my fault. My brothers told me to stay away from you, but I didn't because I couldn't resist that phat ass." His snicker was an attempt to ease the blow, but it was in vain.

Tears blanketed my words. "Messiah..."

"Don't cry, baby." His words were soft with masculine energy.

"I can't help it." I inched over to a hallway that was out of view of those who could see me as they sat or stood in the baby shower.

"I don't want Shauka to see you crying because I don't want him to know any of this yet. Not with Jah being so sick."

Despite his gentle orders, I still began to weep.

Messiah sighed with regret. He always hated to hear my tears. Ironically, he felt responsible for them.

"You can't take that deal. You can't go to prison, Messiah. I need you. I'm lost without you. This last week has been hell for me. And the kids…" Mentioning them made the tears flow with urgency. "They miss you so much."

"I miss them too. I'm thinking about doing this for y'all too. I'd rather you miss me for a few years than twenty-five."

My head lowered, causing my big bang to fall into my face. My tears traced the blonde strands.

Messiah sighed. "Is Faye there?" He was attempting to change the subject, but I continued to weep. He gently called for me. "Tory…"

"Humph?" I mumbled, my cries causing my voice to crack.

"Talk to me, baby. I don't have that long on the phone."

Every time he called me baby was like being tied down to an electric chair.

I pushed past my hurt and need. "Yes, she's here."

"How she say Jah is doing?"

I cringed, hating to give him bad news. "Worse. It's bad, Messiah."

He groaned a breath. "Shit."

"It's his asthma. COVID is worse for asthma patients. That's why they encouraged people with pre-existing conditions to get vaccinated. It's his lungs that are the problem at this point. He's having a lot of trouble breathing. Faye says that all he does is sleep."

Messiah scoffed. "Jah thought like most Black folks that the vaccine was a set-up or some shit."

"Yeah, I know. He'll be okay, though," I spoke positively.

"Yeah, he will." Coupled with a sigh, he asked, "Can you take the phone to Shauka?"

"Okay."

"No. I mean, *can* you? Are you still crying?"

I patted my face dry, trying not to mess up my makeup. "No."

"Good girl."

Hearing that, my loins quivered, yearning for his touch, his penetration.

"Take him the phone so I can holla at him."

"Okay."

I hurried into the room. My eyes scanned it for Shauka. I found his thick, long, curly mane standing at the bar. I inched over the slippery stone flooring toward him. Once in arm's reach, I handed him the phone. "It's Messiah."

He took the phone as he took his drink from the bartender with his other hand. As he walked away, Queen approached me with sternness in her eyes.

"Hey, Queen."

"Come here," she said, motioning for me to follow her out of the room. "I need to talk to you."

SHAUKA DISCIPLE

"What up, bro?"

I took a relaxing breath as I sat on a bench in the lobby. "*Shiiid*. At this baby shower in disbelief."

"Why is that?" Messiah asked.

"I'm about to be a father. It just got real."

"It *just* got real?"

"I guess since me and Yaz had been hiding it, it didn't feel that real. But with everybody talking to me about being a father and watching Yaz open all these gifts, it got real as fuck."

I had been connecting with my baby. The safest, most calming place on earth for me was right up against Yaz's belly. I talked to her belly, hoping that my baby could hear my voice. As she got bigger, the baby would even move, proving that it did. But being at this shower, having everyone congratulate me, getting the pep talks from the men in our lives, it was really hitting me that I was about to become a father.

"You good?" Messiah probed.

"Yeah."

"I mean, are you *really* good with the Sariah bullshit."

I shrugged as if he could see me. "It is what it is. I feel stupid. But I'm not heartbroken. I don't even miss her."

With a laugh, Messiah replied, "I still can't believe Najia beat her ass like that."

I chuckled. "I can. They say the quiet ones are the most dangerous. Guess it's true."

Messiah scoffed humorously in agreement.

"Plus, she got a lot of pent-up anger because you're gone."

"I know," he responded sadly. "I call her every day to help her cope. I know it's still not the same as me being there, though. Is she still fucking with Nardo?"

I shook my head, grinning at his persistence. He was locked up with no bond facing a murder charge, but he was still obsessed with Nardo linking with Najia.

"I assume so. But since your arrest, she's been at home a lot more."

Anger seeped into his tone. "Have y'all hollered at that nigga yet?"

"You already know he's good with me and Jah."

"But he ain't good with me," he griped.

"He *should be*, Messiah," I pressed.

"Man, fuck that. Our sister tried to kill herself, and he didn't even tell us."

"But he saved her. He took care of her. He gets mad respect from me for that."

"He should have told us."

"No, *she* should have told us, especially you. So, your frustrations are pointed toward the wrong person."

Messiah sucked his teeth. "So, we're still going to serve that nigga?"

I groaned. "I'm not thinking about that shit right now, Messiah. I got a lot on my mind with you locked up and Jah being so sick."

"And with your baby coming," he added.

"Yeah." The mention of my child caused my lips to curve upward. It felt so unfamiliar to smile since it had been so hard to for the last week.

"So, now that Sariah is out of the picture, did you tell Yaz how you really feel?"

I shook my head at my reluctance. "I had the chance to. She asked me how I was so calm about what had happened. I wanted to tell her that it was because I always preferred to be with her, that I would rather marry her. But I just couldn't say it."

"Why?"

Suddenly, I felt an anxious feeling when I thought of Yaz. I had previously been so certain of how I felt about her. Now, I was unsure. "I don't trust my own judgment anymore. Despite her being my second choice, I could have sworn that I knew Sariah. Nobody could have told me any different about her. And I was so wrong. I can be wrong about Yaz, especially since she was cool with us ending things sexually."

"I feel that."

Talking to Messiah was a reminder that he was away. The distance was crippling. Me and my brothers had purposely been tight because of the destruction of our family after our parents' death. Now, it felt like I was mourning the loss of Messiah *and* Jah.

My next breath came out hard and long as I brought my elbows to my knees. "Jah is in bad shape."

Messiah sighed. "Tory told me."

"We need to take him to the hospital."

"It's that bad?" he pried, reluctance in his tone.

My heart ached as I revealed. "He can't breathe, bro."

"*Fuck*," Messiah barked in desperation.

"But I'm scared that if we take him to the hospital, they are going to intubate him. And that's the one thing we don't want. People don't come back after that shit."

"Aye, stop talking like this. He's strong. He got this, man."

I shook my head, attempting to shake off the truth. Because it was facts that Jah was declining rapidly. During the pandemic, I had been exposed to the different types of COVID cases. Queen and Buck had contracted it, and so had many of my friends. Most of them were asymptomatic. Queen and Buck were the more concerning cases since they were older and not the healthiest, considering their age and eating habits. But they had gotten through what felt like a severe flu to them. But through grapevines and social media, I had heard of the different types of COVID cases. Jah's case was similar to the ones that ended untimely.

"Anyway," I sighed, pushing past the grim reality. "Enough of that bullshit. How you holding up in there?"

"Man, besides wanting to be with my family and my bitch, this shit is a cake walk. I'm in here with all the homies." His chuckle was so light and airy that I feared he was getting way too comfortable behind bars. "Shit, even some of the correctional officers fuck with a nigga. We can do some business in this bitch."

"You ain't gon' be in there long enough for that shit."

His silence was deafening.

"*Right?*" I pressed.

His deafening silence lingered, but he eventually answered, "Right."

CHAPTER 6

JAH DISCIPLE

O pening my eyes was as painful as every breath that I took. But when I did, the vision before me made me inhale with boisterous fear.

"Dad?! Mama?!" I called out, my words trembling.

My father's tall, wide build strolled toward the foot of my bed. My mother glided next to him, holding his hand.

Taking in the sight of my father was prodigious. I had seen him in my dreams so many times over the years. But to see him now, in what appeared to be in person, was momentous. I was a reflection of him, and that made me proud. I was his twin, despite our drastic difference in skin tones. We shared the same dark, bushy brows, and thick, curly hair. He and I kept ours in a low cut, layered with deep waves, when Shauka had traditionally kept his long and wild since he was little because that's how my mother liked it. My father's beard was as lustrous and full as mine, with the same dark, curly hair on our heads.

We shared the same mass as well, which caused the mattress to shift as he sat at the foot of my bed. Smiling, my mother sat on his lap. She was so beautiful that my eyes began to water. Just as in my dreams, seeing her was like looking at Najia's big sister. My mother's smooth dark skin made her brown eyes glow. Her hair was still in the long box braids that she had worn during our last family trip to Mississippi. They hung low, stopping at the curve of her hips.

"I missed you, Mama." My eyes began to tear up.

Her smile was so loving and adoring as she sat on my father's lap and looped her arm around his neck. "I missed you too, baby."

I looked up at Faye. She was sitting next to me with tears streaming down her face. But I turned away from her and looked at my parents with pride blanketing my eyes.

"Mama, Dad, this is my girlfriend, Faye."

"She's beautiful," my mother beamed.

"Yeah, she's a winner," my dad added. "She loves you unconditionally."

I scoffed with a smile. "How you know?"

My dad's head tilted dramatically. "C'mon. I'm always watching."

I cringed with a playful, guilty smirk. "Always?"

"*Naaah*," my father sang lowly as he shook his head with an uncomfortable smirk.

My mother giggled. "We're watching when it counts. It was so hard to watch you suffer in the streets, baby. I'm sorry that we weren't here to protect you from those awful foster parents and homes that you ended up in."

The mention of it made my father's eyes grow dark with sadness and rage.

"But you took such good care of Shauka. We were so proud of you," my mother said.

My father nodded in agreement, the darkness of his eyes immediately growing light. "You did good, son."

"*So* good," my mother insisted. "But I wanna tell you something."

My eyes widened with interest. "What?"

"Don't feel so responsible for them. You need to live your life, baby," my mother said softly. "You've done your job."

"And you did a great job," my father injected. "Admittedly, a better job than I would have done."

"Exactly," my mother agreed. "You were an exceptional guardian to Shauka. You ensured that you all kept in touch with Messiah and Najia."

I kissed my teeth, interjecting, "I failed Najia."

"*No*. No, you didn't," my father insisted.

"Predators are everywhere, baby," my mother told me. "They lie in wait, hunting for vulnerable prey. Najia was vulnerable. She was soft-spoken and quiet. You could not have saved her because she would have never told you. But you see how she bossed up on that mother-fucka?!" My mother's full lips spread into a pleased smile. "My baby popped that ass!"

The three of us laughed. Yet, as my eyes wandered up to Faye, she was still sadly crying.

I looked back toward my parents, noticing that my father's laughter had been replaced with a stoic expression. "And you and your brothers got her justice. You all did the same thing I would have done. I'm so proud of you, son. You're handling this family and our business like I would, *exactly* like I would. And don't let not nary a motherfucker tell you any different."

That made my heart swell with pride.

FAYE SINGER

"Please stop crying," Chloe softly begged.

"I can't. It's getting bad, Chloe." My voice cracked as the words found their way out around whimpers. "He hardly opened his eyes since last night. He only moans because it's so hard for him to breathe. Each breath looks like it hurts. His chest literally caves in with every painful intake of air. He barely speaks, and when he does, he sounds confused and disoriented."

I sat on the top stair, a few feet outside of Jah's room. My elbows were on my knees as one hand held my face, my tears saturating my palm. With the other hand, I held my phone close to the side of my face so that I could speak without Hattie hearing me as she sat with Jah.

I'd had to leave Jah's bedroom. When I'd walked into his bedroom after returning early from the shower, I was so happy to see his eyes open. But when he began to speak, he was talking to his parents as if they were in the room with us. He was smiling with light in his eyes. He'd even reached for them.

That was only confirmation that he was declining into a state that many COVID patients didn't return from.

"He's going to be okay."

"He's having delusions, Chloe. He was just talking to his parents. He had a full-blown conversation with them."

She sucked her teeth. "Shit."

I wanted to believe that he would be okay. I *needed* to believe that. But I knew what his current symptoms meant. It had been almost two weeks since he'd fallen sick. It was the time that most COVID patients' symptoms began to subside. Yet, Jah was only getting worse. It was so bad that I hadn't wanted to attend the baby shower that day. But Hattie assured me that she would be by Jah's side until I returned. I believed her because she had remained by his bedside since he started to decline. She catered to his every need. So, I got dressed reluctantly and went to the baby shower. But I had left before it was over because I was so worried about Jah.

Now, his symptoms were coupled with delusions, making the outcome potentially catastrophic.

"His room... this house... everything feels so morbid," I cried.

"That's because there is a lot of fear and loss in that house. I'm sure Messiah's absence and Jah's sickness are very scary for everyone, especially for his siblings. They've already been through so much loss and tragedy."

I cringed. She was right. And every time I thought about it, my heart painfully went out to them. Najia was a mess. She had hardly said a word at the baby shower. That ass whooping she had given Sariah wasn't even meant for Sariah. That was anger and resentment that was boiling over in Najia because she felt like she was losing her brothers. Shauka seemed to be operating on auto pilot. He was physically at the baby shower, but mentally, he was very absent.

Suddenly, the front door opened. I watched as Shauka and Najia fought their way through the door with a plethora of gift bags. Shauka had been stocking his bedroom with so many baby clothes that it was mirroring a nursery at this point.

They headed toward the stairway, but when they realized that I was there, when they saw my tear-soaked face, they froze.

"Let me call you back, Chloe."

"Okay," she said reluctantly.

I hung up, my heart hammering against my chest fearfully.

"What?" Shauka asked, nostrils flaring.

Najia's eyes bore into mine with reluctance and terror.

"It's... it's..." My cries caused me to stutter. A gate of fear and resistance suddenly appeared at the base of my throat, making it difficult for me to get the words out. "It's time to take him to the hospital."

Their shoulders sank. Their heads lowered. The gift bags dropped to the tile of the foyer.

We had all regretted this. We knew that in Jah's state, if he was admitted, he might not come back.

YAZMEEN HILL

The next day, I was clinging to Shauka's hand as we stood leaning against the wall in Jah's room in the ICU. Since he had surpassed the window of contagiousness, we had been allowed to visit him. The waiting room was filled with his crew, family, and loved ones. Since only three people were allowed to visit at a time, Shauka and I were taking our turns because Faye rarely left his side.

Since I had been a nurse during the height of the pandemic in this very hospital, looking at Jah, I knew that his prognosis was grim. His oxygen level was dangerously low. His delusions were haunting.

As Shauka had been telling me the details of his symptoms the last few days, I knew that Jah would need to be hospitalized soon. So, I was grateful when Shauka called yesterday after the baby shower and let me know that he was trailing the ambulance that was carrying Jah to the hospital. He was admitted right away, and oxygen therapy was started immediately.

Since then, we had been clinging to the hope that he would respond to the therapy so that he wouldn't have to be intubated. The benefits of intubation outweighed the risks. However, during the pandemic, it was as if intubation sealed the ruinous fate of the patient.

"Mumph," I groaned, getting Faye and Shauka's concerned attention.

Shauka's head whipped toward me, concerned. "You still having contractions?"

"You're having contractions?!" Faye blurted.

"They are only Braxton Hicks contractions." I winced, rubbing my hand soothingly along my pelvic.

"But you've been having them since last night," Shauka reminded me as if I didn't know.

"Shauka, I'm a nurse. I'm telling you that... *Oh!*" Suddenly, a crippling pain caused me to yelp. I bent over, bracing myself with my hands on my knees.

"Oh my God," Faye shrieked, springing to her feet.

"I'm okay," I insisted.

"No, you're not," Faye said desperately as she rounded the bed. "You're bleeding, Yaz!"

NAJIA DISCIPLE

Luckily, Nardo hadn't been able to attend the baby shower. But unfortunately, he was now walking through the door of the family waiting area of the ICU.

"Shit," I mumbled under my breath.

I lowered my head as if that would prevent him from seeing him. Despite the news playing loudly on the mounted television in the room, I heard him speak to Frey, Chris, Codey, and Koop. Peeking while slightly lifting my head, I watched as he hugged a somber Queen. Since entering the waiting area, Buck had been tight-lipped. But I saw the shame in his eyes, which he deserved. He had been treating my brother like shit for months. And although we all played the middle because we wanted our makeshift family to stay intact, I took offense to his sudden sympathy now that my brother was in the hospital.

Finally, Nardo began the short distance toward me. Suddenly, rocks of anxiety formed in my throat, leaving me speechless. Realizing that the chair next to me was free, I cringed inwardly.

I had missed him over the week that I hadn't been under him. But the fear of what his eyes had promised me the last time I'd seen him outweighed my desire for him.

Nardo sat down in the chair next to me, looking at me with an expression that was unreadable.

"Hi," I spoke hesitantly.

"What's up? What are they saying about Jah?"

"We're waiting to see if he responds to the oxygen therapy."

He nodded. Then he looked around, scoping the room, until he leaned into me. "Why have you been dodging me?"

"I haven't been dodging you. I've just been busy. I have a lot on my mind."

He scoffed quietly. "C'mon now, Najia. Don't play me."

"What?" I acted innocently. "I'm not."

He shook his head. "Okay."

"I'm dealing with a lot, Nardo."

Suddenly, my phone, which I was gripping in my hand, started to vibrate. I looked down at it and rolled my eyes when I saw that it was Karen.

I declined the call, hoping that Nardo hadn't seen her name on the screen.

Thankfully, it seemed that he hadn't. "I know that you're going through a lot, but you don't have to go through this alone."

"It's not your responsibility to help me through this. We're not in a relationship. Fuck buddies don't help each other through a crisis."

His eyes showed his offense. "Oh, so you're only on some fuck shit. You're cool with me using your body, but when I try to connect with you outside of the pussy, you're good?"

"I didn't say that."

Nardo chuckled sarcastically. "You might not have said it exactly like that, but it's definitely what the fuck you mean."

I couldn't breathe. The hurt in his eyes was unbearable. He sat back, jaws tight, nostrils pulsating with frustration and anger.

Why did he care this much? Why did he want to be there for me?

The anxiety was too much to bear. I suddenly stood up and marched toward the door.

"You good, baby girl?" Buck asked behind my back.

"I'm fine. I just need some air." My steps were long and swift. Once I was outside of that room, breathing and the ability to focus were much less complicated.

I felt so immature for abruptly leaving. But I didn't know any other way to handle Nardo. He was too much for me. I wasn't used to the overbearing presence of care and attention. I had only gotten that from Karen and my brother. I had never received it from a man I was intimate with.

As I rounded a corner, I wondered where the hell I was going. I looked back to see if Nardo had followed me and was relieved that I only saw an empty hallway behind me.

"Oh, God!" The sudden wailing screech caused my head to whip ahead of me. My eyes narrowed, trying to take in the scene of Shauka holding Yaz up as she was barely able to walk.

I ran toward them. "What's going on?"

Shauka appeared so scared and helpless as he looked toward me. "She's having contractions, and she's bleeding."

"Shit!" I gasped.

"We need to get her to the emergency room," he rushed.

Suddenly, Faye jutted from around a corner, pushing a wheelchair with frenzy contorting her face. She and I met in the middle and rushed toward Shauka and Yaz. I shrank when I saw the blood smearing Yaz's jeans. She cried as Shauka and I helped her into the wheelchair.

"It's going to be okay, Yaz," Shauka persuaded her as he began to bolt down the hallway with the wheelchair. "Okay? You hear me?"

She only offered him cries and whimpering in response.

CHAPTER 7

YAZMEEN HILL

Uterine bleeding had caused me to go into labor early. An ultrasound had revealed placental abruption. The placenta had completely separated from my uterus. That had caused the bleeding and triggered preterm labor.

"*Arrrrgh*!!" The scream that exploded out of my throat was so powerful that I could feel my tonsils rattling. "Oh *shiiiiit*!"

"Breathe, Yaz," Shauka coached me. Standing beside me, he was dabbing my dewy forehead with a cold towel.

"*Fuuuuuck*!" I growled.

"You're doing so good, Yaz," my nurse, Mona, told me as she held my legs wide open. "Push, push, push, push, *push*!"

"*Arrrrgh*!!"

Mona peered between my legs, where Shauka refused to look. Then she brought her eyes back to me and smiled. "I see hair!"

"Okay, Yaz. The contraction is subsiding, so you can stop pushing for a few seconds," Dr. Alexander said from her seated position between my legs. The OB tech stood closely by, ready to assist if needed.

"Mumph!" I slumped with a grunt. I was heaving as I reveled in the relief of the pain easing.

I looked up at Shauka, who was wearing such a proud smile. He had been terribly upset when I was bleeding in the ER that I thought he would get kicked out of the trauma room. They had been able to quickly identify what was happening. I was indeed in labor. They then rushed me up to labor and delivery. Faye and Najia had gone back up to ICU. Since I'd arrived in my room and changed into my gown, Shauka had been very attentive, catering, and encouraging. My heart swelled with more love for him with every inspiring word. With each massaging touch to my neck, I fell deeper in love.

"All right!" Mona exclaimed excitedly. "Let's get this baby out. Push, Yaz!"

Shauka helped me sit up a bit just as the next contraction began to stab my pelvis and back.

"*Fuuuck!*" I growled.

"Push, Yaz! Push!" Mona encouraged me.

I held onto my knees, closed my eyes, bit down on my bottom lip, and pushed with all my might while roaring like an enraged beast.

"You're doing great!" Mona said.

"The shoulders are out," Dr. Alexander announced. "Push, push, push, push, *push*!"

I could feel Shauka's large hand on my back, rubbing it soothingly as he spoke into my ear, "You're doing a good job. You got this."

"*Arrrrgh!*" I howled.

Then, suddenly, I felt such an amount of relief that it made me collapse onto my back.

My baby was out.

"What? What is it?" I was short of breath and weak.

"Dad?" Dr. Alexander addressed Shauka with a smile. "Why don't you come cut the umbilical cord so that you can tell Yazmeen the gender of you all's beautiful baby."

Shauka's smile was boyish and adorable. I had never seen him so timid. Our child was already humbling him.

He was still reluctant as he left my side to stand next to the doctor. He had always told me that he would be in the room during my delivery, but he didn't want to see the baby coming out. However, as soon as he stood next to Dr. Alexander and looked down on the baby in her arms, all that recollection went out of the window. His smile was so bright that his cheeks pressed against his eyes.

"It's a *boy!*" His words cracked as if he were holding back tears.

Immediately, I began to sob. A roller coaster of emotions barreled through me. Shauka looked at my tears with admiration, still wearing that prideful, boyish grin.

Dr. Alexander handed him the scissors and instructed him how to cut the umbilical cord. I smiled weakly, still barely able to breathe. He followed her instructions with such care and determination. His eyes glazed over with unshed tears once he clipped the cord.

He shot a wide grin my way. "He looks like me."

"He... He..." The shortness of breath was starting to worsen. "He doesn't look like anything yet." I then giggled faintly.

Shauka watched with protective intent as Mona took our baby boy from Dr. Alexander. She then wrapped him in a blue blanket and began to wipe him free of birthing residue covering his head and face.

"Here you go, Mom." Mona smiled from one ear to the other as she inched toward the bed, holding my baby carefully.

Tears clouded my vision as she nestled him between my arm and chest. Weeping, I kissed the top of his head. The unwavering bond between my son and me formed while I was carrying him in my womb. I immediately wondered how my parents could have ever abandoned me. Now that my baby was here in my arms, I most definitely couldn't fathom how any mother or father could look into their child's eyes and do anything except go over and beyond all efforts to be in such an innocent soul's life forever.

I was already in love with my son.

Shauka stood next to me, bending over so far that he might as well have gotten in the bed with me. Witnessing his adoration for his son submerged me deeper into the infatuation and love I already had for him.

But I couldn't focus on him or my son anymore. I was a nurse. I knew when something was wrong. And there was nothing right about the way that it was becoming more and more difficult for me to breathe.

"Something's wrong." I began to panic. "Here. Take the baby."

Shauka's brow furrowed with worry as he took the baby from me.

"Damn it!" I heard Dr. Alexander spit. I then felt her hand inside of me. "She's bleeding from the uterus!"

Dr. Alexander watched me, eyes narrowed with deep interest. "Yaz, what's—"

Insistent beeping interrupted her concern. The monitors I was connected to started to wail in alarm.

Mona and Dr. Alexander rushed toward the machines, forcing Shauka away from my side and toward the foot of the bed.

"Her blood pressure is way too low," Dr. Alexander said, raising everyone's anxiety.

"What's wrong with her?!" Shauka barked.

Suddenly, I felt faint. My heart was pounding against my chest as my anxiety exploded. Something was terribly wrong.

I tried to communicate what I was feeling, but I couldn't speak. Suddenly, my limbs began to twitch wildly just as everything became dark.

SHAUKA DISCIPLE

"Seizure!" Mona alerted frantically.

Watching Yaz in a medical crisis was crippling. I felt so helpless. I could only stand there, clinging to my son.

The OB tech, doctor, and nurse quickly surrounded Yaz, making it hard for me to see her. They repositioned her on her side. Mona then put something in her mouth.

"Do something!" I ordered. "Help her! Make her stop."

They ignored me, tossing medical terminology between one another that I couldn't understand. I could only stare on frantically, waiting for them to tell me something... any damn thing.

Without warning, the door barged open. Two other nurses rushed in as more beeping erupted from Yaz's monitors. I put all of my weight on the wall behind me, trying to remain standing. But the sight of so many people surrounding Yaz and the sounds of the monitoring devices were grim. It gave me anxiety that I recalled feeling when I was a little boy when I thought of my parents dying in that crash and whenever I would hear my abusive foster mother coming. It was like the dread I experienced when the biting wind and snow surrounded me and Jah as we wondered where we would sleep for the night.

"Sir!"

Blinking uncontrollably, I realized that a nurse was standing in front of me wide-eyed. "Huh?"

"We need you to leave the room," she urged.

Scowling, I sucked my teeth. "Hell no! I ain't goin' nowhere."

"Please, sir, you need to leave the room so we can help her."

All the supportive and protective senses that defined my manhood were disabled as she took my son from me.

"We're going to take the baby to the NICU," she explained.

"NICU?!" I panicked. "Something's wrong with him too?!"

She breathed impatiently. "Since he is premature, its protocol to monitor him in the NICU. But he looks healthy. Please go to the waiting room, and we will update you as soon as we can."

"What's happening to her? What's wrong?" I asked with my eyes fixed on a now unconscious Yaz. Blood was pouring from between her legs that had fallen out of the stirrups during her seizure.

"As soon as we figure that out, we will let you know. Now, *please* go to the waiting area."

I kept my eyes on Yaz as I reluctantly inched toward the door. But all I could see was people surrounding her, frantically moving and speaking as if they were trying to save her life.

"What the hell is an amniotic fluid embolism?" I hadn't meant to be so direct with Mona, but I was far past frustration at this point. I had been sitting in the waiting room for what felt like forever, but it had actually only been about fifteen minutes before Mona finally hurried in.

"It's a birth complication, most likely derived from uterine bleeding. It is an allergic-like reaction to the amniotic fluid that enters the mother's bloodstream."

I blinked rapidly, trying to understand everything that she was attempting to explain. "Is she going to be okay?"

"We had to give her an emergency blood transfusion, and now Dr. Alexander is rushing her to surgery."

"Surgery?!" I repeated with bucked eyes. "Why?"

"Her heart stopped—"

"What the fuck?!" I sprang to my feet, causing Mona's eyes to bounce around in concern.

She lifted her hands, palms facing me in an effort to stop my rage-filled outburst. "But we were able to resuscitate her."

"So, she can die?" I asked, breathless.

Mona exhaled hesitantly. "Amniotic fluid embolism can be fatal in some patients, but—"

I collapsed down into my chair, feeling like my heart wouldn't make its next beat.

"But we are doing everything that we can. We need to stop the bleeding."

"What? I mean... how..." My head was in shambles. I had so many questions, but fear kept me from forming a coherent sentence.

"I really have to go assist Dr. Alexander. I will be back with an update as soon as I can."

Frozen in my dismay, I was only able to nod extremely slowly. She pressed her lips into a reluctant stripe as she nodded and then darted out of the room. I lowered my head. Suddenly, a wave of nausea rumbled through my stomach.

"Shauka?!"

My head shot up when I heard Najia's voice. Once I was put out of the delivery room, I called Najia but didn't get an answer. So, I had sent a text message telling her where I was and that I needed her. I assumed that she had finally gotten it.

"Oh my God!" she said pitifully as she stalked toward me with worry all over her face. "What's going on? Have they told you anything?"

"The nurse just left. They are taking her into surgery."

Najia's eyes stretched dramatically as she slowly sat in the seat next to me. "Surgery for what?"

"To stop the bleeding." I could hear the fear in my shaky tone. "After having the baby, she couldn't breathe. The machines started going crazy. Then they said her blood pressure was too low. She was bleeding so much." My spheres were blurry as I looked at Najia.

Sympathy poured from beyond her long lashes. She put an arm around me and assured me, "She's going to be okay."

"Her heart stopped," I sadly revealed.

Najia's jaw dropped as her hand went to her chest. "Oh, God."

"They were able to resuscitate her, but Mona admitted that her condition could be fatal."

Najia sighed and looped her arm with mine. She then leaned her head on my shoulder. "We gotta think positive. She's going to make it out of this."

But it didn't feel like it. With so much grief and loss unfolding in this family, it was hard to be positive that this wouldn't be yet another burden that I would have to bear.

"Did I tell you it's a boy?" Tears came to my eyes as I looked at my sister. Then I began to sob in a way that I hadn't since I was a young boy. I had just been embarrassed in front of all of my friends and family by the woman I was willing to give my last name to. Yet, I hadn't shed a tear. My heart never ached.

Now, I could feel each painful rip as my heart broke into a million pieces.

DETECTIVE FREEMONT

"Freemont!"

I cringed when Captain Martin belted out my name from the doorway of his office.

"Yeah?" I called out without taking my eyes off my computer.

"Get in here!"

Shit.

I reluctantly stood from my desk and made my way. I knew I hadn't done anything wrong. But I was investigating so many murder cases that I was backlogged. I knew he was about to tear me a new one because I wasn't closing these cases fast enough.

"Yeah, Captain?" I asked as I walked into his office.

"The DA called. They want to solidify the evidence for the Disciple case next month. Have you been able to locate the informant?"

I cringed inwardly, but on the outside, I remained indifferent. "Not yet."

Since Messiah's court case was next month, it was imperative that I locate Moe so he could testify. However, each stone that I had turned over had only proven that Moe had gone missing. He hadn't answered any of my calls. His wife hadn't seen or heard from him since the day I took his statement.

Sucking his teeth, Captain Martin sat back in his big reclining chair behind his desk. "Isn't the Clark girl coming in to talk to you?"

"Yeah, in a few minutes, actually."

I was surprised when I got a call from Tory telling me that she wanted to meet with me today.

"I'm sure that Moe won't testify against him. So, let's hope that she provides some solid evidence to hold up this charge."

"I doubt that. She's beyond loyal to Messiah."

"Well, get her to turn!" he roared. "We need something solid."

"I have footage of him going to the house soon after the murder." Finally, I had convinced one of Tory's neighbors to provide me with footage from their Ring camera of Messiah coming and going from Tory's house soon after Kidd's murder. He was only willing to because he felt that it was safe since he was moving back to his homeland of Jamaica soon.

Captain Martin's beady eyes rolled. "That's not enough to win the case."

"I'm still scouring the surveillance footage from all of the businesses in that area on the night of the murder."

Captain Martin jeered. "That'll be like finding a needle in a haystack. Most of those shoddy businesses don't even have cameras." He blew out a frustrated breath. "Get the girl to talk and then talk to the DA. We need to offer Messiah an even better deal so we can close this case."

I managed to hold back my grimace until I agreed and excused myself from his office. The politics of the police department often made it very hard to thoroughly do my job. The higher-ups were always more concerned about numbers than real police work. It was more important to get a suspect to take a deal than to get the real evidence to put them away for the time they truly deserved.

No sooner than I sat back down at my desk, the phone rang. Looking at the Caller ID, I saw that it was reception.

"Yeah, Tracy?" I answered.

"Tory Clark is here to see you."

"Put her in investigation room three."

"Okay."

I lingered at my desk a bit before going to the investigation room. I had given up getting any information from Tory. I was fine with finding other concrete evidence to secure the DA's case. But since she had requested this meeting, there was a small chance of hope that she had finally come to her senses.

When I opened the door, I actually sympathized with Tory. The life that was once in her eyes was now gone. Her expression was filled with despair and sadness. It was clear that Messiah's arrest had taken a toll on her. But that was the life these women chose to suffer when falling in love with street guys.

"Tory," I greeted stoically as I closed the door behind myself.

"Hi," she spit with irritation as if *I* had summoned *her*.

The tension between us was suffocating. I sat down in it, across from her on the other side of the table. Her eyes defiantly bore into mine. She despised me. I was the woman who had been adamant about taking her boyfriend away from her. But I felt no sympathy for her. She wouldn't be in that chair had she made better choices with her vagina.

"What can I help you with, Miss Clark?"

"I'm ready to make a statement."

I fought to remain aloof, but my insides were jumping for joy. "And that is?"

She exhaled long and hard, nervously bouncing her foot as it crossed over her leg. "You were right all of this time. I knew that Messiah killed Kidd."

I could no longer feign casualness. My eyebrow rose as I sat up, resting my elbows on the table. "And you're willing to testify to that?"

"Yes. Kidd used to beat the shit out of me. Everyone knew it, including his friends. Messiah was one of them. That night, he came over to my house to pick Kidd up. They were supposed to go somewhere together. I'm not sure where." She shrugged. "Anyway, he walked in on Kidd beating the hell out of me. He had me against the wall, choking me. I was about to pass out until Messiah came in and pushed him off of me. Kidd was high off of pills, so he was even willing to fight Messiah too. Messiah was getting the best of him. That's when Kidd pulled his gun, but Messiah was quicker. He shot Kidd before Kidd could shoot him."

My head tilted. That story smelled like grade-A, top-tier bullshit. I scoffed with a chastising chuckle.

"When I first interviewed you, you said that there were three men that came in that night."

"I made that up," she explained.

"So, if it was self-defense, why wouldn't he wait for the police to get there? Why didn't you just tell me the truth?"

She sucked her teeth. "C'mon now. Messiah has never been in trouble as an adult, but he is still a Black man who is the product of the streets. We were scared of what is happening to him *right now*. I'm only telling you the truth now with the hope that it will downgrade his charge and his sentence. He killed Kidd in self-defense."

I sat back, taking in her disposition. She looked sincere, but this all felt like a lie. "Is that *really* what happened?"

She nodded confidently. "Yep. And it's what I'm willing to testify to."

SHAUKA DISCIPLE

Yaz had thankfully survived the embolism.

"Because she is so young, I attempted every measure possible to avoid performing a hysterectomy. Thankfully, the blood transfusions and a procedure to compress the arteries to the uterus saved Yaz's life and her uterus." With that, Dr. Alexander smiled.

"Thank you," I barely said above a whisper as I stared at a sleeping Yaz.

"I'm on call tonight, so if there are any issues, I will be right in. But I don't foresee any."

I nodded as Dr. Alexander smiled and left out of the room.

Despite the good news, my heart was still racing as fast as it had been as I waited for her to come out of surgery. It felt like my heart was about to burst out of my chest. My hands were shaking, and I couldn't seem to catch my breath. I was standing at the foot of Yaz's hospital bed, looking at her still form, and I couldn't shake the feeling that something terrible was about to happen.

I knew that she had just come out of surgery, and her doctor had said everything went well, but I couldn't help but feel like she was still in danger.

I couldn't lose her.

Not now.

Not ever.

My vision started to blur, and I felt like I was about to pass out. I tried to slow my breathing, but it felt like I was suffocating. I needed to get out of there, but I couldn't leave her side.

I was trapped, and the panic was overwhelming.

I closed my eyes and tried to focus on something, anything, but my mind was racing too fast. I was spiraling out of control, and I didn't know how to stop it.

Then, a soft hand touched mine, and I opened my eyes to see her nurse, Mona, standing beside me.

She looked at me with kind eyes." She's going to be okay. Take deep breaths and just focus on the fact that she's okay. She needs you. You can do this."

She squeezed my hand before letting it go and walking toward the monitors. As she checked the vitals on each one, I allowed her words to ground me. I took a deep breath, trying to slow my racing heart. I looked at Yaz, reminding myself that, unlike Jah, we were certain that she would be okay.

She needs me. I need to be strong for her.

But that was the problem. Suddenly, everyone around me was leaning on me. Suddenly, I was the head of two families because everyone else was falling apart.

"She's going to be heavily medicated for a day or so to help with the pain," Mona explained as she walked away from the machines. "But, other than that, she's okay."

Mona smiled into my eyes as she left the room. I fought to keep my composure, holding on tightly to the rails at the foot of the bed.

But no sooner than the door latch closed, I crumbled.

I was gasping for air, my heart pounding so hard I feared it would stop beating. I couldn't breathe, and my hands were shaking so badly I couldn't hold on to anything. So, I dropped to my knees.

I didn't know what was happening. I'd never felt like this before. Sure, I'd been scared at times, but this was different. This was like my brain was short-circuiting, like I was losing control.

I tried to calm myself down, but it was like I was suffocating. And then, when I thought it couldn't get any worse, it did.

Unable to withstand the pressure anymore, I hollered and groaned into my hands until tears came to my eyes.

The constant thoughts of the loss of my parents, of potentially losing Jah, of Messiah being gone made the panic explode. I couldn't lose anyone else, not after losing my parents. I felt like I was drowning, like I was being swallowed up by my own fear.

The visions of Yaz's having that seizure danced in my head, causing fear to grip me like a vice.

What if I lose her? What if Jah dies? What if Messiah loses his case?

The thoughts were too much to bear, and the panic kept hitting me over and over again, harder each time.

A FEW DAYS LATER...

CHAPTER 8

SHAUKA DISCIPLE

"He's such a cutie pie to only be a few days old."

Sitting next to my son's bassinet in the NICU, I was approached by one of the NICU nurses, Brenda, ogling him. Over the last few days, I had gotten to know all of the nurses in the NICU since I had been hanging around so much. I had even gotten them something to eat and other treats to ensure that they had a special interest in taking care of my son. Thankfully, he was healthy, but because he was born prematurely, he was in the NICU for monitoring.

"Yeah, he is." My lil' homie was already a replica of his dad. He had a head full of dark hair. He had the same heavy-lidded eyes as I had. He currently was a bit brighter than Yaz's pale skin. Yet, another nurse had looked at his ears and assured me that because of the color of them, his skin color would possibly be as chocolate as mine.

"Have you figured out a name yet?" Brenda asked.

"Nah, not yet." I hadn't been able to come up with a name without Yaz. I had never imagined that I would have to. Yet, things had taken a drastic turn. Life had been proving to me over and over again that I could prepare for the worst, but the unimaginable could still come out of nowhere.

Brenda's head tilted as a sympathetic frown graced her lips. "Well, you better hurry up. We're going to need a name to put on the birth certificate. I hear he will be able to go home soon."

"Really?!" That excited Yaz, who was sitting on the other side of the bassinet. She was leaning out of her wheelchair and into the bassinet, stuffing her finger into his tiny fist.

"Yes. I heard the doctor suggesting that he should be able to go home next week. His weight looks good, and so do his vitals. As long as his temperature remains normal, he should be able to get out of here." Then the nurse smiled brighter as she watched Yaz. "And since his mom is a nurse, we are sure that you can watch out for any unforeseeable issues."

I watched tears pool in Yaz's eyes.

Brenda's frown deepened. She reached over and gave Yaz's shoulder a slight squeeze. Then she walked away.

My eyes couldn't find a target to focus on. Between Yaz and my son, I didn't know which one of them was a more inspiring and beautiful sight.

For the first two days after her surgery, she had been heavily medicated. So, I'd had to be a single parent, something I had never imagined I would have to do. I had even refused to come up with a name for our son until Yaz was awake. That hadn't occurred until today, the first time that Yaz had been able to lay eyes on our son since giving birth to him.

My ringtone pushed me to leave the ping pong game that my eyes were playing between my son and Yaz. There hadn't been much of anything that could pull me away from Yaz and the baby. I had only stepped away from them to lay eyes on Jah, who was a few floors above us. Other than that, I had been all in with fatherhood. It had been days since I had even conducted any of the crew's business. But, thankfully, Nardo and Frey had willingly stepped up in my absence.

Since the call was from Messiah, I stepped out and into the hall.

"What up, bro?" I answered.

"What up, *Pops?*"

I chuckled, pride all over my face.

"How is Yaz?" Messiah asked.

"She's up today. She's in the NICU with the baby right now."

"That's what's up," he said excitedly with relief.

I hated to have to tell Messiah everything that had happened when he called the night of the baby's birth. His absence from his family had been the main source of his bitterness while being locked up. We may not have been raised in the same household, but our bond was strong and unbreakable. Thus, it was devastating to Messiah that he couldn't be here for all of the torment that had unfolded since his arrest.

"Yeah, I'm so relieved." I sighed, feeling the ease return in my heartbeat. "I ain't never been that scared in my life. I didn't even have these feelings when I found out about Sariah."

"Because you were settling for that girl, but your heart longs for Yaz."

My brow wrinkled. *"Longs for?"*

"Yeah, I've been in here reading romance novels and shit. That's all we really got to pass the time besides playing cards. I've been reading all those hood love stories."

I chuckled. "Wow."

"You should tell Yaz how you feel, man."

"The pain that I felt in that waiting room, I never want to feel again. Loving somebody this much is too fucking painful when you can potentially lose them." A balloon expanded in my throat instantly. Saying those words made me think of Jah. "I can only afford to love my family this much. I can't take feeling this way for nobody else."

"Look, man, take it from me. Tomorrow isn't promised. One day, you can think you have all the time in the world. The next, your life can be taken away from you. You gotta live life like there is no tomorrow."

PROPERTY OF A RICH NIGGA 3

My eyes squinted inquiringly. He was speaking with such finality in his words that it worried me. "Aye, you good? When is your next court date?"

"Next week."

My eyes narrowed even more. He had been tight-lipped about his case for the last week, but I had been too engulfed with Jah, Yaz, and the baby to give it my attention. Now that some of my burdens had been lifted, I was able to see that Messiah was being way too lackadaisical about fighting a murder charge.

"What's your lawyer saying? Is she sure you will beat this?" I asked.

"Don't worry about me. You have too much to deal with out there. It'll all work out, bro."

FAYE SINGER

"I'll be back. I need to get some air."

Queen didn't pull her eyes away from Jah when she nodded slowly. "Take your time, baby. I know you're tired."

That was an understatement. I had been at the hospital since Jah was admitted. I had only gone to me and Chloe's condo to shower and change my clothes twice.

"I am," I told her with a sad, tired chuckle. "But I'll be back in a few. I'm going to go get something to eat. You want anything?"

She shook her head, eyes still on Jah. She had pulled a chair up next to his bed and was clinging to his hand with both of hers. "No, baby. I'm okay."

I nodded and left the room. Stepping out, I welcomed the untainted air. Even though the entire hospital smelled of the iodoform that they disinfected every surface with, the air outside of Jah's room was different. Inside, I felt suffocated. The air was drenched with despair and morbidity.

When Jah was first admitted, he had a revolving door of visitors. But after a few days, it was only me, Najia, Queen, Hattie, Greg, and Buck that took turns staying by his side. Everyone else had to go back to their regular lives. Shauka would come down whenever he managed to tear himself away from Yaz and the baby.

I had nowhere in particular that I wanted to go. I just needed air. So, once outside of the hospital, I welcomed the bitter February winds. Though it was nearly the end of the month, Chicago still wasn't in the clear. We often got snow in March, so there was no telling when spring would come. However, the cold was better than being in that depressing room with Jah. Every update from the doctor was grim. Jah was hardly responding to the oxygen therapy. Intubation had been mentioned. Since Jah wasn't married and didn't have any parents, it was up to Shauka, Messiah, and Najia to make that decision. But they wanted to give him time to respond to the therapy because we had all heard that intubation for many COVID patients led to eventual death.

I was drowning in misery. Watching Jah's demise was gut-wrenching. He was conscious, but he was submerged in confusion and delirium. He slept a lot. He was no longer the gentle giant that had rescued me. It was heartbreaking to witness him succumb helplessly to feebleness.

I walked slowly to my car, unfazed by the freezing temp. I welcomed the bite of it on my skin because I needed something to remind me that I was alive, to remind me of life.

Once I climbed into my car, I crumbled. I rested my forehead against the steering wheel and allowed myself to wail as loud as I wanted to. I cried out to God, asking him why this was happening. Selfishly, I was upset that I was being threatened with the loss of another man. Even though I was miserable with Doon, I'd had to mourn the loss of what we were when we first met so long ago. I had started grieving his loss way before he had died. Now, it was hard to believe that I wouldn't be grieving again.

Sudden ringing from my phone blared through the once-quiet car, causing me to jump out of my skin. I reached for it and answered quickly, just to stop the ringing. Looking at the phone, I saw that I had actually answered a call from my Instagram DM from a profile with no picture and a name I didn't recognize.

"Who the fuck is this?" I spit.

"Faye, don't hang up."

My eyes narrowed when I heard the female voice on the other end. "Who. Is. This.?"

"It's Mia."

I groaned, not worrying about if she could hear my reluctance. The only thing positive about Jah being so sick was that it kept me from obsessing over Mia and this baby she claimed was Jah's. Every now and then, the destructive thought would fight its way through my worry for Jah. But I was so consumed with praying for him to get better that I could hardly focus on the possibility that he could have fathered a child with my arch nemesis.

But now, she had all of my attention. I was more than happy to take my frustrations out on this hoe.

"Bitch—"

"Wait, Faye..." Her softness and sincerity quieted me. "I'm not on any bullshit. I promise." I had never heard her sound so humble.

"I've been trying to get in contact with Jah about doing a paternity test," she explained in a panicky voice. "But I can't reach him."

No one can.

"Why do you need a paternity test? I thought you said that it was Jah's baby," I quipped. "Oh, you just said that to fuck with me."

"It's a possibility, Faye. I'm sorry, but it is. I didn't think that it was. But now that the baby is here and growing, my guy started to question paternity. Me and my guy were on a break when I fucked Jah."

Her sincerity was ending me. Usually, her antics were full of hostility and resentment. Now, she just sounded desperate and afraid.

"And when was that?" I pried in an effort to catch her up in a lie. "When did you fuck him?"

"Last year—"

"*Obviously*, Mia," I spit.

"I was going to say last year in May," she carefully told me. She actually was trying to prevent me from getting angry, when back in high school, that had always been her motive. "It was May 28th, to be exact. I remember specifically because it was the day after I saw the prom send-off for his sister and brother."

I inhaled sharply. "So, you follow my nigga online?! How many times did you fuck him?!"

"Everybody follows him online, Faye. We only fucked once."

"May 28th?" The date kept ringing over and over again in my head. It felt so familiar.

"Yeah."

Shit. Dread flooded my heart.

The day that the blog released those photos Sam took of me.

My eyes were sealed together tightly.

"He came into the club. To be honest, Faye, he was drunk as hell. He asked me into the champagne room and—"

"*He* asked you?" I probed, my heart beating feverishly.

"Yes."

My face got hot.

"He offered me a lot of money. And, to be honest, I did it to spite you. Yes, I did. And I was being a bitch when I sent you that DM because I had been honest with my man about the possibility of Jah being the father, and he left me. But I am not on bullshit right now. I want my man back, so I need to prove that Jah isn't the father—"

"So, just test your man."

She frustratingly sucked her teeth. "He won't take it. He's being an asshole. He won't even talk to me. So, I need to do a paternity test so that, hopefully, I can prove that the baby isn't Jah's. I was calling because I will be in town in a few days, and we can get this shit done then, but Jah won't answer."

"Because Jah is in the ICU fighting for his life. He has COVID, and it's pretty bad."

Her end of the line went eerily silent. Finally, she replied with a soft, "Oh."

My head returned to the steering wheel. Being ravished with a yearning for him to live and despising him at the same time was jarring. Yet, I kept telling myself that Mia could still be very much lying.

At least I hung on to hope that she was.

"But..." I gritted, hating to assist this bitch in any way, shape, or form. "I can help you."

TORY CLARK

"You think it will work?" I asked, feeling desperation in my soul.

"It should. If not, it will at least give my lawyer a better motive to fight this."

I sat in my bed with my back on the headboard and my knees to my chest, biting my nails nervously. My conversation with Detective Freemont was replaying in my mind over and over again. Giving that statement to her had been one of the hardest things I had ever done. And the thought of taking the stand had me petrified. But I was willing to do whatever Messiah had told me to do in order to help his case in any way.

"Now I'm really going to have issues with Seretta and Monique," I grumbled.

Since his bail hearing, I had been getting text messages from Monique and Seretta that accused me of having something to do with Kidd's murder. There had been so many that I eventually blocked their phone numbers.

"I'll have somebody in the crew go holler at them and let them know what it is."

"Won't that cause even more trouble?"

"Not if they are hollered at in the right way."

His protection made me smile weakly. "I love you, Messiah," I breathed into the phone.

"I love you too, baby. You already know."

Oddly, it felt as if his arrest had drawn us closer together. When chaos would usually tear a couple apart, it felt like our bond and dedication to each other had grown stronger.

"I'm riding with you," I promised him. "Whatever you want to do, I understand, and I'm riding with you."

"You don't have to. If I end up doing time, please don't wait for me."

I recoiled, closing my eyes with regret. "Don't say that."

"Listen to me, Tory."

I stubbornly quieted.

"We already know that people have been found guilty with circumstantial evidence. I'd love to think positively, but that's not rational. It's a strong possibility that I will be in here for a long time. And I don't want you to wait for me. You're a good woman and a great mother. Do what you gotta do to be happy, and I'll never judge you for it."

"Fuck you," I softly replied. "I will never leave you, especially at a time that you need me the most. You are willing to make a sacrifice to save your family. That's so mature and admirable. You were a dope guy when I first met you, Messiah. But now, you are a great man. I would be a fool to leave you now. So, stop telling me that shit before you make me spazz out and do something that lands me in there with you."

"You'd like that."

I smiled, crazily imagining myself in jail with him. The thought actually gave me comfort. That's when I knew that my heart and body belonged to him. "I'd *love* that."

CHAPTER 9

NARDO DAVIS

With Shauka being wrapped up in Jah, Messiah, and the birth of his son, he had asked that I help him with some things that he needed to take care of in the crew. I was more than happy to oblige him.

That day, he had tasked me with a couple of errands. The first was riding down on. Monique. She was a bartender at a local hole-in-the-wall, The Family Den, so I rode down on her there.

She thought nothing of it when I walked through the door. She was familiar with me since Kidd and I were a part of the same crew and had partied together a few times.

The bar had just opened, so very few patrons were inside.

"Hey, Nardo," she greeted. "You're drinking this early?"

"It's five o'clock somewhere," I said as I sat on a stool in front of her. "Let me get a shot of Don Julio."

She nodded and moved about the back of the bar, looking for the Don Julio. As she did, I scoped the scene. Since it was four in the afternoon, most of the patrons were over sixty and minding their own business.

After she sat the shot in front of me, I sat back, staring at her.

She blushed and lowered her eyes shyly. "What are you looking at?"

"You're done threatening Tory."

Instantly, her face washed with rage. "She calls herself telling on me?"

"Word has gotten around about the things you and your mother have been saying."

"I know that she is lying about what happened to my brother. Her story keeps changing. She had something to do with it."

"Leave the investigation to the police."

"That's my brother."

I threw the shot down my throat. Then I stood. Looking around, I ensured that all of the patrons had their attention elsewhere. Most were staring at their phones or the flat screens that were replaying highlights of games. So, I discreetly pulled my gun from my waist. Her eyes widened, and her body stiffened as I sat it on the counter in front of me.

"Like I said, leave the investigation to the police. If I hear that your family is threatening Tory in any way or getting involved in the investigation of Kidd's murder, his death won't be the only one that your family will mourn."

She inhaled sharply, but she didn't say a word as I reached into my pocket. I pulled out my wad of cash and peeled off a twenty-dollar bill. I then threw it on the bar and grabbed my piece.

"It was good to see you, Monique." Then I winked with a smile and strolled out.

THAT NIGHT, OBLIGING SHAUKA HAD LED ME TO THE DISCIPLE estate a few hours later. Because of the frenzy that was occurring within their family, Shauka had left some work and money in his bedroom closet that he needed me to transport to the stash house.

I grimaced when I pulled into the driveway and saw Najia's Hellcat sitting pretty. That woman had been the bane of my existence for the last week.

When we first had sex, I wanted it to be the one and only time. I had never planned to allow anything to jeopardize my relationship with the Disciple brothers. I could have easily found another plug. But we trusted each other. We knew how one another worked. The loyalty and respect between me and the brothers were never a question. All of that was a rarity in the streets. Some hustlers were grimy. They easily would rob the next nigga or snitch. I was so comfortable with my position with them as my supplier. But no matter how many times I'd told myself all of these things, I couldn't resist her. Najia had shown me that a woman could stimulate your mind, along with your dick. For the first time, I felt as if the woman I was fucking was also my friend.

Slowly, the other women in my life began to fade. Keisha, who had been on the yacht when Najia attempted suicide, couldn't understand why I hadn't seen her in months. I had unconsciously dropped my entire line-up and solely focused on Najia. But it seemed as if that had only scared her away. I hadn't even expressed the half of what I felt for her. Because of her past, I knew that I had to be gentle with her. I couldn't be too aggressive physically or mentally. But it was fucking me up that even the effort in showing her that she was more than a piece of ass to me was pushing her away.

Groaning, I climbed out of my ride. I regretted even being in the same space as Najia since she had walked out of that waiting room on me. When she'd described us as fuck buddies, I was shockingly offended. I felt like so many women must feel whenever a man reduces her existence in his life to only sex. Since then, I'd had to give her space as well. There was no way that I was going to let her little ass play me.

I used Shauka's key to open the front door. The sound of the soles of my shoes walking through the foyer caused Najia to pop her head out of her bedroom door. Her light skin was red with sorrow. Her eyes were overshadowed with pain. Tears lingered in them as she peered at the source of the noise questionably.

"Oh," she said barely above a whisper. "I thought you were Shauka."

My heart went out to the despair weighing her down. But I forced myself to mind the business that had brought me there. "He sent me here to handle some business for him."

"Oh, okay." She inched backward into the room.

I could guess what she was upset about: Jah, Messiah, or both, most likely. I naturally wanted to protect and comfort her. I wanted to take her into my arms and wipe her tears away. But shorty didn't want that. So, I gave her a sharp, quick nod and headed to the stairway.

My masculine energy was yearning to be there for her. But my ego couldn't take another blow. So, I forced my legs to climb the stairs, rather than rush into her room to comfort her.

Once up the stairs, I went straight into Shauka's room and into the closet where he had directed me. Behind the rack of jeans were two duffle bags. I knew what was inside, but to be thorough, I checked anyway. One duffle was filled to the brim with bricks, and the other with bundles of cash held together with rubber bands.

After zipping them back up, I headed out. On my way to the stair-case, I noticed that Jah's bedroom door was open. It looked as if he had simply left out to run an errand. The bed was still unmade. Remnants of the medicine that he had been taking were on the nightstand.

I had to pull my eyes away and jog down the stairs. It was eerie that Jah was so sick. He had always treated me as if we were equals. But for me, he was older and wiser. I mimicked his ability to be a beast in any situation. So, to see him so helpless was a reality check. I had heard of so many people who had experienced hard battles with COVID and those who had lost the fight. But when a loved one was suddenly in a life-threatening situation, it was a reality check that any of us could lose our lives in an instant.

As I stalked through the foyer, Najia's door swung open. There were even more tears streaming down her blanched cheeks.

"So, you're just going to leave?" she cried as her eyes showed the offense she felt.

She was used to me being there for her, being her support system. She felt like I should have comforted her just as I did.

"What else am I supposed to do, Najia? You keep running from me. I'm not going to keep chasing you."

"I thought we were friends," she tearfully mumbled.

"I don't fuck my friends, baby girl, especially not the way I fuck you."

She inhaled sharply. My words had her in a chokehold. But the offense was still all over her expression.

"You dodged me for a whole week and then walked out on me when I tried to talk to you in the waiting room. That shit don't feel good."

She fell into an uncontrollable sob. "I'm sorry." As soon as she said the words, her head hung low.

I immediately dropped the duffle bags and took long, quick steps to her. I took her into my arms, and she buried her face in her hands.

"I miss you," she cried.

I kissed the top of her head while gently cupping the back of it. "I miss you too."

"I just... I... I've never been this close to this close to a man, besides Messiah. It scares me."

A painful expression covered my face, causing my eyes to squeeze together. "It's okay. If it scares you, I'll slow down." I pushed back to look her in the eyes. "But stop treating me like I'm only good for one thing, especially if that's not what you want in return."

FAYE DISCIPLE

The next day, things went downhill for Jah.

"Loooord, fix it for me. Anybody know that ooonly Gooood can do it. Ooooh fix it for me. Because Lord, I have a problem. That only you can solve." Queen's eyes were anchored on Jah as she slowly rocked back and forth while singing Lord Do It For Me. *"So Loooord, do it for me –"*

She immediately stopped singing when the door to Jah's room opened. When I saw his doctor coming in, I cringed. Every time this damn doctor came into his room, I unraveled into a frenzy of anxiety.

He never had good news.

Hattie, Queen, and I sat upright, reluctantly waiting for him to speak.

He sighed before speaking, solidifying that he didn't have anything good to say.

"My grandma used to tell me that if you don't have anything nice to say, then don't say anything at all," I quipped, rolling my eyes.

Dr. Ross' face slowly turned pink as he pursed his lips.

"Faye," Hattie warned softly while putting a hand on my leg to shut me up.

I sat back, folding my arms tightly across my chest as I glared into the blue eyes of the doctor.

"Go ahead," Queen told him.

"Unfortunately, Jah is not responding to the oxygen therapy. There is too much stress on his lungs, which can cause cardiac arrest. It's best that we intubate—"

"No," I quickly blurted out.

"His hypoxia is worsening. His lungs are working too hard. Both of these issues are life-threatening. He keeps going in and out of consciousness, which has an unclear prognosis for neurologic recovery. It's best that we put him in a medically induced coma and put him on a ventilator."

Queen's head tilted to the side as she gave him stern eyes. "Dr. Ross, you and I know that there's a very small percentage of people who recover from COVID after being intubated."

"Exactly," I spit, frustration coating that one simple word.

"Are his siblings visiting today?" Dr. Ross asked.

The three of us scoffed at his dismissal of us.

"I'll call them and get them up here," Hattie said.

Dr. Ross gave her a small smile. "Thank you."

Once Dr. Ross left the room, Queen let out a frustrated sigh.

"Jesus," Hattie softly called out, shaking her head slowly.

I couldn't respond. I could only stare blankly at Jah. My emotions were all over the place. I missed his eyes being on me. I missed his touch. I felt like as soon as we had rekindled our relationship, he was taken from me again. But I was pissed with him! The conversation I'd had with Mia kept playing over and over in my head on a loop. His potential betrayal was pushing me toward hating him. The only thing keeping me from walking out on him, even in this state, was the possibility that Mia could be lying. Though she sounded sincere on the phone, considering her past, it was hard for me to trust anything she said.

Hattie's heavy sigh brought me out of my trance. I pulled my tired orbs away from Jah and saw Hattie standing.

"I need a cup of coffee." There was so much frustrated grievance in her tone. "Faye, I'll call Shauka and tell him what the doctor said."

"Thank you." I was so relieved. I couldn't take calling him or Najia with any more bad news. Shauka and Najia would usually be planted in his room. But with both Jah and Messiah being out of commission and Yaz having had the baby, Shauka and Najia were very busy handling family business.

"I'll come with you," Queen said, standing as well.

Finally.

"You need anything, Faye?" Queen asked.

"No, I'm good."

Since Jah had been admitted, I'd had very little appetite. I forced myself to think and speak positively. But I couldn't help but allow the vast amount of death that surrounded COVID to impact my hope. The fear of his death changed me. My eyes were different. I could barely eat. But after my conversation with Mia, I rarely felt the hunger or cared to feed it.

"Okay. We'll be right back," Queen said as she followed Hattie out of the room.

Once I heard the door latch closed, I blew out a tired breath and reached down between my legs for my purse. My hand started shaking as I fished through it, looking for the envelope that Mia had given me that morning in the hospital parking lot.

Since I'd offered my help, she had jumped right on it. She'd purchased the DNA test from Walgreens. As soon as she had gotten into town that day, she called me and agreed to meet me. After handing me the test and instructions, she told me she would be back to get it later that evening to pair it with her baby's DNA and send it off for the results.

After reading the instructions, I stood on trembling legs and inched toward the bed. Jah was sleeping, per usual. Though the door to the room was closed, I still glanced toward it to ensure that no one was coming. Then I took the Q-tip from its packaging and carefully slipped it into his mouth, rubbing it along the inside of his jaw.

SHAUKA DISCIPLE

"Hey, Asa," Yaz purred. She was bending down in the crib next to my bed. Since they had been released from the hospital that day, she hadn't been able to pull herself away from him.

Sitting on the foot of my bed, I admired how her ample butt cheeks spread apart as she bent over. That motherfucker was opening up like a broken heart. Biting down on my bottom lip, I fought the urge to ram my dick into her from the back, despite the fact that she wasn't cleared for intercourse and we were just two friends co-parenting our child.

We had decided on the name Asa Tamir Disciple. Yaz had actually wanted to name him after my father. I loved my father and wished he was here, especially now that I was trying to figure out how to be a father. But there was no way in hell that I was naming my son no fucking Frank. And that nigga didn't even have a middle name, so Yaz was SOL.

Surprisingly, Yaz turned away from the baby and started walking toward me.

"He's sleeping." She actually looked sad.

I laughed. "It's okay. He'll wake up soon. Don't panic."

She giggled. "Whatever."

"You're obsessed with that lil' nigga."

"So! That's my baby."

I shook my head while holding a smile. "God, I'mma have to make sure you don't turn my son into a spoiled, lil' bitch."

She cracked up. "Shut up! I'm not going to spoil him, I promise. I just gotta get my obsessions out of my system."

"It's okay. I love the kind of mother you are. You're already so attentive and careful with him. I have no doubt that you're going to be a great mom."

She leaned over, slightly nudging my shoulder with hers. "You're going to be a great father too."

My head lowered as I shrugged my shoulders. I wasn't sure of that. But I knew that my father was great because of what others had told me. I barely remembered his influence on me. So, I didn't have a father figure to mimic besides Buck. But I had no interest in exposing my son to the game or raising him to be a boss as Buck had raised us. The only type of boss I wanted him to be was in a boardroom or as an entrepreneur. I hadn't had a choice whether I wanted to get into the game or not. It had been automatically handed down to Jah, and it was my duty to be his right hand. Besides, we hadn't had a choice if we wanted to eat. But Asa would have more choices than he could handle.

"You are," Yaz insisted. "Anybody would think that we would be the last two people who should be parents. We'd had to raise ourselves in some fucked-up situations, so no one would trust us to raise a child. But I feel that because we didn't have parents, we will work very hard to be to Asa what we didn't have."

Turning my head, my eyes met hers as my lips slowly curved upward. "You're right."

There was nothing more that I wanted than be everything to Asa that I had wanted so desperately back then and even now. He would always be protected. He would never go hungry. He would never need for anything.

As Yaz and I stared at one another, thick tension grew between us. I thought I was the only one who felt it because I had so many unspoken words on the tip of my tongue that I was too timid to release. But she must have felt it too, because she sighed and shook her head as if she needed to change the subject.

"Are you sure you want me to stay here?" she asked sheepishly.

When Yaz was preparing to be discharged, she started to freak out. She was scared that she couldn't handle Asa alone, and she was under a lot of restrictions due to her surgery. Of course, I had planned to be with her as much as I could. But I couldn't be there full-time since I had a crew to run by myself. I had offered to hire a nanny, but Yaz didn't like the idea of a stranger caring for her baby and being in her home. So, I told her to stay with me. That way, she would be surrounded by my family, that wouldn't hesitate to help her with Asa.

"It's cool. I wouldn't have the two of you be anywhere else." Those words made the tension suddenly reappear.

She smiled softly. Appreciation danced in her eyes as she looked at me. Her smile was so contagious. I lost myself in it, staring at her in appreciation. I had always loved this woman. But as of late, she and my son had been the only light in my days.

"What?" she asked, shying away from my stare.

"You're amazing."

Stunned, she blinked slowly.

"I love you," I finally admitted.

"I love you too," she easily returned.

Suddenly, I wanted her to know just what that meant. I couldn't hide it anymore. She was more than my best friend. She was the love of my life and the mother of my child.

"No, *I love you*. I'm *in love* with you." Surprisingly, those words had been much easier to say than I had thought.

"Shauka," she breathed. But that was all she could say. She was taken aback.

"I always have been, probably always will be. And don't think it's because of what Sariah has done. I've felt this way since I ended things between us. I had my reasons, and I thought I knew what I was feeling. But I've missed you since I cut us off. You've been in my life since, but I miss the potential of us being more. I thought that because I wasn't willing to leave Sariah to be with you, that my love must not have been real. But that was just fake loyalty that I was giving to the wrong person. I soon saw that it was wrong. I want you." Her breath hitched. "I had to see you the day of the wedding because it should have been you walking down the aisle toward that altar so I could officially give my heart to you for the rest of my life." Tears pooled in her eyes as her bottom lip quivered. "But I felt like you didn't want me since you were cool with us just being friends."

"Because I thought that if I was willing to share you, that my love for you must not have been real." Her words were choppy, caused by a sudden shortage of breath. "But I soon learned that that actually proved how crazy I am about you."

Our need for one another brought us together like magnets. Our faces collided. We were nose to nose as she sucked my bottom lip. Her tongue hesitantly pressed between my lips. I sucked it, taking the reluctance away and swallowing it as our tongues made the love that we couldn't just yet.

CHAPTER 10

MESSIAH DISCIPLE

I was sitting in the interview room at the county, waiting impatiently. I had been brought there and told that someone wanted to talk to me. I hadn't been locked up for long, but since I'd been on the inside, a lot of old heads had schooled me. Because I had been called into the room unexpectedly, they had told me that the DA most likely wanted to holler at me.

My shackled hands were folded on top of the table. My body was covered in the orange county-issued jumpsuit. The boots that they had given me to wear were way too tight, but nobody cared enough to give me a pair that was my size.

Finally, I heard heavy footsteps approaching the open door, where a correctional officer stood on the other side, ensuring that I stayed put.

First, Brian, the DA, rounded the corner and sauntered into the room. Julia followed. My eyebrow rose inquiringly when Detective Freemont entered last with a satisfied smirk plastered on her pale face.

Julia rounded the table and sat in the metal chair beside me.

Brian and Detective Freemont sat beside one another. Detective Freemont placed a manila folder in front of her.

Opening it, she pulled out a photo and spoke first. "Messiah, this image is a still from video footage from a gas station two miles from Tory's home about fifteen minutes before Kidd's murder."

Reluctantly, I peered at the photo. I recognized my frame and the hoodie that I wore that night. My insides curdled. My jaw tightened as I fought to keep a grimace from forming on my face. Jah had told me to sit my hyper ass down, to wait to get the blunt until we were done with the job. But I just had to get a blunt.

"Is there a crime to go to the gas station?" Julia quipped.

"No." Detective Freemont smiled wickedly. "But coupled with the Ring Camera video of Messiah returning to the scene of the crime multiple times after the murder and Tory's testimony, I believe we have a strong case."

"Excuse me?" Julia spit. "Tory's testimony?"

Julia's eyes burned into the side of my face. She was well-informed of my relationship with Tory, so she was obviously very confused. But I kept my eyes still on Detective Freemont.

"Look, Messiah," Brian said in a stern tone as he leaned on the table. "Tory's testimony sounds like you were defending her. But the self-defense case is weak. But we can reduce the charge to second-degree murder, which carries a sentence of four to twenty-five years, depending on the leniency of the judge. But we are willing to offer you a deal of six years. Maybe with good behavior, you can get out even sooner."

"Otherwise," Detective Freemont pressed. "You will go to trial and open a can of worms that will put your brothers under investigation as well. Tory's initial statement was that there were three men that night. I'm assuming they were in the car waiting for you in this image. I mean, it's a little blurry, but we can get someone to clear that up for us."

All I saw in my peripheral was Julia's blonde hair swinging between me and Brian as he and the detective went back and forth.

"I'll take the deal."

"Wait a minute!" Julia interjected. "I need a minute with my client!"

Grinning, Detective Freemont stood. Brian slowly followed, grunting along the way as if his knees could barely hold his weight.

Once they were out of the room and the door was shut, Julia turned her chair toward me. "What are you doing, Messiah?!"

I finally broke my blank expression and smiled. "It's all good. This is what I wanted."

Once my bail was denied, I knew what I needed to do. I just had to get the courage to break Tory and my siblings' hearts to do it. I wasn't going to risk a lengthy trial that would bring attention to my brothers and our organization. I also couldn't live with myself if Jah and Shauka were to suffer because of my wild behavior. Detective Freemont wouldn't have any leverage had I simply listened to Jah and Shauka that night and afterward. They have always protected me. Now, it's my turn to protect them.

I had only been honest about what I wanted to do with Tory and Queen. They were scared and hurt, but they understood. Therefore, Queen had helped Tory come up with the story of self-defense.

"Why?!" Julia spat.

"I'm not trying to have our kingdom crumbling because of my immaturity and dick."

"Messiah, we can win this." She was so frazzled that she was turning pink.

I slowly shook my head. "Not without putting my family under a microscope. Jah and Shauka being in here with me isn't an option."

"Messiah—"

"It's all good, Julia," I firmly interjected. "Call them back in here and tell them to write up the offer, and I'll sign it."

Grimacing, she swallowed hard and nodded.

"And since you and I have attorney-client privilege, I'm assuming that I don't have to ask you more than once not to tell my brothers."

Her expression flushed with anxiety. I hated to be deceitful to my siblings, but I knew that they would only try to stop me or even attempt to take my place, and I wasn't having that shit. I had made this bed as a child, and I was going to lie in it comfortably like a man.

SHAUKA DISCIPLE

It had been very taxing, juggling my attention between the crew, Jah, and Asa. I was starting to realize why older men with families and careers walked around with a permanent scowl. This was exhausting.

"Hi, Shauka!" Michelle excitedly waved as I approached Jah's room.

I smiled at the nurse sitting behind the desk. "Hey. How are you?"

"I'm good." Her smile was seductive and flirty.

"I got y'all for lunch today. Get everybody's order and let me know what you want."

She blushed. "Okay. Thank you, Shauka."

"No doubt."

All of the nurses on the floor had flirted with me a time or two. Besides me being a handsome dude, it was obvious that I had money because I showered them with food and anything else they needed. I wasn't trying to impress anyone, though. I just wanted them to take special care of my brother.

Michelle was still eye-fucking me as I turned my back to her and opened the door to Jah's room. The usual doom came over me as I stepped inside. I walked around daily with this relentless feeling of grief. But when I laid my eyes on Jah lying helpless in that bed with a tube inserted in his throat, it was unnerving. Jah had always been the strong one, the decision maker, our rock. Now, he was lying there helpless, clinging to life.

That reality was unbelievable. It all felt like a nightmare that I couldn't wake up from.

Opening the door, I heard whispers and sobs. I froze, straining to listen.

"I'm sorry. I take it all back. I love you like you're my own son."

My eyes narrowed as I listened carefully. I recognized Buck's voice, though it was in a whisper. I left the door open and tiptoed into the room. Poking my head around the corner, I saw Buck seated next to Jah's bed, clinging to his hand as he wept. His forehead was pressed against Jah's.

"I'm so sorry," he cried.

Hearing Buck's sorrow was emotionally taxing for me. I had never heard him sound so feeble. Yet, he deserved this pain for how he had treated Jah.

"Lord, please bring him back," Buck began to pray. "Please let him live."

Sighing quietly, I tiptoed back out of the room.

Buck needed privacy to say the things he should have said months ago. I just prayed that he would have the chance to say it to Jah when he was able to hear him.

❦

I had finally been able to meet up with Gabriel and Angel Astro that morning. I hadn't expected the Mexican cartel to be patient because my family was falling apart. But they had surprisingly shown some compassion.

They were willing to sell to us on the same terms that Saudi had. So, it was the same game, just a different boss to work under. The only stressful part about it was learning their personalities to ensure that things would run smoothly. But, so far, so good.

After the meeting with the cartel, I headed to the estate to holler at Nardo and Najia.

When I walked in, they were sitting next to one another in the den. When they saw me crossing the threshold, Najia's eyes got big. She sat straight up and swallowed hard as if she was in the principal's office.

Before saying a word, I went to the bar and poured a shot of tequila. Though Jah was the capo, he never treated me and Messiah like we were beneath him. Our crew was as much ours as it was his. We were all bosses. But with Jah and Messiah not being in it with me to help me run shit, I felt the difference in the pressure of being the capo for the first time. Coupled with that was the stress behind the reasons why my brothers weren't with me. Najia, Messiah, and I had been under the pressure of choosing to intubate Jah or not. I was starting to lose hope that he would make it through this. But I was clinging to hope that he and Messiah would be home soon.

After gulping down the shot, I left the shot glass on the bar and sat on a barstool.

"So, I met with the Mexican cartel today." In the past, I would never have discussed business with Najia. But without my brothers, I had been forced to confide in her. "It went smooth. No worries on that end. I called y'all both here because, with Messiah and Jah out of commission, I need your help."

Najia was instantly relieved but intrigued.

"I need you to be my right hand, Nardo."

He nodded, accepting the task.

"I know there's some beef with you and Messiah because you've been hooking up with my sister."

Najia cringed.

"But Jah and I appreciate you being there for her in her time of need," I added. "I'm not going to act like I'm cool with knowing that you're piping down my sister," I said with disgust. "But she's grown. She can make her own decisions. You've been loyal to this family and organization, so you'll always have love from me and Jah."

Nodding, Nardo said, "I appreciate that, bro."

"You ain't never gotta get a new connect as long as you're running with the Disciple family. We'll just have to ignore Messiah until he grows the fuck up."

We all chuckled halfheartedly because there was a layer of grief in this house that left us too sorrowful to find much humor in anything.

"Najia, Jah already taught you how to manage our largest property. But I'm going to need you to manage them all, including the businesses that we use to wash our money. I also need you to help out with my role at the record label. I might even use you to pick up money here and there from our network of distributors. But you are never going to touch any drugs."

Nodding, she said, "Okay."

"All right, now let me holler at Nardo about some shit."

She was still under pressure, as if she was in trouble. She was stiff as she stood up.

"C'mere," I softly demanded.

I stood as she padded her way toward me. Once she was within arm's reach, I wrapped my arms around her in a firm hug.

"I don't want to bring up anything that makes you uncomfortable or that brings up bad memories. But you can always talk to me, to all of us. You ain't never gotta suffer alone. And if you ever need some help, please ask." I then kissed her on her cheek and pushed back to look her in her eyes. Holding my wrist, she nodded but didn't say a word. I didn't understand why she was tight-lipped with me and my brothers, yet so open with Nardo. But that was why I appreciated their relationship, rather than forbidding it. "Ah'ight, get out of here. I'll be in there to talk to you soon, though."

She eyed me questionably.

"We gotta make a decision about Jah," I said. "Messiah said he'd call at five o'clock so we can talk about it."

She cringed and moped out of the room. I understood her frustration. Making the decision to intubate Jah was like deciding whether to pull the plug or not. Yaz had educated us on the risks of intubation. It all sounded like a death sentence.

FAYE SINGER

"Any news yet?" Chloe asked as we walked the halls of the ICU.

Often, I would pace the entire unit just to exercise my legs.

"No. I haven't heard from her. But the instructions said that the results may take up to thirty days."

"I bet that bitch was lying," she seethed.

"I doubt it, Chloe. Why would she go through all of this just to hurt me?"

"Because she's fucking diabolical!"

Even my laugh was tired. "Girl, she wouldn't waste her time driving in town just to hurt me."

"You see all that Sam went through to hurt you."

I scoffed sarcastically. "True. Well, I hope I'm right about this."

"You and me both."

This had been truly a test of my love for Jah. I was so angry with him that I wanted to leave this hospital and never come back. But Jah's next breath wasn't guaranteed.

He was now suffering from hypoxemic respiratory failure. He didn't have enough oxygen in his lungs. This had given him the appearance of the walking dead. His lips, fingertips, and toes had turned blue.

That morning, he had been diagnosed with pneumonia, and there was a threat of him going into septic shock.

His doctor had been stressing the need to intubate him, and I was starting to agree. But the decision was up to his siblings.

"You want me to bring you something to eat when I bring you a change of clothes?" Chloe asked as I rounded the corner, heading back to Jah's room.

"Yeah. That'll be nice. I'm so tired of hospital food."

"Girl, that pasta was bussing when I was there with you the other day."

"Yeah, but they don't have anything good on their menu to—" The chaos going in and out of Jah's room tied my tongue. Nurses and other staff were rushing in and out with one machine after the next. Cries and whimpering mixed in with the stabbing alarms that were sounding inside his room.

When Queen rushed out of the room with her face flooded with tears, I gasped. I hung up on Chloe mid-sentence of words that I hadn't even heard. I then took off running toward Queen.

"What happened?!" I shouted.

Queen could hardly speak through her tears. "He's.... He's..."

"What, Queen?!" Instead of waiting for an answer, I tried to run past her and into the room. But she stuck her arm out, stopping me. When she looked at me, I had never seen so much remorse in a person's eyes.

"His heart stopped, baby," she whimpered.

The room started to spin. Suddenly, the floor felt like it was swaying beneath my feet. "What?! *Noooo!*"

I continued trying to fight my way past her, but she was strong for her age.

"Let me go!" I shouted.

Queen's tearful orbs were full of regret. "They don't want us in there. They're trying to get his heart beating again. We can't be in their way. We need to stay out here and pray. We need to pray *hard*."

Without permission, she took hold of both of my hands and bowed her head. She began to talk to God from the deepest part of her heart. It was a powerful prayer, and I felt every word of it moving all over me. I could hardly form words. Fear was assaulting my every limb and every nerve in my body. I had only had Jah in my life for a moment compared to everyone else. Yet, he had impacted it in a way that I could never imagine or forget.

SHAUKA DISCIPLE

"*Shiiiit.*" Yaz had my dick deep down her throat. She was sucking it with so much hunger that I was whimpering like a bitch. "Gawd damn, girl."

My head tilted back with my eyes staring at the ceiling. I didn't want her to witness the way that her mouth had me unraveling like a virgin.

Since our confessions to one another, we hadn't bothered to make anything official. It didn't feel necessary to either one of us. It was hard to put a title on what we were because we were so many things to each other.

She purred with a mouthful of me. "I want this dick inside of me so bad."

I gnawed down on my lip until pain shot through me. "I want that pussy just as bad," I groaned.

It had been so hard to resist her, but I didn't have a choice. Six weeks felt like a jail sentence. And I was already ready to break out.

She started to jag my dick with both hands while keeping her wet, juicy lips on the head of it.

"Fuck!" That shit was making me melt like a bitch.

She started to moan, causing my shaft to vibrate.

I hated the way that she was making me unfold. I slipped my fingers into her bob and gripped its strands. Then I started to fuck her mouth.

Her nasty ass didn't run. She took every stroke eagerly.

"That's it," I encouraged her. "Just like that. Fuck!"

To my annoyance, my phone rang. "Shit," I grumbled. But I wanted to cum, so I kept stroking.

Yaz pushed back, causing my wet, thick member to fall out of her mouth with a heavy thud. I shot confused, hungry daggers into her.

"It might be the hospital," she told me. Still on her knees, she crawled over to the nightstand and grabbed my phone. Looking at it, she told me, "Its Faye." She tossed it to me.

After catching it, I answered. "What up, Faye?" Concern made my eyes squint as soon as I heard all of the commotion in her background.

But the frenzy made that concern grow into panic. "Shauka, you need to come up to the hospital!"

I hopped out of the bed, pulling my sweatpants up along the way. "I'm on my way. What's going on?"

"It's Jah." Her voice trailed off as the sobs got heavier. I could barely make out her words as she said, "He... he went into cardiac arrest."

"Fuck. I'm on my way right now. Is he okay?"

"They got his heart started again, but it's bad, Shauka. His heart is so weak. They need to intubate him. They can't wait until you get here. They need your permission now."

"Fuck," I growled lowly with a grimace.

Messiah, Najia, and I had tried to make the decision. I was for it if it would help him. But Messiah and Najia were totally against it. I hadn't been able to convince them to come to a unanimous decision before time ran out on Messiah's call.

"Shauka?!" Faye blurted frantically.

"Fuck it," I spit with regret. I held my head as I paced my bedroom floor. "Tell them to do it."

"Okay." There was uncertainty in her tone as well. Our call fell silent. We both knew that this needed to be done, but it could lead to Jah never being the same again.

I swallowed the grief and guilt, blinking my way back into reality. "I'll be there as soon as I can."

"Okay."

As soon as I hung up, I started to quickly move around the room, looking for a shirt and shoes to throw on.

"What happened with Jah?" Yaz asked.

I suddenly realized she was still on the floor, looking up at me with a worried stare.

"His heart stopped." I could barely breathe. The fear was suffocating me. "I told them to intubate him."

"Okay."

She watched sadly as I slipped my foot into a shoe. But before I could put on the other one, I crumbled. I squatted and held my face with my hands. Out of the blue, I became sick to my stomach, and my legs were so weak that I figured I would fall soon.

I felt Yaz beside me. But I kept my face hidden in my trembling hands.

"He's strong. He'll make it through this," I heard her say.

That was hard to believe. I didn't see the light at the end of this tunnel, only pain, suffering, and guilt because it felt like I had just engraved my brother's name on a tombstone.

A WEEK LATER...

CHAPTER 11

MESSIAH DISCIPLE

Blowing a heavy breath, I reluctantly took the phone off the hook. This was the worst call that I'd ever had to make in my life. I waited for the operator to go through the collect call prompts. Then I nervously rubbed the back of my neck as I waited for Shauka to answer.

"What up, bro?" His question was already full of concern. He had asked me so many questions when I'd told him the day before that I would call at this time and needed everyone to be with him when I did.

"What's up, Messiah," I heard Buck greet.

"What up, Unc?"

"You still good in there?"

"Yeah, I'm good, man." My words were so uneasy. I hadn't cried in years, so when my eyes started to pool with tears, it surprised me.

"Hey, 'Siah!" Najia's greeting was loud, as if she had taken the phone from Shauka. "Why didn't you call me this morning?"

I called her every morning right after I called Tory. It had become our routine. I went out of my way to keep it up so she could continue to feel our bond.

"I was a lil' busy, sis."

"Busy doing what, nigga? You in jail."

My chuckle was breathy as I fought not to unfold in front of all the other prisoners next to me on the wall having their own conversations and the ones waiting on their turn to use the phones.

"My bad, sis. You know I would never forget about you."

"You bet' not."

"Where y'all at?"

"We all up here with Jah."

I cringed, knowing that I was about to multiply their pain. But I hoped that now they could stop worrying about me and put all of their focus on Jah. He needed them way more than I did.

"Oh, okay." My tongue stabbed the inside of my jaw as I tried to force the words out. "I'm on speaker phone, right?"

"Yeah," Najia answered.

I began to pace amongst the two squares that surrounded my space. "I gotta tell y'all something."

Their end of the line went completely silent. I could hear the beeps from the machines that were keeping Jah alive.

"I had a court case today," I spit out.

Najia gasped. "Why didn't you tell us?!"

I cringed at the offense I knew she would feel.

Shauka then asked, "Why wouldn't you let us know, bro—"

"Aye, y'all, just listen to me." Once they were quiet, I reluctantly continued. "I didn't tell y'all because I didn't want you to be there because... um... I took a plea deal today."

The sound of Najia unfolding with a hysterical scream was gut-wrenching.

I cringed, hating to hear my sister in such distress. That was another reason why I hadn't told them about the court date. Had any of them been in that room, I wouldn't have had the courage to take that deal. I would have fought the case to ease their burdens. So that morning, I appeared at the plea hearing, pled guilty, and received a six-year sentence.

"You did what?!" Buck barked.

"Buck, please," I heard Queen say, trying to quiet him.

"Why the fuck would you do that, bro?!" Shauka snapped.

"Because I needed to."

"What the fuck you mean you needed to, my nigga?!" Shauka scolded me. "You trying to put this family through more shit?!"

"I'm actually saving y'all from extra shit on top of what we already got goin' on. A case would only draw more attention to everything we've built. Besides, this is on me."

"How? How is it on you?!" he snapped with Najia's wails in the distance.

Sighing, I lowered my head and rested it on the phone's base. "They had videos of me going to that gas station and after the murder when I kept going to Tory's house. No one else needed to get in trouble for this but me. You just had a baby. And Jah..." I couldn't even finish my sentence. It had been so hard on me to hear that my brother's heart had stopped, and I wasn't there because of my own immaturity and stupidity. Though he had only died for a few minutes, I was overwhelmed with shame that I hadn't been able to be there. "I did this for y'all because it was what I needed to do." When I heard my voice cracking, I stopped talking and swallowed hard.

"I understand why you did it." Buck's voice was close to the phone as if he had taken it from Shauka. "You did what you had to do. Shauka and Najia will understand soon enough."

"Is she okay?" I reluctantly asked.

Buck released a heavy breath. "She will be."

"Look out for her for me." My heart had never ached so much.

"You know I will."

"How many years did they give you?"

"Six."

That ignited wails from Najia.

"Queen, get Najia out of here. Calm her down," Buck said sternly. Then he addressed me. "You only gotta do seventy-five percent of that."

"I know."

"You did good, son. The rest of them will understand soon enough. I'm proud of you, though."

That made the tears fall. I had hoped that my father was proud and wished that he would come into my dreams to assure me that I had. But all I heard at night was the chaotic wrestling of the prisoners who couldn't or were too stubborn to sleep. However, hearing confirmation that I had done the right thing from Buck was good enough.

NAJIA DISCIPLE

I was numb.

It was weird, but I was actually appreciative that I had been so young when my parents died that I didn't have memories of them to grieve. Now that Messiah was gone, I was exceptionally grateful for that. I was sure that it felt ten times worse than the pain that was ravishing my body. I knew that, unlike my parents, Messiah would eventually come back. But we had been by each other's side for nineteen years. We had survived being adopted together, and we'd battled high school together. Messiah had been more than a brother to me. Without him by my side, I wasn't the same. I felt as if I was missing a limb.

"What are you doing?" Nardo was rightfully confused. We had just been silently lying in his bed. My head had been on his bare chest as I cried my eyes out. But I was tired of feeling this pain. I wanted to feel something else, so I'd kissed him.

"I want you to fuck me," I spoke into our kiss.

As my tongue began to tango nastily with his, I finally felt some relief. So, I got hungry for it, wanting more.

I didn't wait for him to oblige. I pulled his athletic build on top of me as our tongues performed a raunchy dance. I then reached down between our bodies. My hand dove inside his shorts, searching for my medicine.

Once I pulled it out, I pushed it past my panties and put each knee nearly under my arms. I wanted him deep inside of me, touching what hurt.

As he slammed into me, I gasped. We had fucked so many times, and each time I reacted to him pressing into me as if it were the first time.

He started to slowly ride me. His hands clasped down on the inside of my knees as he stared down at me. "You know I got you," he promised, never taking his eyes off mine.

Reluctant whimpers were my response.

"You won't need for shit. I'll be here for you."

I pulled my eyes away. Instead, I stared down between us, watching him plunge in and out of me with the grace of a dancer. "Fuck me," I demanded lewdly.

He was making love. I wanted to fuck.

"Look at me, Najia," he appealed.

I frustratingly disobeyed. I didn't want to hear his sweet nothings. I didn't want to be treated like a treasure. I wanted to be fucked like a slut.

"Look at me," he begged once more.

Sucking my teeth, I gently pushed him, causing him to fall back on his knees. "Stop."

"Why? What's wrong?"

A groan left my throat as I rolled over onto all fours and climbed out of the bed. I felt silly for running from his constant nurturing. Though I had the sense to know that it was what I needed, it wasn't what I wanted. I wasn't comfortable with it. It made me feel so suffocated.

"What's wrong, Najia? Where are you going?" He sounded so over me and my emotional roller coasters. But I also knew that telling him how I felt would be a bad idea. Any woman would pay for the treat-ment that he gave me without me even asking. But that was just it; I hadn't asked. I didn't know how to be intimate with a man. I wasn't experienced in that, so it made me feel insecure at a moment I wanted to feel confident.

"I can't be here right now," I simply told him. "My head is every-where. I'm sorry."

His eyes told me that he wanted to say more. Yet, he bit back and simply nodded.

I was sympathetic to his confusion and frustration. But I knew no other way to handle the flood of emotions surging through me. At ten years old, Miguel's assaults began to carve out who I would become. I just didn't know that it was something erroneous about the woman that the trauma had turned me into until now.

I couldn't even look at Nardo after slipping into my pants and shoes. "I'll call you tomorrow." I tucked my tail and left out of the bedroom, not even waiting for his response. I knew that he wouldn't follow me out because I always locked up behind myself.

I hated that I was being this ridiculous. But I had no other way to deal with my trauma on top of all of the dismay happening in my family.

There were experiences in life that transformed us. Miguel's abuse had been one of them. Having to grieve both of my brothers would be another. There was nothing that I could do to stop it. And it felt like the woman it was changing me into would be one that I feared.

MESSIAH DISCIPLE

"*Yoooo'*, Messiah!"

I pulled my eyes away from the book I was reading and gave the correctional officer, Romello, standing on the other side of my cell, my attention. I knew him from high school, though he was three years older than me. It had been so odd to see him delivering mail the first time I had received some. We had been familiar with each other, but we ran in much different crowds, which was why he was on the right side of the bars, and I was fighting a murder conviction.

"Mail!" he announced while pushing envelopes through the bars.

A small grin formed through the beard that I had begun to grow out. The highlight of my day was getting letters from home. Najia and Tory wrote me the most. I wasn't surprised that the testosterone of my brothers hadn't led them to pen a four-page letter to their little brother.

I left the bed and took the short walk to the bars. "Good looking," I told him as I took them from him.

He gave me a respectful head nod and continued to push his cart full of mail down the unit.

As I'd assumed, Tory's name was on the letter at the top. But the next had been written in penmanship I didn't recognize.

"*Whaaat?*" I shockingly sang as I read the sender's information.

I rushed back to the bed and tore the letter open. I wondered how Karen knew that I was in jail. My brows were wrinkled curiously as I kept my guard up, recalling the conversation that she'd had with Najia in Starbucks some time ago.

Hello Messiah,

I learned of your incarceration in my attempts to locate where you and your sister were living. I asked the detective over Miguel's case to look into it for me. I was so saddened when he informed me of your arrest and charges. I know that I raised you and your sister to walk the right path, and I looked down on the things that your brothers were into. However, nothing would ever make me stop loving you. I hadn't tried reaching out to you before because I was so very hurt when you moved. But since learning the truth about Miguel, I realized that nobody is perfect, especially me. I don't care what life you choose to live; I just want to be in it.

I've always prided myself on being a great mother. I did not look at you and your sister as children that needed me. When I adopted you guys, I was so grateful to God because I'd needed the two of you. But I failed you and Najia. The moment that Miguel went missing, I allowed the detectives in his case to convince me to keep my distance from you. I also allowed them to convince me to ask Najia when we met if she knew anything. Of course, you know that I have no experience with investigations and the police. So, I was easily manipulated. But when I saw the hurt in her eyes when she walked out, I knew that I had allowed them to convince me to deepen her hurt. I don't care where Miguel is. He destroyed the family that I had begged God for. So, I told the police the truth; that he had most likely fled to Mexico to avoid the charges against him.

I may not be your biological mother, but I love you and Najia with every fiber of my being. I pray that one day we can mend our relationship. Please put me on your call and visitation list so that I can support you during this time in your life, not because I feel like you need me, but because I desperately need you.

I love you,
Karen

TWO MONTHS LATER...

CHAPTER 12

SHAUKA DISCIPLE

"**H**ey, man." I had to laugh at the way I was cooing in Asa's face. My son had softened my heart. I was now one of those men who freely spoke baby talk in public.

As I grinned at the FaceTime call, Asa smiled.

"Oh shit!" I spat so loud that a nurse sitting at the station darted warning eyes at me above the rim of her glasses.

Respectfully, I inched a little further down the hall.

"You smiling at Daddy, man?"

"He's been smiling all day," Yaz said from behind the phone.

"What you smiling at, dude? Huh?"

The way Asa smiled back at me and how his eyes lit up with every word I said had my chest swelling. I had needed this call. It gave me the energy I needed to push through. That's what Asa and Yaz had been to me. They had been my energy, my sunshine, my happiness in one of the darkest times in my life.

They still lived with me, and I was grateful to have them to wake up and go home to. Initially, the plan was for Yaz to stay with me until she got acclimated to being a new mother. But as time passed, I had gotten accustomed to them being there. I had developed an addiction to them being there at the beginning and end of my days.

I knew it would be premature to ask Yaz to live with me since we still hadn't put an official title on us. We had simply been enjoying being parents, getting to know Asa, and enjoying each other intimately. But at her six-week checkup, she'd been medically cleared. She was given permission to perform normal duties, like lifting heavy weight and going back to work. She was okay to live on her own, which gave me grief that I couldn't afford to add on my shoulders. So, I had asked her to stay, and she had gladly obliged.

Living with Sariah had felt like a routine. Jah had always mimicked our father. Buck thought like our father as well. So, growing up, they both had instilled in me that real men took care of their women and made a home for them. Therefore, that's what I'd done with Sariah. Yet, the excitement that I felt coming home to Yaz and Asa was exhilarating. It gave me the push that I needed to fight the demons in the outside world.

As I continued my one-sided conversation with Asa that Yaz kept chiming in on here and there, she put the camera on herself.

"What the fuck?" I frowned. "My son and I were talking."

She sucked her teeth. "Boy, whatever! I wanna know how Jah is."

Just like that, I was snatched out of my happy place. My smile disappeared, and my shoulders sank. The heavy burdens returned, and I had to lean on the wall behind me for support. The reminder caused stabbing pain in my chest. It had been a little over sixty days since Jah had been intubated. His condition had yet to improve. There had been days when there were teases of hope. His stats would improve for so long that Dr. Ross would assume that he could decrease the levels of ECMO and ventilation. Then Jah's stats would fatally drop, and the levels were raised again.

It had been a traumatizing game of ping pong for weeks. All of us were exhausted. Najia was at her wit's end. Faye was inconsolable most days. Messiah had asked that we no longer update him because it was the only way he could keep from spazzing out in prison and earning more time. He was just waiting for the chaplain to come to get him out of his cell to notify him that Jah had passed away.

Before I could respond to Yaz, I heard shouting coming from the direction of Jah's room.

"No! Get out!"

As soon as I recognized Najia's voice, I told Yaz, "Let me call you back." I hung up before she could respond and took off toward his room.

Running into the room, I nearly collided with Dr. Ross, who was being forced to back out of the room by Najia because she was shouting at him angrily while marching toward him.

"Fuck you! We ain't doing shit!" she seethed.

"Aye! Aye! Aye!" I barked, getting their attention. "What's going on?"

Dr. Ross spun around, relief flooding his eyes.

"He's trying to kill my fucking brother!" Najia snapped.

I blinked slowly, staring at Dr. Ross. "Huh? What's going on?"

"Shauka, can we talk outside, please?" he asked with pleading eyes.

I looked behind him at Najia, who was so enraged that her face had turned as red as the lipstick that she was wearing.

I nodded at the doctor while I gave him room to exit. Then I told Najia, "Be cool before you get us kicked out of here. This is the ICU floor. We can't be in here nuttin' up."

"Then check that motherfucka!" she gritted while stabbing a finger toward Dr. Ross.

I stepped out of the room and closed the door.

"I apologize, Shauka," Dr. Ross said as I gave him my undivided attention. "That was a sensitive conversation that I knew would garner that type of response, but it needed to be said."

I folded my arms tightly, glaring at him. "And what is it that needs to be said?"

"As you know, it's been two months, and Jah has not been responding to curative treatment."

"*Okaaay...*"

"It's my recommendation that he is transferred to hospice care."

My eyes bucked. "The fuck? Why the fuck would we do that? He's not dying!"

Dr. Ross raised his hands in an attempt to stop me from exploding. "He's not dead because the machines he's attached to are keeping him alive. But they are *only* keeping him alive. His condition has not progressed in two months."

"Then we'll give him two more months," I said through clenched teeth as I stepped into the doctor's space. "We'll give him two fucking years if that's what he needs. What? You think we can't afford to keep him here?"

Dr. Ross shook his head as I reached into my pocket.

Pulling out a wad of cash, I threw it at him. "Here! Now, do your fucking job."

Dr. Ross stepped back over the bills scattered on the floor. He then began to look around with wide, fearful eyes. But none of the nurses was at the station, and no visitors were in the halls. "That's not the case at all, Shauka. And it is with my deepest regrets that I have to make this recommendation. But your brother is not getting better, and the longer he is on the vent, his body is susceptible to even more life-threatening issues. I strongly suggest hospice care so he can receive the attention and comfort he needs as he approaches the end of life."

My hands balled into fists. Yet, I gnawed into my bottom lip to keep them at my side, instead of crashing them into the doctor's face.

"And I strongly advise you to get the fuck up outta my face before I send *you* to hospice care, Doc."

His expression flushed crimson red. His lips mashed together tightly as he made an about-face and scurried away. I then did my own scurrying down the hall, eyes darting around frantically, trying to find privacy. Suddenly, I couldn't breathe. I had an overwhelming sense of dread and fear that was making my stomach do summersaults.

Finally, I found a bathroom and threw myself inside. After slamming the door and locking it, I slid down the metal until I was sitting on the floor with my face in my hands.

The overwhelming since of dread was catastrophic. My heart started racing, and each breath was becoming more laborious, almost impossible to draw in. My hands were shaking, and I started sweating profusely. I felt like I was going to pass out or die right there on that floor. I tried to calm myself down by taking deep breaths, but it only made things worse. The more I tried to control my breathing, the more panicked I became.

My mind was racing with all sorts of irrational thoughts.

What if I'm having a heart attack?

Am I going crazy?

What if this is the beginning of the end of my family?

I was losing my fucking mind. I felt completely out of control and helpless. It was like all the worst fears that I had been carrying around with me for years had suddenly come crashing down on me all at once.

TORY CLARK

"Messiah!" As soon as Honor saw Messiah, he snatched his hand out of my grasp and took off running. Since there weren't many people in the visitation room, I let Hope's hand go as well. She took off after her brother, who was already being scooped up by Messiah.

Once he'd accepted his deal, Messiah had been transferred to a prison in Ohio that was a five-hour drive away. And, every weekend, I packed up the kids, and we hit the road to visit him. I never let a weekend go by without seeing his face. Selfishly, it was for me, not him. He had preferred that he did not have any visitors, especially not his siblings. Being separated from his family for a second time was unbearable for him. The only way he could cope was if no one visited. But I refused to obey his wishes. There was no way that I was going to survive the next six years without seeing his face. So, out of fear of what I might do, Messiah reluctantly added me to his visitation list.

As I made my way to the table where he was standing, I admired my man. Prison had glamorized a man who already had unrealistic beauty. The lack of alcohol had brightened his skin. He used weights to make the time go by, so he had begun to bulk up. Every time I saw him, I imagined those big arms throwing me up against the wall like a poster as he fucked me into ecstasy.

Once I was near him, he put Hope down and pulled me into his arms. Closing my eyes, I relished every second that he held me. I had missed this the most, him simply holding me.

He pushed back because it was against the rules of visitation to embrace for too long. He looked down at me, grinning from ear to ear. "You look nice."

I smiled like a little girl who had gotten her daddy's approval. "Thank you."

It excited me to get dressed for him on visitation days. There was a dress code for visitation. So, I couldn't wear the seducing outfits that I wanted to. But I made sure to sex it up as much as the rules allowed. So, my jeans were molded to my phat ass, and so was my short-sleeved top that stopped right at where the high-waist jeans began. Since it was now May, I had my pretty, white toes out, and I had on a long, deep wave, thirty-inch wig.

Messiah and I fell into a trance as we stared at one another. I allowed his eyes to swallow mine and relished his eyesight. Any moment of intimacy was like sex with him since I hadn't had it in months.

But then my hating-ass kids had to interrupt it.

"Mommy, can we get some snacks?!" Hope asked.

"Ooo, Mommy, I want a honey bun! Can I have a honey bun, please?!" Honor begged.

I lightly groaned, lowering my eyes. Before I left Messiah's arms, he was sure to rub my belly. Something he did every time he saw me.

"Yes, you all can have some snacks," I groaned. I stuck my hand into my back pocket and pulled out the ones that I had gotten from the bank for this very reason. "You want something?" I asked Messiah as I peeled bills off for the kids.

"Hell yeah," he answered with a greedy grin. "I want some honey buns and a burger."

I frowned, still disgusted at the fact that he actually ate those White Castle burgers from the vending machine. But I understood that they tasted every bit like a Five Guys Burger in comparison to the meat that the prison served.

"Here, Honor. Go ahead." I gave him a few bills, and he rushed away. He was now almost six, so I trusted that he could get everything they wanted. The vending machine was the highlight of the visit for them, outside of seeing Messiah.

"You don't want anything?" Messiah asked me as we sat across from each other.

"No, I'm good."

Messiah's eyes glared a warning at me. "Don't be starving my baby."

I blushed, and the reminder made me place a hand on my growing belly.

I was three months pregnant. In the past, I would have been infuriated to find out that I was pregnant. Prior to Kidd's death, the last thing I'd wanted was another child. Kidd was barely physically in the kids' lives, so I would have been a single mother of three. But when I realized that my period was late soon after Messiah took his deal, I was thrilled to have a connection to him. I feared that Messiah would hate the idea, and he would have had every right to be. He would miss the first six years of our child's life. He had a lot to worry about, so stressing about a child on top of it all would be too much. But surprisingly, he was elated with the idea, which only showed how he had truly matured so much more since being arrested.

"I'm not starving your baby," I insisted. "Your baby had me craving pizza before we left the hotel, so I ordered one. I'm full."

"I got the picture of the crib. It's nice." He smiled with approval.

"Isn't it? I can't believe all of the dancers gifted it to me at my farewell party."

Then a sly grin graced his lips.

"What?" I quizzed.

His slick expression deepened. "Told you I was gonna get you to quit dancing."

I giggled, shaking my head. I had already known that I would need to quit dancing once I found out I was pregnant. I waited as long as I could. Messiah was taking great care of me, but I still wanted my independence. However, he was right. He had definitely forced me to quit one way or the other.

Finally, Honor and Hope returned with the snacks. The three of them dove in as Messiah and I caught up. There wasn't much that we had to talk about because we talked multiple times a day, every day. I knew everything about the prison, and he hadn't missed a beat in my life. The only thing we didn't talk about was Jah. He couldn't handle it, and I respected that.

"You all moved in now?"

His question caused a radiating smile to invade my expression. Messiah had done more for me while in prison than any man had in my life. Once he'd decided to take the deal, he had always assured me that he would still take care of me even if I didn't want to wait for him. When I told him that I was pregnant, he told Najia to use some of his stash to buy a house for my kids and me. I had chosen a beautiful two-story brick home merely minutes from the Disciple estate. My kids finally had their own rooms and a safe backyard and front yard to play in. When I first moved in, I was sort of uncomfortable with the silence. I was used to the chaotic city noises. The peace and stillness of the suburbs had given me an uneasy feeling. For the first two weeks, Najia and my mother had come over to keep me company at night because I was too scared to be alone.

"Yeah." I smiled. "It's decorated beautifully. That interior decorator Shauka recommended was the shit. The house looks like its straight out of the magazines. I printed off pictures and sent them to you. They should be here soon."

"I got a Black Panther room, 'Siah!" Honor told him excitedly.

"Yeah? That's dope, dude."

"Mine is Frozen," Hope added.

Acting as if I hadn't told him all of this already, Messiah's eyes bucked with impression. "I bet that's pretty."

"Mommy, did you send him pictures of it?" Hope asked.

"Yes, I did. He just hasn't gotten them yet."

I hated how slow the prison's mail system was. Though my letters arrived quickly, it took forever for them to be inspected before giving them to the prisoners.

Messiah and I held hands while the four of us chatted and laughed. Often, we gave each other googly eyes that made my pussy wet. This moment with him made me regret any time we'd taken for granted. I hated the time that I had lost with him because of our immaturity. I regretted the smallest things, even allowing him to talk me out of doing anything for his birthday that year because we had gone to Miami for New Year's Eve.

"Have you had any more problems from Kidd's family?"

Hearing their names made me instantly roll my eyes. "No. Thank God."

During one of our many conversations, Messiah had told me that Nardo had rode down on Monique. However, I had held my breath, wondering if that would be enough. Apparently, it had been because I hadn't heard anything else from them.

Messiah nodded once. "Good." Then he told me, "I don't want you on the road every weekend, especially once you get big."

I rolled my eyes. "I'm coming. I don't give a fuck what you say. And if you don't accept the visit, I'll just move here and get a job as a correctional officer."

He scoffed with a laugh. "You so crazy."

"For you, hell yeah, I am." I reached over and held his hand. "You're not going to do this time alone. I know I'm not inside with you, but I'm going to be here as much as I can to make the time a little better. I got your back better than your spine."

YAZMEEN HILL

"*Yeeees*, Shauka!" I was whimpering as he pounded this pussy. He was fucking me so rough. But it hurt so good. Since I had been cleared by my OBGYN, Shauka had been murdering this pussy. He had been so consumed with the stress of filling Messiah and Jah's shoes, all while dealing with the anguish of Jah's declining condition. If he wasn't hustling, at the hospital, or being a father, he was destroying this pussy. When he called that day and told me what Dr. Ross had recommended, I knew that my body was in for a lot of punishment the moment that he made it home.

"Oh, God. Oh, *God*!" I panted. There was so much pressure in his strokes. But I wanted each inch of him so bad that I was welcoming the challenge. "Mumph! God!" I began to convulse as an orgasm exploded. He tortured me with continuous strokes through the frenzy. My legs trembled as they rested on his shoulders. My toes curled as I fought to handle the intensity of the climax. My pink toes were signing my lewd moans out in ASL. He saw that I was unraveling wildly and had absolutely no mercy on my throbbing center.

"That's it." The way that he advocated for my orgasm made me leak even more. "I love the feeling of you cumming on this dick."

"Ooo shit!"

"Yeah, let it out. Cum hard for me."

"Oh, God!"

"Look at you." He had the audacity to give me an adoring smile. "You look so beautiful when you cum."

He watched me with daunting intensity as if it was turning him on to see that this dick was making me completely unravel.

He licked his lips and removed my legs from his shoulders. He then rolled me over on my stomach. My sweat and makeup smeared his fitted sheet. He then straddled my ass and held it wide open. The cool air flowing from the vents made the perspiration on my ass tingle. I gripped the sheet as I felt his large head press against my center. I was bracing myself for his intense penetration.

"Mumph!" I yelped as his throbbing member stretched my slick walls.

He then put all of his weight on me, lying on top of my convulsing body. He fisted a handful of my hair and yanked softly until my head was up and my ear was level with his mouth.

"You take this dick so good." His encouraging dominance made me melt into his California king. "Tell me you love this dick." Each word was so fucking addicting.

"I love this dick," I panted. "You know I love this dick."

Still gripping my hair, he slipped his other hand around my throat. Squeezing, he asked, "You gon' let me cum down your throat?"

I nodded so eagerly that it was almost pathetic.

"Come here," he breathily ordered.

He released my neck and hair. I then felt his body weight lift off of me. I hopped up on all fours and then spun around. He was on his knees, jagging his impressionable length fast and hard. His bare chest was heavy. His naked, chocolate body was saturated with sweat.

"Come catch it, baby."

I fervently brought my mouth to his head and sucked him down my throat.

"*Aarrrgh!*" he barked as his body went stiff. I loved him so much that his cum tasted as if it was spiked with maple syrup as it shot down my throat.

Spent, his butt dropped to the bed. His hand left his dick. He was done cumming, but I was an over achiever. I grabbed his length with both hands and resumed jagging him off as I sucked the tip.

"Fuck!" His obscenity bounced off of the walls of his bedroom. I feared that it would wake the baby. "Ah'ight, ah'ight, ah'ight," he panted. "Stop! *Please.*"

I giggled at his rare moment of submission and obliged. I released him from my grip and throat. Just as I collapsed on my back, panting from our kinky, vigorous workout, Asa started to cry.

"I knew you were going to wake him up," I said with a chuckle.

"You shouldn't have been gnawing on my dick like a chihuahua."

"A what?!" I cackled.

He joined in on my laughter as he climbed out of the bed. "I'll get him."

Still attempting to calm my racing heart, I admired his bare perfection, dick swinging between his thick legs. My heart began to sprint.

As he took Asa out of the crib, I envied the way the baby immediately stopped crying. He was already in love with his father.

"Me and Asa are going to go home tonight."

Shauka spun around. Expectantly, he immediately questioned me. "Why?"

"Because I miss my house, my bed, my kitchen."

"What's wrong with this house, this bed, and this kitchen?"

I smiled, shaking my head. Since giving birth, Shauka had placed very tight leashes on me and Asa. At first, I thought it was admirable that he wanted us in his home so much. Now, I felt sorry for him because, obviously, he just wanted us there to ensure that nothing happened to us.

"I've lived alone for the past couple of years, Shauka," I explained. "Being here is different. Sometimes, I miss the solitude of my place."

Shauka shrugged as he kissed Asa's forehead. "Then close the bedroom door."

I sighed inwardly, deciding that this fight wasn't worth trying to win.

Motherhood had been a fantasy. When I had first found out I was pregnant, no one could have convinced me that it would be this blissful. During my pregnancy, I was so elated about becoming a mother. I assumed that it would come with hardships, though, since I was a single parent of a baby that had been created in betrayal. However, fate had been kind, and it hadn't turned out that way. I wasn't alone. Shauka was by our side at every moment when he wasn't hustling or at the hospital with Jah. The Disciple family doted on Asa as if he were the prince of the family. Hattie and Greg treated him like a grandson.

However, this leash that Shauka had around my neck was getting tighter and tighter. Dealing with Messiah's imprisonment and the potential loss of Jah had turned Shauka into a man that now obsessed over his loved ones and who often lost his cool. Unfortunately, since I was closest to him, I got the brunt of it. But I was happy to take the blows because I finally had the man that I had been pining for most of my life.

I loved being Asa's mother. But the icing on the cake was me and Shauka finally telling each other how we felt. It would have made more sense to be honest when we were teenagers or as we started to mature, or most definitely when we ended things the first time. It would have been way less toxic. However, had we connected back then, there was no telling if we would have made it this far. We didn't have a title yet. But at this point, our connection was so intense and powerful that we could survive anything and remain friends and great parents. Our relationship and minds had matured enough that what would have ruined things for us back then would be lightweight now.

Things happen when they are supposed to. The hardest thing about "everything happens for a reason" is waiting for that reason to show up. But, with my eyes fixed on Shauka smiling into Asa's slobbering grin as he held him in the air, I realized that my reason had finally made an appearance.

CHAPTER 13

NAJIA DISCIPLE

A week later, Nardo and I were at one of the crew's staff houses. I was counting money while he divided up the current shipment from the cartel to transport to our network of distributors. The back room that he and I were in was sadly very quiet. Tension had formed between Nardo and me that I regretted and took responsibility for. As time passed, I realized that I simply wasn't the type of woman who could handle intimacy. I constantly ran from Nardo's caring nature because all I knew intimately was the complete opposite.

We still had sex here and there because, despite what I knew and his frustrations with my stubbornness, we couldn't resist each other. Our bond continued to draw us together, and the business kept us in one another's presence. So, some days we would be inseparable. Then he would get too close, and I would put distance between us by making excuses as to why I couldn't spend time with him. Things had been going like that with us for two months, and each time I pushed him away, his comeback was weaker and weaker.

It had been much easier to put all of my focus on business than my reality. I still had yet to shake off the grief of hearing that doctor suggest that we send Jah to hospice care. Luckily, Shauka and I had stood firm on our decision to give him more time. Days later, his stats started to improve. It was as if Jah had heard what the doctor had recommended, and he'd decided to fight even harder. Each day they were reducing the levels of ECMO and oxygen, and his stats either remained level or continued to improve. Yesterday, he was taken off of sedation. Yet, he had yet to wake up. We were all holding our breaths for the moment that he did because that would tell us if he had suffered any neurological damage.

Finally done with counting over half a million dollars, I blew out a relieved breath and pushed back from the table. I then stood and traveled over to the wall where the stash was. My brothers had cut out parts of the drywall so that they could hide money inside of the wall.

As I removed the drywall, I heard Nardo say, "Ah'ight, I'm 'bout to bounce."

His voice was so dispassionate that it broke my heart. But that was my fault too. I had run away from his affection so much that he feared giving it to me at this point. But I found comfort in the distance because I was only accustomed to men being in my presence pretending as if they had no sexual desire for me, when in reality, he loved fucking me.

I turned around, feeling my center pulsate in response to his distance. "Can I see you later?"

Reluctantly, Nardo halted in the doorway and gave me his eyes. He scoffed cynically as he held on to the handles of two large duffles. "I'll let you know."

I pouted. "You've been saying that all week."

"I'm supposed to jump when you say so because now you feel like being bothered?"

My eyes blinked rapidly in response to his sudden aggression. I recoiled as I leaned against the wall. I shamefully lowered my head, unable to look at the frustration in his dark eyes. "You know I've been in my head for the last week."

He angrily clicked his teeth. "Najia, tell that shit to some lame nigga who doesn't know any better."

My eyes rose, questioning the disdain in his tone.

Scowling, he told me. "You always wanna blame the way you act on everything but what it is."

"You have no idea what it is," I mumbled.

His chuckle was so bitter. "Oh, I do, because I was there with you, remember? I was there when you jumped. I snatched the nigga up that made you jump, that made you this way."

The frown on his face brought tears to my eyes. He usually spoke of my trauma with care and support. Now, it was as if he despised it.

"I understand that you got a lot of shit to work out in your head, but I'm not about to keep chasing you, Najia."

"I've never asked you to chase me," I snootily told him.

"You don't have to. Your actions do!" he fussed. "One week, I can't get you out of my bed, and the next, you're making weak excuses for why we can't link. I'm far from one of these lame-ass niggas who's gon' chase you because I ain't never had anybody better. I'm a rich nigga with a big dick. I got options, and I don't have to chase you."

"Then don't." Folding my arms, I hated that the potential of his chase ceasing actually gave me reprieve.

He shook his head with a disappointed glare at me. "And *that's* your problem."

I rolled my eyes. "What is?"

"That you don't want me to chase you." He continued to shake his head as he turned and strolled out.

"I can't help what my trauma turned me into!" I stalked after him. "Do you think that I wanna be this fucked up?! That I only know how to function intimately with a man when he treats me like shit because that's how I was groomed?" Stubborn tears fell from my eyes as he finally halted in the living room.

When he turned to face me, I hated what we had become. What had started out so magical and dreamlike was now a toxic mess.

"I wish that I can be like other girls." Tears raced from my eyes. I could taste the saltiness of them as they slid into my mouth. "I don't want to freak out from what other women would run toward. I swear to God, I wish that Miguel hadn't adopted me just so he could have in-house pussy because he was only attracted to little girls!"

Nardo's disposition softened, as well as his eyes. It was obvious that he wanted to comfort me, but he no longer had the energy. "This is why I said we shouldn't fuck with each other. I knew better."

I inhaled abruptly as his words stabbed my heart. My teeth slid over my bottom lip as I nodded slowly. "Yep. I guess you were right."

The disdain for my stubbornness returned to his eyes. Glaring at me, his jaws tightened. He opened his mouth to say something but changed his mind with a disappointed shake of his head. His large stature then made an about-face and strolled toward the door with a defeated gait.

It felt like I had finally pushed the man who had supported me in one of my darkest times to the brink of no longer caring. I feared that the next time I saw him, that man would no longer exist. I couldn't watch the first man who had ever unconditionally cared for me, outside of my brothers and uncle, walk out of my life. So, I ran back into the room, weeping into my hands.

I rounded the table and collapsed into the chair I'd occupied earlier. With each sniffle, Nardo's masculine scent wafted into my nose and made me despise myself even more. Yet, I couldn't deny the sudden comfort that I felt now that it seemed as if Nardo and I were officially over. I could breathe now that the man who had chosen me and wanted to adore me was now tired of me. That realization made the tears nonstop.

Thankfully, my phone rang, and it was Messiah. I would have never missed a call from him, so I held back the tears and tried to put on a happy disposition as I answered and went through the operator's prompts.

"Hey, brother."

"What's wrong with you?"

I grimaced, realizing I hadn't been able to hide my sorrow. "Nothing."

"Stop lying."

I sighed deeply. "I think I pushed Nardo away."

"Why you think that?"

Messiah had slowly become comfortable with me talking about Nardo to him. Time and situations had forced him to be less obsessed with me and Nardo. But since I was his sister and his twin, his possessive nature still preferred that I didn't fuck with one of his homies.

"I'm still struggling with being comfortable with him...." I paused, finding it hard to say the words.

"Loving you?" he offered.

"He doesn't love me," I insisted.

Messiah clicked his tongue with a chuckle. "Ain't no nigga gonna fuck with his plug's little sister and deal with her trauma for all this time unless he *loves* her. That's the only reason why I'm okay with him being with you. He obviously truly cares about you."

I cringed. "That only scares me even more. I don't want to be like this."

"But unfortunately, the hand life dealt you made you this way. It's a bunch of people that prefer unattached connections over intimacy and feelings. When sexual assault happens within an emotionally intimate relationship like a parent, it makes sense that when sex and intimacy come together later in life, the victim is uncomfortable with it."

I rolled my eyes. "Nigga, you in there reading books and think you a gawd damn therapist."

His words were shaped with pride and happiness as he boasted, "I've been reading up on that shit so that I can counsel yo' ass."

Finally, I laughed, which reminded me that I needed my brother. He ensured that we talked every single day. However, I was longing for his presence so desperately that I feared how I would make it for the next six years. Regretfully, to make his time easier, he refused to take visits from family. But he didn't realize how that made it was more difficult for us.

"But in all seriousness, you gotta stop playing with his feelings. You know I hate to admit this shit, but he fucks with you. He cares about you. He risked his position in our crew to be with you. If your emotions aren't ready for him and for what he brings, then let him go, sis. Because fighting it will only make things worse."

MESSIAH DISCIPLE

I was shocked when I was called for visitation. Visitation was on multiple days during the week, but Tory specifically came on the weekends because the drive was so long. I knew that it wasn't any of my family members because I hadn't put them on my visitation list.

"Oh shit." I smiled when I saw Karen.

Her eyes were wide with impatience as she scanned the line of inmates entering visitation.

She and I had been in heavy communication via letters and phone calls. At first, I was leery of her attempts to mend our relationship. When I got the first letter from her that requested that I call, I was still hesitant. It took weeks of more letters for me to finally call. When I did, I heard the sincerity in her voice. I honestly felt like it was necessary to rebuild our relationship. She and I had our differences, but she had always been a good mother. And I needed the support and care of a good mother.

I was cool with adding her to my visitation list because my bond with her wasn't as nearly inseparable as mine with my siblings, Uncle Buck, and Queen. I knew that I could survive her visits. But she was still finding the courage to make the drive alone to visit a prison full of degenerates that she would usually completely avoid, so she had yet to visit.

Our eyes finally landed on one another's as I broke the line and walked toward her.

"Surprise!" she happily exclaimed with her arms outstretched.

I felt confused eyes from other inmates and visitors on me as this older white woman took me into her arms.

"Oh my gosh! Look at you!" She pushed back, holding on to my arms as her striking blue eyes scanned my frame. "Jesus, you're big!"

I smiled cockily. I had been heavily relying on lifting weights to pass time.

Chatter and chaos around us caught her attention, pulling her eyes away from my smile. She scanned the room that was full of prisoners and rowdy loved ones. Some of them were crying. Some were already arguing. Most of the kids were acting up. A lot of prisoners and visitors were of a lower class than she would ever willingly be in the same room with. And all of them were Black. The only Black people Karen had been around were the uppity ones who lived in suburbia with us. She had never been surrounded by the danger and filth of the criminals and ghetto personas of the people who were eyeing the only white woman in the room.

She suddenly blinked rapidly, as if she were trying to bring herself back to reality. She then looked up at me with a forced smile. "Let's sit."

Miguel had always been distant when Najia and I were growing up. He had been a dispassionate father who spent most of his time at work and left the housework and kids to his wife. I had no idea that his distance was actually because he was raping my sister. However, Karen had always been a mother who was ten toes down. She was deeply involved in every aspect of our lives. But, as we grew up, it was very obvious that we were Black and she was white. There were certain elements of the Black culture that she wanted our family to stay away from. So, I found it funny that she was clearly perturbed with her surroundings as we sat. But the fact that she was there spoke volumes.

"You want anything?" she asked as she watched people going to the vending machines.

"I'm good for right now."

Her smile spread as she reached over the table for my hands. She took both of them into hers. "It's so good to see you. I've missed you and your sister so much."

I recoiled when she mentioned Najia. No matter how much I passed on Karen's explanation for her actions at Starbucks that day and her love and apologies, Najia refused to hear it.

"She still won't answer?" I asked.

"I stopped calling," she admitted reluctantly. "I just pray that she will come around one day. But I miss her so much." She looked up at the ceiling, briefly closing her eyes. "Gosh, I miss my baby. I had always been preparing myself for the day you two left the nest. Nothing would have prepared me for it being under these conditions, though. I would have never imagined that I wouldn't have a relationship with either one of you. But..." She forced a bright smile. "I'm appreciative that I at least still have you."

"I'm sorry she's being so defiant," I told her. "But you gotta understand that her mental is not stable right now. And I have no idea when it will be. She's been through a lot."

The reminder made Karen shutter. Her expression tightened as she lowered her head. Her hands released mine. She then placed her chin onto one palm and rested that elbow on the table. She began to stare out of the nearest window as a tear escaped.

I sadly watched her. I knew that her remorse was real. In the short time since Miguel's arrest, she had aged so much. Wrinkles had appeared, and so had gray hairs in her traditional bob that she kept at her chin.

Thankfully, because of what she told the police, there had been no further investigation into Miguel's disappearance.

"I *cannot* believe that I was married to such a terrible man." Tears teetered at Karen's eyelids. "I spent so much time protecting you all from danger when I was married to it. I'm so sorry."

I reached across the table and held her hand. "You have nothing to be sorry for. You had no idea. Neither did I."

Squeezing my hand, she finally brought her sorrowful eyes to me. "I know what really happened to Miguel," she said in a whisper. "His father told me about the man that came into his house and took him that night."

My brows furrowed as I sat back, but she held my hand so tight that I couldn't take it out of her grasp.

"I thank whomever it is that did it. Rotting in prison wouldn't have been enough punishment," she seethed. "And I, nor his father, will *never* tell a soul."

Finally, she released my hand, and a small smile appeared amongst her tears.

The night that Miguel was kidnapped, Nardo threatened Miguel's father into silence. I had assumed he had never told anyone about the man who had broken into his home and took Miguel that night, since those details had never been shared with the police.

"I thank them too," I coolly replied.

"After his father told me that was when I went to the police and convinced them that Miguel had most likely skipped town to avoid those charges. I also went to Mexico and used some of his credit cards. So, we never have to worry about his case being opened again.".

Though she now sat across from me silently, simply staring at me with that weak smile, I understood every word that she wasn't saying.

TORY CLARK

Our shared burdens, stress, and love felt for the Disciple brothers had forced a bond between me, Yaz, Faye, and Najia. Yet, we had never been able to hang out without the guys because as soon as our bond formed, Messiah went to jail, Jah got sick, and no one could focus on anything outside of that.

However, Jah's improvement had given us all a reason to finally relax a little bit. That evening, we met at Chemistry in Hyde Park for some good food and drinks. We were seated at the bar as we waited for our entrees.

"Ooo, I'm so mad that I can't drink." I pouted as I watched the waitress sit the other's cocktails in front of them.

Najia scoffed with a humored scowl as she shook her head. "I still *cannot* believe that Messiah is about to be a father." As we all giggled, she added, "Like who would let that crazy motherfucker knock them up and be somebody's daddy?"

"My crazy ass!" I spat as I cracked up, causing the rest of them to follow suit.

"But I gotta admit that he has matured so much," Najia said.

Everyone nodded.

"He really has," Faye agreed.

Per usual, whenever Messiah was brought up in conversation, I was blanketed with yearning and weariness. Messiah and I did all that we could to help each other deal with his incarceration. But there was only so much that those weekend visits and daily phone calls could do. We hadn't missed a beat in one another's lives, but the yearning for his presence was suffocating. Many days, I managed to keep myself busy in order to prevent the depression from setting in. My kids kept my mind on other things. My pregnancy was a light in each day. And being a part of the Disciple family kept my spirits high. However, I longed for his touch, and, at random moments, the reality sunk in that he was going to be gone for six very long years.

"Yaz, Shauka has Asa?" I asked to change the subject.

Yaz sucked her teeth with a wave of her hand. "No. Hattie is watching him for me."

"What's wrong?" I asked with an arched brow.

"Shauka is wearing me out. The smallest things send him over the edge, and he refuses to let me go home. All of the things that have happened have really changed him." Sighing, Yaz sadly shook her head.

"Yea, I've heard about him spazzing out on some of the crew," Najia added.

"Everyone deals with loss and pain differently," Faye replied.

"I know," Yaz said, still wearing her weary expression. "Don't get me wrong. I love being at the estate and with Shauka. Having Hattie and Najia around to help with the baby has been a lifesaver. But I miss my house, and, sometimes, I need a break from Shauka's imbalance."

Najia and Faye nodded in agreement while I sipped from my cup of water with lemon.

"Well, I hope Hattie will be available to help me with mine when it comes," I said, rubbing my belly.

"I'm sure she will be," Najia said with a smile.

"That's a shame we gotta rely on Hattie instead of our baby daddies because they some street niggas," I said.

"Why can't we just be normal twenty-something-year-old chicks that are in college getting romanced by athletes and being taken home to meet their parents?" Yaz asked.

Faye scoffed with a roll of her eyes. "Because that shit is boring as hell."

"Facts!" I laughed.

"Speaking of college, when are you going, Najia?" Yaz asked.

Since graduating from high school, Najia had pushed back starting college. She didn't think that she could focus on her studies while her mind was consumed with the trauma that her adoptive parents had caused. And for the last two months, she had been really busy managing the crew's finances and multiple properties, as well as assisting at Disciple Records.

"Now that I'm working for my brothers, I doubt I ever will," she answered before taking a sip of her drink. "In addition to the money that I'm making, I'm realizing how much I can make through investments, rather than spending years in college."

Yaz nodded slowly. "I feel that. I still think you should go, though."

"You didn't go," Najia fussed.

"Nah, I didn't, and look at me!" Yaz countered. "My life is good now, but I went through some shit that I wouldn't have had I been on somebody's campus. The streets ain't all fun and games. Don't get too comfortable living that life."

"It ain't like she's selling drugs, Yaz," Faye said.

"True. She's just the drug secretary," Yaz quipped.

Najia groaned. "Can we change the..." Suddenly, she froze. She was staring straight ahead, grabbing all of our attention. We followed her eyes to the vestibule where the hostess stand was. I gasped inwardly when I saw Nardo speaking to the hostess with his hand in the small of a woman's back.

I reluctantly looked toward Najia, who blinked slowly a few times before giving her attention back to her drink.

We all knew of the toxicity of her and Nardo's relationship. It was obvious that Nardo cared about her, but Najia didn't want all that he had to give. Usually, it was the woman who was chasing the man, trying to get him to commit. But we also knew of Najia's trauma and treaded lightly when it came to how she dealt with Nardo.

"You okay?" Yaz asked softly.

Najia shrugged. "We aren't in a relationship."

"So," I spat. "Y'all been fucking for a minute. That's your dude."

Najia lifted her hand to stop my ranting. "He's not. And it isn't like he hasn't tried. It's *me*. I don't want to be in a relationship, so he has every right to date whoever he wants to."

FAYE SINGER

Najia was trying to sound tough, but I could see the hurt in her eyes. I was hurt for her. Nardo was clearly on a date. The woman he was with was smiling up into his eyes. The anticipation in her orbs was that of a woman looking forward to what was next with him. He was even dressed differently. The joggers and hoodie had been replaced with jeans and a fitted short-sleeved collared shirt. The lights in the chandeliers bounced off of the diamonds on and around his neck and wrists.

Tory and Yaz continued to watch Najia sympathetically as she forced her eyes to stay on her drink. I watched Nardo to see if he would ever look this way. But as he and his date were taken to their table on the other side of the restaurant, he never did.

"*Anyway*," Najia pressed. "What do you want to have, Tory?"

Despite her attempt to change the subject, the rest of us wore uncomfortable and disappointed expressions. The way she had stubbornly rejected Nardo was sad to watch. But we understood.

Clearing her throat, Tory forced a smile and allowed the subject to change. "I don't care since I already have a boy and a girl. As long as it's healthy, I'll be happy."

I groaned discreetly. Every time they mentioned anything about pregnancy or baby, I got sick to my fucking stomach. I had been hitting Mia up for the DNA results for weeks, but she wouldn't answer. Chloe was convinced that it meant that Mia had been lying. But I needed a definite answer so I could finally let go of this rage and resentment.

It had been such an unnerving experience to sit by Jah's bedside, praying for him to get better while despising his existence. I never expected Jah to be faithful. He was a rich nigga and a beautiful man. Women threw pussy at him all the time. But I had specifically only asked that he stay away from Mia. That was a violation that I could not stop thinking about, even while he had suffered over the last two months. I couldn't even wholeheartedly fight for him because I was hurting because of him. I felt so guilty that my prayers had been laced with hostility.

I had even felt reluctant when his health started to turn around last week. If he remained unconscious, I would never have to confront him.

"Faye," I heard Tory call.

I pulled my eyes away from my drink. "Humph?"

"You okay?"

"Yeah," I answered softly.

However, Tory continued to look at me suspiciously.

I hadn't told anyone except Chloe about Mia's baby and the DNA test. I didn't want to add this drama to their worry for Jah. For them, I knew it would be so trivial in comparison to what he'd been going through. But for me, it had overshadowed everything.

"You sure?" Tory asked.

I forced a smile. "Yeah, I'm—"

My ringtone impaled the air, interrupting the lie on the tip of my tongue. I glanced down at the bar where it sat next to my drink. It was a FaceTime call from Jah's nurse, so I quickly picked it up and answered.

"Hello?"

"Hey!"

My eyes narrowed curiously at the wide grin on Amber's face. I could see every tooth in her mouth as her thin, red lips curved up to her ears.

"What's up?" I asked.

"I tried to call Shauka and Najia. Are they around you?"

"Najia is."

Hearing that, Najia sat up to look at me. "Who is that?"

"Amber."

Immediately, Najia hopped off of her barstool and hurried toward me.

Standing next to me, she placed her face next to mine and stared into the phone. "What's up, Amber? Is something wrong with my brother? How is he?"

Her eyes began to dance. "Ask him yourself."

Our heads reared back curiously. We looked at one another as Amber's camera turned around.

"Oh my God!" I screamed excitedly.

"Ah!" Najia belted.

Tory and Yaz scrambled toward us to see what had caused me and Najia to overreact. Patrons and bartenders darted their curious and warning eyes toward us as me and Najia's shouts interrupted the quiet atmosphere of the quaint restaurant.

"What?" Tory asked as she forced space between Najia and me so that she could see the phone. "Oh my God!"

I couldn't speak. I could only cry as Najia yelped, "Hey, brother!"

Jah couldn't speak either. He was still intubated. But his eyes were open, and he was smiling.

CHAPTER 14

JAH DISCIPLE

I was so happy to be alive when I opened my eyes a month ago. I could hardly remember much of what I had suffered once I was admitted. The last thing I recalled was the delusions and wild, vivid dreams and being sure that I was going to die.

Yet, a month after opening my eyes, I was recovering from COVID. But when they removed the ventilation that was when the real fight began.

It had taken me awhile to get back to my normal self. For the first week, I had suffered from hospital delirium. I had been sedated so much and on so many different medications that my mental status was delayed, and I wasn't myself. I was in and out of consciousness. When I was awake, I suffered panic attacks because the trach and NG tube were so alarming.

Slowly, I began to become myself. Physiotherapy had helped to improve my breathing and lung capacity, decrease anxiety and phobia, as well as increase the muscle strength that had been affected by COVID. I was being discharged to a rehab facility in a few days to improve my physical and functional recovery from the virus' damaging effects on my body and mind. My strength had been significantly depleted. The nerves and muscles in my body weren't performing the same. I had weakness in my legs, hands, and fingers that made it difficult to complete regular activities that I once took for granted. I could hardly walk or do simple things like dress myself and shower.

Since I'd opened my eyes last month, I had had a revolving door of visitors. But that day, as Faye and I heard footsteps coming into the room, we were surprised to see Renee.

Faye's shocked irises whipped toward me as Renee sheepishly walked toward the foot of the bed.

"Hi," she softly spoke.

"H-hey," I returned, unable to hide my surprise.

Since Faye had barely left my bedside, she had been filling me in on everything that had happened since I was admitted, including every single person that had visited me. So, I was aware that Renee never had.

"Hi," Faye spoke as well. "I'm–"

"Faye," Renee interjected with a smile. "I've seen pictures of you on social media. Nice to meet you."

"Nice to meet you too."

I hesitantly looked at Faye, hoping that she wouldn't react to the recollection of Renee trying to kiss me. However, when I told her some time ago, she understood that Renee was just going through a lot.

Sighing, Faye stood. I held my already weak breath until she finally gave me a small smile. "I'm going to give you two some privacy. I'm going to get something to eat. You want something?"

Slowly, I had been able to eat normally with the tracheostomy, although swallowing was difficult at first. I started by taking small sips of water before gradually moving on to soft foods, followed by regular food.

"Just get me whatever you get yourself."

She nodded before grabbing her purse from the hook on the wall and walking out. I watched her longingly. Though she had never left my side, Faye was obviously different. There was a tension between us that I couldn't put my finger on. However, I had to remind myself that I hadn't gone through this alone. She had suffered as well, along with my family. When they told me that my heart had stopped and that the doctor had suggested that I be put in hospice, my heart went out to the grief that they had suffered.

Clearing her throat, Renee inched toward the seat that Faye had just been occupying.

"How are you?" she asked nervously.

I chuckled sarcastically. "I'm alive. So, I won't complain."

She gave me a small smile while her eyes took in the NG tube, trach, and countless machines that I was attached to.

"I'm so happy that you survived," she said. Her eyes were fighting weariness as she looked at me. "I hated hearing what you were going through. I'm sorry that I never visited. I just..." She took a shaky, deep breath. "I was scared to show my face, knowing all of the grief that Moe caused."

"No one blames you for what Moe did—"

"He was an informant."

"I know."

"For Messiah's murder case," she admitted with reluctance and guilt painting her expression.

My body grew rigid as her eyes lowered.

"Detective Freemont called me over and over again, looking for him. He had given her a statement. He told her that Messiah killed Kidd. She was looking for him because he had promised to testify, but she could never find him."

As she spoke, my heart began to pound in my chest as anxiety washed over me.

"I'm so sorry," she said with tears in her eyes. "I'm sorry for everything he did, and I'm so sorry for trying to kiss you."

I reached for her hand, and she reluctantly gave it to me.

"You don't have anything to be sorry about. My mind was still reeling from her confession, but I was able to push past that to soothe her. She wasn't to blame; drugs were at fault here. "I'm sorry for not looking out for him. I should have been there for him so that he never got hooked on that shit."

"He was a grown man, Jah. He knew what he was doing." Then regret filled her eyes. Her lips parted but then closed as if she didn't want to say what was coming out next. "Jah... Moe's body was found a few days ago."

I blinked slowly. No amount of sedation and medication could have made my mind so foggy that I forgot that I had killed my own brother. The guilt had often found me in my dreams and delusions as the disease engulfed me. I remembered seeing Moe standing at the foot of my bed many times when I opened my eyes at the height of my suffering. However, each time, he told me that he forgave me.

"His remains were found in an abandoned house."

I then made my own confession. "I know where he was."

I had too much respect for Moe and her to sit in her face and lie.

Renee gave me a knowing expression. "I assumed you did."

"You..." My voice cracked, so I cleared my throat to push past the guilt and sadness of his demise. "You did?"

"Yea," she nodded sadly. "And I don't blame you. He was a loose cannon. He was going to destroy everyone's life around him. He may not have been able to ever testify, but he had something to do with Messiah being in jail. He was a snitch. I don't blame you. And his death actually helped me and Ariel." Finally, she smiled brightly. "His insurance policy is going to get us back on our feet, help move us into a safe neighborhood, and set us up for a prosperous future."

I grinned, nodding. "Good. But you know I'll always take care of you and my god baby."

Her lips still curved upward, nearly touching her ears. "I know."

"When is his funeral?"

"I'm not having one," she said, waving her hand dismissively. "I'm going to cremate him and turn his ashes into something memorable for Ariel. Maybe a necklace or something."

"I'd like some of his ashes, if you don't mind."

"Of course, I don't mind."

❦

RENEE AND I WERE STILL CATCHING UP AN HOUR LATER. RENEE HAD shown me picture after picture and countless videos of my god baby. I was amazed at how much Ariel had grown.

Soon, Faye returned with Buck on her heels.

"Renee?" he called out in surprise as soon as he noticed her.

She grinned while standing. "Hey, Buck."

He quickly galloped toward her with his arms outstretched. When he took her into his arms, she closed her eyes as if she needed the embrace.

"How are you doing?"

"I'm good, Buck. You?"

"Can't complain." Then he looked at me, saying, "God is good."

"Yes, He is," she said, glancing back at me as well. "And how is Queen?"

"She's great."

"That's good. I'm so sorry about what happened to her."

"Hush," he said as he took his arms from around her. "That wasn't your fault."

She pursed her lips but said, "I appreciate that."

We all conversed for a while as me and Faye ate the tacos she had brought back with us. Soon, Renee said her goodbyes.

"You bet' not be a stranger," I told her.

"She better not," Buck added.

Renee smiled sheepishly as she put her purse over her shoulder. "I won't. I promise."

Relief flooded me. I was grateful to have her around again because it made me feel Moe's presence and forgiveness.

"I'm going to walk out with you," Faye announced as she stood. "I need to go home to shower and change. Let me know if you want me to bring you anything back," she told me.

"Cool," I returned.

She followed Renee without her usual "I love you", which made it hard to believe that our tension was solely because of my hospitalization.

After they walked out, Buck rested back in his chair, staring at the game on the television mounted on the wall. It was still so odd to have him in my life again. There hadn't been an emotional kumbaya between us. But Shauka had told me what he'd secretly heard Buck praying and saying as he cried at my bedside. That was all that I needed to accept his presence when my eyes opened again. As men, a handshake was as good as any apology. And that's what he had done the moment he'd come to see me once I was conscious again. He'd paired it with an "I love you," that spoke volumes. That was all that I needed to hear to know that he wanted my forgiveness and that I already had his.

SHAUKA DISCIPLE

That afternoon, I was in the hood, standing in the bed of a pickup truck amongst a plethora of food and toys.

"Aye, everybody stand in a single file line. You don't have to push. It's enough for everybody!" I bellowed over the raucous that the crowd was causing.

Heavy and Tank reiterated what I'd said to the crowd as they forced everyone into an organized line. One by one, they eagerly walked up to the truck to receive either a bag of toys for their kids, a box of food, or both. Whatever they asked for, Nardo and Frey gave them. Every few months, my brothers and I would give away food, clothes, shoes, and toys in the hood to those in need to keep up my father's tradition of being the ghetto's Robin Hood. It was surreal that I was now doing it without them. But I was grateful that soon, Jah would be by my side again.

"Aye, Shauka!" Recognizing Coop's voice, I looked around and spotted him parked in front of the pickup truck. "I need to holla at you."

Nodding, I hopped over the bed of the truck onto the sidewalk. Coop then started to frantically hurry toward me.

"What's going on?"

"White Boy Mark is MIA," he unloaded with frantic eyes.

Last month, Coop had agreed to transport fifty bricks to a hustler, White Boy Mark, that I knew in Minnesota who needed a new plug. Last night, I had sent Coop back to collect the money Mark owed me.

I shrugged. "Then find him."

His eyes ballooned. "Find him? He's *your* people. I was simply doing you a favor by making the drop and going to collect. I got my own hustlers to keep up with."

I had resented having to rely on other members of the crew to take care of my responsibilities. But I had to because Nardo and I were spread so thin.

I sighed, frustrated with being brought yet another problem to fix. "I ain't got time for this shit."

Coop scoffed at my audacity. "Neither do I. But he's *your* people, bro. I don't even know him, so how am I supposed to find him?"

The constant barrage of words was sending me into a spiral. Suddenly, a wave of anger washed over me, a seething, boiling rage that I couldn't control. I felt like I was about to explode, like I needed to unleash this fury on someone, anyone. And then I see my homie, standing there, looking at me, waiting for me to make another big decision, to be the leader, yet again.

"I said I ain't got time for this shit right now!" I bellowed into his face, causing sudden quiet around us. It was as if the entire block had gone completely still as I exploded on Coop. "Nigga, I got an entire crew to run, grown ass niggas to look after, and you steady chirping—"

"Chirping? So, you're calling me a bitch?" he asked, chest swelling.

I closed the space between us, jaws tight. "You must be a bitch if you can't handle one white boy! Do I have to do everything?! You can't handle him?! If not, then what the fuck I need you in the fold for?!"

"It don't look like I'm the one that's acting like a bitch." Then, Coop chuckled, sending me flying over the edge.

Before I even knew what I was doing, my hands were around his throat as I hurled insults and accusations like they were weapons.

"Yo, Shauka, chill." Nardo was behind me, gently grabbing my elbow.

But the sudden rage that engulfed me had convinced me that he had snatched me up as if I was as weak as I felt. Letting go of Coop's neck, I swung around, snatching my arm out of his grasp and throwing my hands into his chest so hard that he stumbled back.

I bolted away, storming off.

"You lucky you my nigga, and I know you're going through some shit!" I heard Coop threaten behind me. "That's your last time, though, my nigga!"

People in my way fearfully scattered the other way as I stalked down the block. I kicked objects in my path, causing a glass bottle to soar into the air and come trashing down the windshield of an SUV.

"Shauka!" I heard Nardo call me in warning. But thankfully, his voice had come from afar.

I could feel my heart racing in my chest, pounding like a drum as my breath became erratic and shallow. My mind was a jumble of thoughts, each one more overwhelming than the last. The weight of all the new responsibilities I'd taken on was crushing me, suffocating me. I tried to take a deep breath, to calm down, but it felt like there was a vice around my chest.

Over time, I found myself unraveling more and more, left alone with the wreckage that my lashing out had caused.

As I charged down the street, feeling boiling rage rise to the surface, my phone rang. I pulled it out of my pocket and only answered because it was Yaz.

"What?" I barked, answering.

"Excuse me?" her offense responded.

Clicking my tongue, I rushed her, "What's going on, Yaz?"

"What the hell is wrong with you?"

I began to pace. "I just lost it on Coop."

"Why?"

"I sent him to Minnesota to get my money from White Boy Mark, but he couldn't find him. He told me it was my problem to deal with because White Boy Mark is my people."

"*Weeeell*," she sang reluctantly. "That's true."

"You don't think I know that, Yaz?!" I yelled.

"Aye, don't yell at me!" she returned angrily.

"Well, *you* called *me!*"

"You're right! That's *my* bad!" she spat before her end of the line went completely dead.

Realizing that she'd hung up, I hurled my phone into the street. "Fuuuuuck?!"

I didn't know what was happening to me. Since my wedding, I had turned into a loose cannon that people tip-toed around and watched with uncertainty. Fear and panic exploded out of nowhere, so powerful that I didn't know how to handle it. So, I succumbed to it by unraveling in sadness or explosive anger.

As I continued to pace, I caught a glimpse of the crowd up the street, where the pickup truck was. Everyone was staring at me in wonder and bafflement. Embarrassment made me turn my back on them. Regret moved my feet further away from them and around the corner.

Before my wedding, I barely remembered what fear was. Now, it was in my rearview mirror, taunting me. I feared losing my brothers, my sister, Yaz, and my son. I feared Yaz seeing in me what Sariah did that made her so comfortable deceiving me. And now, I feared losing everyone around me for good because I had completely lost control.

FIVE MONTHS LATER...

CHAPTER 15

FAYE SINGER

"*oooooh* shit!"

I shook my head at Messiah's dramatic antics while dabbing Tory's forehead.

Panting tiredly, Tory growled at Najia, "Hang up on his ass!"

"You betta fucking not!" Messiah threatened Najia.

Poor Najia looked so torn as she stood at the foot of the bed. She was holding her phone up so that Messiah wouldn't miss a second of his child being born while on FaceTime. At this point, he was a boss in prison. He had power and a crew. That power had given him the perks of paying a guard to slip him an iPhone inside.

"One more push, Tory!" her OB encouraged.

Tory began to growl so loud and push so hard that I cringed as if I could feel her pain.

"Good job, Tory," I encouraged her.

Tory's mother had chosen to stay home with Hope and Honor when Tory went into labor that morning. Najia was always going to be in the delivery room with Tory so that Messiah could watch the birth of their baby. Yet, she had also asked that I come along in her mother's place because she needed someone to comfort her.

Yet, I felt as if I were doing a poor job. It had been nearly a year since I'd learned of Jah's disloyalty. But every time I saw a pregnant woman or a baby, anger consumed me.

"*Arrrgh!*" Tory howled as she pushed with all of her strength.

I couldn't bring myself to look toward the foot of the bed. I didn't want to witness what was obviously sickening to Najia, because, while holding the phone next to the OB's head, she continued to look away with a disgusted expression painting her face. However, peeking just a bit, I saw as the OB pulled the baby out.

Tory blew a heavy, loud breath of relief as she flung her body back onto the bed. She panted as delirium covered her expression.

"It's a girl!" Messiah could be heard exclaiming with excitement.

Immediately, Tory began to cry.

"Take the phone over to her, Najia," he told her.

Obediently, Najia rushed over to the other side of the bed. She then aimed the camera at Tory, who was too weak to look at it.

"I love you, baby." Messiah's words cracked. "You did so good. Our baby is beautiful, just like you."

Hearing a once immature, all too playful boy now speak to his woman like a grown man brought tears to my eyes.

Sobs prevented Tory from being able to say a word. The nurse appeared next to me with the baby swaddled in a blanket. She was now clean of after birth, revealing her perfect face. I gushed as the nurse nestled the baby under Tory's arm, causing emotions to burst out of Tory in more uncontrollable sobs.

Messiah cried. "I wish that I was there with you."

"Me too," Tory exclaimed with uncontrollable tears.

"Thank you for being the mother of my child."

Tears poured from my eyes. Even the doctor and nurses in the room began to show emotions of sympathy and adoration.

"I love you so much," Messiah told Tory.

In return, she cried, "I love you too."

OVER THE LAST FEW MONTHS, I HAD REMAINED BY JAH'S SIDE AS HE completed physical therapy. The wonder behind the truth of Jah's deception was in the back of my mind as I drove him to each session, as I showered him, while I fed him, as I aided in nursing him back to health. But I could never part my lips to ask the question because it felt so selfish to bring up something that was obviously so minuscule in comparison to what he was going through.

But after witnessing the love and devotion between Tory and Messiah, I could no longer resist.

As I paced outside of the delivery room, I nervously waited for Jah to answer the phone.

"Hey, baby."

I cringed when the loving sound of his voice disgusted me. "Hi," I forced.

"Is the baby here?"

He was so curious that he completely ignored the bitterness in my tone.

"Yea. About thirty minutes ago. It's a girl."

"That's dope. How is Tory?"

"She's resting now."

Then he finally heard the mood that I was in. "What's wrong? You okay?"

"No."

"What's going on?"

"I need to ask you a question, Jah."

"What's that?"

I cringed, forcing myself to open this can of worms. "Did you fuck Mia?"

The deafening silence told me what I needed to know. Then his deep sigh, riddled with guilt, made it official.

I cringed. "*Shit*, Jah."

"I'm sorry, baby."

"Why would you do that?!" Realizing how loud I was, I began to bolt towards the exit of Labor and Delivery.

"I was drunk. It was the day that those pictures of you were leaked online-"

"And you purposely went to the club to fuck her so that you could hurt me!"

"Wait... How do you know all of this?"

I was spewing through gritted teeth as I barged through double doors. "She called me while you were sick. She told me because she had a baby and realized her boyfriend might not be the father. He left her because wasn't sure if it was yours or not. I helped her get your DNA."

"What the fuck, Faye?! Why didn't you tell me?"

"Why didn't I tell you?!" I mocked cynically. "Why did you fuck her?!"

"Was the baby mine?"

"I'm assuming not since she disappeared and is back with her boyfriend."

When he sighed with relief, my anger multiplied because he felt better, while I was still in shambles.

"I'm glad you feel better."

"Of course, I'm happy that the baby isn't mine, but I'm not happy that I hurt you."

"You could have told me."

"I couldn't bring myself to tell you something like that. I knew that it would crush you."

"And, yet, I still ended up crushed, didn't I, Jah?!" That explosion gained the attention of staff and visitors that were in the hall along with me. I quieted, saying, "I have to go, Jah."

"Wait. Faye!"

I ended the call.

JAH DISCIPLE

"Fuck!" I barked as I got Faye's voicemail again.

It was now the next day. I hadn't heard from Faye since she'd hung up on me. She was nowhere to be found. Her car hadn't been parked outside of her building, and she never came back to the estate.

"That girl loves you," Shauka tried to convince me. "She's not going to leave you."

Throwing my phone onto the couch, I shook my head. "I doubt that, bro. I fucked up this time."

Once I was stable, I was released to a rehabilitation facility. But, after a few months of rehabilitation, I was a new man. I had gained my weight back and could, once again, complete normal day-to-day activities on my own. I had my life back. However, Faye thought it was the perfect time to approach the elephant in the room that I'd had no idea was there.

When Faye confronted me about Mia, I was dumbfounded. I wanted to lie. I could feel her heartache through my phone as she waited for an answer. It would have been easier to play on Mia's obsession with humiliating Faye. But I had a new outlook on life. God had spared me, so I couldn't lie.

"I should have lied." I shook my head slowly as I picked up my glass of cognac from the floor of the den.

"That would have only made shit worse," Shauka replied as he checked his phone for the umpteenth time.

I chuckled sarcastically. "Yaz ain't calling you back either, huh?"

Shauka groaned. "Nah."

"She's at work, right?"

"Yea. I'm just checking on her."

I taunted him with a chuckle while turning toward where he sat on the recliner. "You gotta chill, bro."

Though I was back to health, the effects of my condition were still lingering on my people. Shauka was a mess. One minute, he was his old self. The next, he was an unstable, angry version of himself that kept his loved ones on a short leash. Yaz and Asa's leash was the shortest.

"I'm sorry for scaring you," I told him. "And I know that Messiah hates to be away from us. But this isn't the same as our parents dying or foster parents that didn't want us. We aren't going to end up cold, broke, and hungry again."

"But I can definitely end up mourning again," he said so confidently. "We made it out of the streets. We're rich now. We can buy anything, except the certainty that nothing will ever happen to us. We never expected Messiah to end up in prison for murder. We never expected to have to make the choice to send you to hospice or not. I laid with Sariah everyday but had no idea that she was manipulating me. We can't assume that everything will be okay."

"But we'll get through it," I assured him. "We'll survive. If we can survive losing our parents, we can survive anything, bro."

Shauka's expression remained emotionless as he stared at the television. I felt guilty for having a hand in making him this way. My hospitalization had aided in turning him into an anxious man that feared everything.

Suddenly, the front door to the estate opened and the alarm chimed. Shauka and I remained still because we assumed that it was

Najia. But I soon smelled *her*. She had been attached to my hip for so long that I knew her smell.

I stood up from the couch and rushed out of the den. Faye and I met in the foyer. The reluctant look on her face told me that her presence there had been a hard decision to make.

The guilt weighing on me forced my shoulders to sink. I moped towards her. I fearfully stretched my arms out to her, holding my breath.

When she accepted my embrace, I released a breath that I didn't know I was holding.

"Where have you been?" I asked while holding her.

"At a hotel. I didn't want you to find me."

"You're mad at me?"

"I hate you," she whined into my chest.

"I know."

"Why would you do that to me?" Her tiny hands gripped the back of my shirt angrily.

"It wasn't on purpose. I was drunk and irrational. I'm sorry. You've been nothing but committed to me and to my family. I owe you the world, and I promise to spend every day of my life returning the favor, baby. I promise."

YAZMEEN HILL

"Let me call you back, Angela. I'm running in my house real quick."

"*Ooo*, what are you doing at home?"

"I'm not staying. Asa and I need some clothes."

"Mm humph. Shauka is going to kill you."

I clicked my tongue as I turned off the engine. "Shauka better chill the fuck out."

"Yeah okay," Angela returned with a chastising laugh. "I'll talk to you later."

"Okay."

As I climbed out of the car, exhaustion weighed heavily on me. The day after Tory had given birth, Angela and I had enjoyed a quick girl's night out after work with Faye. She needed it because she was reeling with anger after Jah's confession.

Since becoming a mom, I hadn't had the time to drink as much. So, the two Long Island iced teas I'd drunk at dinner with her had me tipsily walking towards my building.

I hated the chaos of living between two places. After a year, I was still living mostly at the Disciple estate. Shauka had been insisting that I give up my condo. It would have made sense since I was rarely home.

But I appreciated still having my condo to escape to whenever I needed some alone time.

Before gathering more clothes for Asa and me, I lay on my bed, relishing in the quiet, relieved that I wasn't in the constant ruckus of the estate and engulfed in Shauka's suffocation. Over time, Shauka had unraveled into a man I didn't recognize. Most days, he was his normal self. Yet, randomly, he would unleash on me in ways that were so odd for him. He clung to me and Asa as if he were losing us.

I loved Shauka with every fiber of my being and every beat of my heart. However, trauma had hardened him over the past year and disloyalty had changed him. He had become increasingly suffocating.

Coupled with the rotation of siblings and crew in and out of the estate, Hattie appearing in our room randomly during the day, music coming from Najia's room, and other constant commotion, I was exhausted.

⟡⟡⟡

I hadn't known how much time had passed when I was jolted out of my sleep by my blaring ringtone. Gasping, I sat straight up, searching my bed for my phone. I found it and cringed when I saw that it was Shauka calling and that it had been three hours since I'd rushed inside.

I had missed ten calls from him.

"Shit!" I exclaimed as I answered. "Shauka, I'm so sorry—"

"Where the fuck are you at, Yaz?!"

"I'm at home. I came here after dinner with Angela to get more clothes for me and the baby. I guess I fell asleep."

"Yaz, that's some bullshit!"

"Huh?"

"I was fucking worried about you! I've been blowing your phone up. If you don't want to be here, then just say that!"

"Why are you overreact—"

"This is not a fucking overreaction, Yaz! I've been calling you for hours!"

"And I told you that I accidentally fell asleep."

"Fuck man!" he barked as I heard a loud thud in his background.

Cringing, I told him, "Calm down, Shauka."

"Don't fucking tell me to calm down, Yaz! Fuck you!"

My mouth fell open. "Fuck me?"

"Yeah. *Fuck you.*"

"I..." Words lodged in my throat when I realized he'd rudely ended the call. Groaning, I held my head in my hands.

One would think that it would be like a fairy tale to be held up in a lavish estate with a chef, housekeeper, and a revolving door of family that catered to my son. And, if I had grown up in that, it would have been ideal. However, I had been alone for so many years that I craved my solitude and peace. The constant liveliness of the estate was overwhelming at times, and I yearned for the stillness and isolation of my condo. But when I'd tried to escape, Shauka was unbearable. Whenever I wasn't in his presence, he called me nonstop. If he couldn't get in touch with me, he would overreact or explode. Many times, he lashed out on me uncontrollably. I had offered that Shauka move into my condo or that we purchase a home together, but he had refused because the moment he had previously stepped out of his comfort zone, he got played.

Sariah had ruined him. Yet, *I* was suffering the consequences.

FAYE SINGER

Jah's truth had ruined us. But unlike the other times, I couldn't bring myself to leave him. I lay in that hotel room for hours, crying while staring at the ceiling. I wanted to leave him, but I got sick to my stomach each time I imagined my life without him.

We had been through too much. We had survived too much.

But I couldn't let the anger go. Though I was still with him, I couldn't stop talking about Mia, asking him questions. I didn't want to be without him, but every time I looked at him, I cursed his existence.

"No, Jah." I frowned, pushing his hand off the inside of my thigh.

I had just returned to the estate after hanging out with Yaz and Angela. I had drowned my bitterness in tequila. My loins were longing for him. Normally, we would be having drunk sex by now. But I refused to give him the satisfaction.

His brows furrowed as he looked down at me. "No? What you mean no?"

Scowling, I looked away from him. "I don't want to."

"Why not?"

"Because I don't want no dick that's been raw dogging Mia."

I would have felt sympathy for the offense in his eyes, but a drunk mind spoke a sober truth, and I was *lit*.

Jah groaned, rolling away from me. "Here you go with this shit."

Drunkenly, I sat up, causing the blanket to fall, revealing my bare breasts. "Yeah, here I go with this shit. If you wanna be frustrated with somebody, be frustrated with yourself for fucking that bitch."

"I'm so sick of talking about a bitch that ain't thinking about us. You think Mia is at home arguing with her nigga about me?!"

"I don't give a fuck what she's doing," I seethed. "I care about you being so fucking manipulative that you would do some dirty-ass shit like that."

"Ah'ight, Faye." Jah threw the covers back and swung his legs over the bed. Then he climbed out and stalked towards his hamper.

"Oh, so you're tired of me?!" I spit as he frustratingly through on a pair of shorts. "Ditto, nigga!"

I glared at him as he angrily stalked out of the room. Blowing out a heavy breath, I flung myself back onto the bed. The liquor had me fuming. Every time I was reminded of his deception, fiery rage bubbled up inside of me, forcing me to vomit pure bitterness toward the man I loved too much to leave.

As I lay there, I wished that I would have never confronted Jah about Mia. I wished that I could rewind time and live in the unknown. Naïveté had been much more manageable than knowing that the man I had prayed back to good health and had helped to learn to swallow again had been so malicious. I didn't want to leave him. I wanted to be his wife. He was my future. But bitterness was a more vicious monster than envy.

SIX MONTHS LATER...

CHAPTER 16

JAH DISCIPLE

I cringed when I saw that Faye was wide awake as I opened the door to my bedroom. I had purposely stayed out all night to avoid her, as I had been doing for the last few months. That was what our relationship had come to. I was walking on eggshells constantly, trying not to irritate her. I didn't want to say anything to trigger her. Often times, I just preferred to stay out of her way. I wanted her near me, her essence in my home, but I knew better than to pair it with my presence because I annoyed her. So, I would try to stay out as late as I could.

But it was two in the morning, and she was wide awake.

"What up?" I asked dryly as I strolled in.

"Hey." She barely opened her mouth. Her eyes remained on the TV, watching an episode of Harlem. "Where you been?"

"Taking care of business."

She scoffed nastily. "Mumph."

I shook my head as I went over to the dresser. "C'mon, Faye. Don't start."

In return, she rolled her eyes.

I didn't hide my disappointment. I jeered annoyingly. "You in a bad mood again, I see." I heard her mumble something that I was sure was derogatory bullshit toward me.

"Is this how its gon' be?" I stared at her through the mirror as I took off my chain. "I gotta keep wondering what kinda attitude I'mma come home to every fucking night?"

"Nigga, fuck you," she snapped.

I clicked my tongue, shaking my head. "I should have fucking lied."

She blew a disgusted breath. "Wow."

"I might as well have if you were going to punish me forever!"

"Who are you getting loud with?!"

I spun around to face her angry irises. "You! Faye, we been goin' back and forth through this shit for six months. One day, we good. The next, we not. I'm walking on eggshells in my own fucking crib because I don't know if you gon' have an attitude when I get here. This ain't no way to live."

"You should have thought about that when you fucked that bitch!"

"You know you got a choice, right?"

She sat up with her brow touching her hairline.

"You do," I said with a shrug. "I told you that I was sorry. I was drunk and pissed off. I was mad at you. I wanted to hurt you like you had hurt me!"

Rage danced in her eyes as she glowered at me. "Mission accomplished!"

"But how long we gotta exist in this shit?! Living like this every day is fucking exhausting! If you wanna be mad, be mad. If you forgive me, then forgive me. But this back and forth is goofy as hell."

"No, you putting your dick in that bitch because you believed some lies is what was goofy as hell."

"You didn't even know what had happened, so how was I supposed to?!"

"What you were supposed to do was not fuck her! You knew my history with her. You knew how she always intentionally hurt me. And you purposely fucked her. That's some calculating shit!"

"Then do something about it, Faye, because I'm tired of living like this."

Faye's eyes narrowed as her head tilted back. The disbelief in my stance deepened her irritable expression.

"I'm serious, Faye." My shoulders lowered. I didn't want to continue to be so dismissive. I loved this woman. She had stuck by my side and by my family during the most trying time of my life and all of our misfortune. She had stayed and stood strong with us through our hard times. She deserved my patience. But I couldn't keep living like this. "We've been doing this for months. You're obviously still hurt. You don't forgive me. You didn't stay with me because you love me. You stayed with me because you didn't want her to win. You are just as obsessed with her as she is with you."

Irreversible hurt covered her orbs.

"You're right." She was so bitter as she swung her legs over the bed. "I don't forgive you."

She stood and padded toward the couch on her bare feet. Quietly, she began to grab her clothes from it and dress. I cringed to see her prepare to leave. But I couldn't deny the relief I felt. The tension between us was foreign. It had caused me to look at us in a different light. I had never seen Faye in any way, except pure love and relief. But for the last six months, our relationship felt stressful and ugly.

She didn't even look at me after she got dressed and threw her purse over her shoulder. She simply walked out of the room, and I let her.

I blew out a heavy breath as I looked at my doorway. I could hear her quickly jogging down the stairs. As I pulled my shirt over my head, I heard her angry footsteps marching toward the front door. By the time I plopped down on my bed, I heard the front door slam.

Sighing, I bent over and opened the bottom drawer on my nightstand. I pushed my boxers aside and reached toward the very back. Feeling the velvet box, I pulled it out.

As I sat back, I opened it. The eternity diamond engagement ring was four carats. I had always imagined it looking way too big on Faye's dainty hand. Releasing a heavy breath, I slammed the box shut and tossed it back into the drawer. I had purchased the ring a month ago. But it had sat in the drawer ever since. Every time I felt the urge to ask Faye to be mine forever, her anger reminded me that she no longer looked at me as her happily ever after. I was a thorn in her side that she loved too much to let go of.

Telling the truth had slowly ended us. I had always felt that she had only stayed with me because she didn't want Mia to win. She had stayed with me out of spite for Mia, not because of her love for me. And every day since, it seemed like her love for me was slowly fading away. We argued about it constantly. But nothing could make me hate her. So, I dealt with the aftermath, hoping that things would change. But that hope was only creating resentment toward her that didn't push me to chase after her, knowing that this time when she walked away, it was most likely for good because I was actually okay with it.

MESSIAH DISCIPLE

Later that day, I was smiling in the face of an angel.

"You're gonna stare at her the entire time I'm here?"

I chuckled at the jealous irritation in Tory's tone, but I never took my eyes off Faith. "Who else am I supposed to look at?"

"Don't play with me," she playfully snapped. Then she reached over the table and punched my arm.

My eyes darted toward the correctional officer on post in visitation. "Stop before you get kicked out of here," I warned Tory.

She kicked me under the table. "Then stop playing with me."

I pushed my chair back, holding Faith close to my chest. "Get kicked out, and I'mma take her back to my cell with me."

Tory's eyes rolled. Her jaws were tight as if she were trying to hold back a smile. "I bet you wish that you could. You're so fucking obsessed with her."

I raised my brow to taunt her. "You jealous?"

"Yes," she pouted.

My eyes went back down to Faith. I couldn't resist staring at her. I was a *father*. My chest swelled every time I reminded myself that I had a little girl. Faith Mariah Disciple was six months old now.

Tory had been such a rider that days after giving birth, she and the kids were on the road to visit me. Tory's dedication had made it possible for me to see my daughter more often than most fathers who were free saw their children.

Hearing Tory sigh, I looked up at her. Her disposition on this visit was different. Her eyes were tired and heavy. She had even left Hope and Honor with her mother.

"You okay, baby?" I asked.

"No," she admitted too quickly.

"What's wrong?" I reached over and held her hand. "What's going on?"

Desperate tears came to her eyes. "I'm lonely, Messiah. I fucking miss you."

My chest tightened. Tory always missed me. She always needed me. But this longing in her eyes was different. It wasn't as superficial as her simply needing me.

She needed *someone*.

Letting her hand go, I sat back. I knew this day would come. She would only be able to take care of three kids and hit the road for hours every weekend for so long before she became tired of it.

"Baby, I told you if you needed to do you, I would understand."

She shook her head, causing her big bang to fall into her face. She pushed it back into place with her index finger as she sat up. "I don't want another man. I want *you*."

"But I'm in here. And I ain't so full of myself that I don't know that another man can't take care of you. Shit, he'll probably be a better nigga than me."

She recoiled sadly. "Don't say that, Messiah."

I shrugged a shoulder. "It's facts, baby. I got years ahead of me. I've had to train my mind to be in here. This is where I am. I got friends. I got work. I'm making money. Shit, even sometimes, I got the nerve to have fun in this bitch. I even get a good nut every night, thinking about your pretty, chocolate, thick ass." Amidst this solemn conversation, my eyes still lowered lewdly, and she managed to sadly blush as I went on. "This is where I am. But you're out there with all kinds of freedoms I don't have. Yet, you ain't living, baby. I want you to live. You ain't no good to the kids if you're stressed or suffering."

A tear escaped her slanted eye. "I don't want anybody else but you. I'll never cheat on you."

Tory's dedication tugged at heartstrings that I hadn't even known were there before I met her. She was worth every year I was spending in prison. No one could have ever told me differently.

I leaned over, extending my hand toward her face. As I wiped away her tear, I told her, "You don't have to devote yourself to me because you feel like I'm in here because of you."

She winced, closing her eyes tightly.

"I'm in here because I didn't listen to my brothers and because of Moe." I had reiterated this to her so many times, but it never completely soothed her guilt. "I had to stop and get that blunt. I had to pursue you. I got what I wanted, and now I gotta pay the consequences. *I* have to pay the consequences for my actions, not you."

YAZMEEN HILL

That evening, I was flying around Shauka's room packing me and Asa's things. Shauka had only gotten more suffocating over time. I couldn't take it anymore. I had to leave before he ruined us completely.

"Where are you going?"

Shit.

I had intended to be gone before he made it home.

I swallowed hard and continued to fill Asa's baby bag, avoiding Shauka's eyes. "Home."

"Why?"

I heard Shauka's footsteps coming closer and closer. "Because that's where I live." Finally, I was done packing the diaper bag. I threw it over my shoulder, feeling the oncoming relief.

"Yeah, okay." Shauka's bitter words were accompanied by a scoff.

My brow rose as I stood over a sleeping Asa in Shauka's bed. "What does that mean?"

Cockily, Shauka leaned on his dresser with his hands in his pockets. "It's real funny how every other week you get this urge to go home."

"Yeah, every other week, I want to be in what I'm used to, *my place* where it's just me and my baby. Not constant ruckus with seventeen people constantly coming in and out."

Shauka's frown mimicked a small child that wasn't getting his way. "You never had an issue with it before. Now you want to run home every few days."

"Because that's where the fuck I pay bills!" I spat. "You had a choice to make a home for the three of us, but you chose not to, remember?!"

"Why can't we live here?" he pathetically asked.

"I want more space than just your bedroom, Shauka! I'm a grown-ass woman who does not have to live like this because *you* have trauma from trusting the wrong bitch."

"Or you want to be free to be with other niggas." He laughed as if he had confirmed his own wild, irate suspicions.

I shook my head slowly, standing. "You can't be serious, Shauka."

"It's not hard to believe."

"You've been acting like you weren't affected by Sariah cheating, Messiah's arrest, and Jah's near-death experience, but you were. And I keep getting the brunt of it all. You need to get some fucking help and heal, Shauka." Tired, I picked Asa up from the bed.

"Put my son down, Yaz."

I angled my head dramatically to the side as I ogled the sternness in his eyes. "Or fucking what?" I challenged him.

Shauka's jaws drew in so tightly that his nostrils flared wildly. The fury in his eyes was very telling. He was no longer the caring, gentle man who handled me with kid gloves. But I knew that it was because he had gone through so much that he no longer saw me as his loving best friend. Now, I was an outlet to let out all of his frustrations on.

"I suggest you remember who the fuck I am before you make this shit worse." My eyes were threatening as I walked toward him, past the dresser, and out of the room.

As I neared the stairs, I instantly felt relief and freedom. I hurriedly trotted down them and hurried toward the front door.

"You're leaving?" I heard Hattie's questioning behind me.

I turned around and forced a genuine smile. "Yeah, we're going home."

Hattie pouted and hurried toward me in her furry slippers. "Well, let me kiss my baby before you leave."

I discreetly took an impatient breath as Hattie moved the wild curls out of Asa's face and kissed his cheek. Out of the corner of my eyes, I saw *him*. I reluctantly looked toward the upstairs landing and saw Shauka standing there, looking down at me with judgmental eyes burning a hole through mine.

"You be careful getting home," Hattie told me.

I tore my eyes away from Shauka and smiled into Hattie's nurturing eyes. "I will." I then hurried out of what now felt like a prison.

CHAPTER 17

NAJIA DISCIPLE

O nce Jah was fully recovered, my brothers didn't want me so involved with the crew anymore. I was still managing their real estate properties and fulfilling some managerial duties at Disciple Records. However, I took my money and invested it in my own real estate. I had just closed on my first six-unit building. It was a total gut rehab that was near completion. I had gotten so engulfed in it that I'd learned how to do some of the renovations myself. I had done some of the painting and designed most of the interior. It had become therapeutic for me. I was so proud of it that I spent a lot of my time admiring the marble floors, modern interior design, and jaw-dropping bathrooms.

"*Ssss!*" My head tilted back. I slowly licked my lips as I stared at the coffered ceiling while Nardo's tongue made circles around my throbbing clit.

Nardo and I spent a lot of time in the units too. He knew he could catch me there, and I would never be able to resist him when that tan, chiseled perfection showed up.

He had positioned himself between my legs after sitting me on the island in the kitchen. His large fingers were clawing at my pussy lips, spreading them wide open. My breathing became rapid as he continued to suck my clit. I leaned back and placed both of my bare feet onto the island, giving him all access to my center.

He chuckled with a mouthful of my sweet epicenter. "Nasty ass..."

An erotic concoction of my juices and his saliva slid from his pursed lips and slid down my ass. Chills overtook me. Nardo's face pressed hard into me as his tongue flicked my clit, causing me to moan so loudly that it echoed throughout the vacant unit. I began to buck my hips against his face, riding his oral fucking. He began to fuck harder, kneading at my nub.

My orgasm began to take over quickly. "Oh, gawd!"

He began to eat me enthusiastically.

"*Ahhh!*"

My juices flowed into his mouth.

"*Grrr!*" As my orgasm subsided, he softened his clamp on my clit. I shook violently.

Finally, he released me and stood upright. I ogled the way his length aggressively reached for my center.

Taking my waist into his hands, he plunged in.

"Shit!" I yelped.

Spent, I wrapped my arms tightly around his neck, holding on for the intense, erotic ride that I was used to.

I love you.

I was *so* in love with him. My heart was his. With each reluctant time he had fucked me over the last year, I'd fallen deeper and deeper. But the deeper I fell, the scarier it got. My anxiety swelled the more I fell in love with him, so I ran faster. His frustration was so high with me at this point that he hated to fuck me, but our chemistry wouldn't allow him to resist me. He dated other people. He courted other women in the way that I refused to allow him to court me, in the way that I *couldn't* allow him. Soon, the woman I had spotted him with at Chemistry had become his main girl.

But his dick belonged to me.

247

Sadly, I was more comfortable being his side bitch than the woman he wanted to commit to.

I love you, Nardo.

I always only thought it. I never told him because I knew that it wasn't fair to him. I was not allowed to love him because I would not allow him to love me.

"You cold?" I felt his hands run over my ass and legs.

"Huh?" My eyes sprang open, bringing me out of my euphoric trance.

"You cold?'

"No."

"You have goosebumps." He pushed back and looked into my eyes.

But I tightened my lock on his neck, bringing him back against me. "I know."

He returned to delivering those sweet, surreal strokes that I often dreamed about but was too traumatized to commit to.

TORY CLARK

I giggled as Ginger's eyes bounced out of their sockets when she saw me approaching the bar. "Buttercup, what'chu doin' in here?"

"Hey, boo," I sighed, sitting on the barstool in front of her. "I just needed to get out of the house."

She eyed me strangely. "And you decided to come hang out up in here?"

"I just wanted to be around something familiar." Oddly, the strip club was so nostalgic for me. It reminded me of better times, when Messiah was free and pursuing me. Then when we fell in love, before all of the drama unfolded.

Ginger's head sympathetically tilted as she watched my somberness. The streets knew that Messiah was locked up, so she was aware of the source of my despair. Pouting, she reached and patted my hand. "What you want? It's on me."

"I don't even care, girl," I told her, blowing out a heavy breath. "Just make me something good and strong."

She nodded and started to pick up bottles.

Looking around the club, I received the comfort I needed. Being at home was torture for me a lot of times. There were no memories in it to remind me of Messiah. So, this particular night, since my mom was willing to give me a break, I had come to The Factory. I hadn't been there since I'd quit dancing. But sitting at the bar was giving me the nostalgic feeling that I had been seeking. I smiled as I recalled the first time Messiah had followed me there and then when he'd showed up the second time. I turned around and looked at the section that had once been reserved for him every night. Tears came to my eyes as I envisioned him standing on the couch with a bottle of D'ussé in one hand as he threw thousands of dollars at dancers.

I was suffering without Messiah. I forced myself to keep my head up for my kids, but nights like this, I was miserable. I missed that man like the desert misses the rain. Yet fearfully, I was starting to miss being with any man. It had been before high school that I was completely single. Being alone was so foreign to me. God meant for a woman to be with a man. I felt empty without serving my purpose.

❦

I got so wasted that night. I was stumbling out of the club.

"You good, Buttercup?" a bouncer named Kirk asked as I tipped into the warm summer air.

"I'm good," I said, giving him a hazy smile. "I took an Uber."

His eyes reflected his relief. I leaned next to him on the building's exterior wall as I swiped through my phone to my Uber app to check my ride's ETA.

"Damn, the motherfucka col'," I heard Rob, another bouncer, say.

Peeling my eyes off of my phone, I looked to see what had attracted their attention. A cherry red Ferrari LaFerrari had pulled into valet.

"*Shiiiit*," Kirk lewdly cursed as if the 1.4-million-dollar sports car was making his dick hard.

My eyes lowered seductively as a 6'5" athletic build climbed out.

The dark-skinned god dapped up valet as if he was already familiar with him.

"Oh, shit!" Kirk's eyes widened like a child. "That's Devin Adams."

I chuckled at his excitement. "Who is Devin Adams?"

Kirk and Rob looked at me like I had five heads.

I bucked my eyes at them. "Who is he?"

"The quarterback for the Eagles who just single-handedly won the Super Bowl for them a few months ago," Kirk explained.

I slowly nodded, and they laughed at my lack of sports knowledge.

My phone's dinging took my attention away from the beautiful athlete, gliding toward the salivating bouncers. The notification read that my Uber was pulling up, so I took a deep breath to get my bearings together.

"Bye, Rob. See you, Kirk."

"Holla," Rob replied.

"Be careful, Buttercup," Kirk protectively told me. "Let somebody know you made it to the crib,"

"I'll text Ginger," I told them as the athlete, and I crossed paths.

"Damn! Well, hello," he greeted me with raw masculinity and confidence.

He didn't have to speak. His masculine, seductive scent had already spoken to my senses.

My abandoned femininity stopped my feet from moving. I looked back and met light brown eyes that were smiling at me. "Hi," I returned.

Up close, he was exquisite. His skin had been touched by God with exceptional melanin. He was black as February 1st through February 28th.

But I forced myself to make an about-face and meet the Lexus that was pulling up to take me home.

"Wait. Hold on," he said as I felt a soft tug on my arm. "Let me talk to you."

"What's up?" I asked as if his mere presence wasn't wooing me.

JESSICA N. WATKINS

"Why are you leaving so soon? The night is just starting."

"I just came to say hi to some friends."

"Friends? You work here?"

"I used to."

"Umph," he muttered deeply as he swallowed me from head to toe with his bedroom eyes. "Can we exchange numbers?"

"No, thank you."

His eyes widened with surprise at my rejection. I imagined that not many women turned him down.

"You in a relationship?" he asked. "I don't see a ring on that pretty hand."

"I'm... I'm ..." Suddenly, I didn't have a witty comeback or quick denial. I didn't have a real answer for continuing to deny myself. I needed someone, and Messiah understood. So, I had no real reason to continue to deny myself. "Yeah." I forced a smile, swallowing that stubborn guilt. "You can have my number."

SHAUKA DISCIPLE

Yaz laughed in my face when she opened her front door. She shook her head at my cocky glare as she walked away.

"What the fuck you laughing at?" I spat as I walked in.

"Yo' crazy ass," she said. She slid into her living room on house shoes. Her ass bounced in the loose oversized University of Chicago shirt that barely covered her butt cheeks.

Lucky for her, Asa was wobbly walking toward me like Frankenstein. He was smiling from ear to ear and flapping his arms. He was so excited to see me that he could hardly keep his footing. So, I hurried toward him and scooped him up.

"What up, my dude?" I asked, grinning into his face.

It had only been one day since I'd seen my lil' homie, but it felt like years.

"You miss your daddy, lil' man? You miss your daddy, don't you?" I cooed. "You ready to come home?"

"He *is* home," Yaz quipped from the couch.

"No, the fuck he ain't," I fussed.

Yaz sighed deeply, shaking her head.

"C'mon. Get your shit. Let's go," I ordered.

"I'm not going," she mulishly insisted.

I felt my body flushing with fiery rage. "Stop playing with me, Yaz."

She sat back comfortably, folding her arms. "Nobody is playing with you. You need to get your shit together before you force this live-in family that you want so bad."

"You're for real?"

"*Yes.*"

"So, you're not coming back any time soon?"

"No."

My eyes bucked. I then slowly put Asa down.

"Shauka, I can't do it no more." Her stubbornness was now sincerity.

"Do what?"

Her eyes grew even more owlishly than mine. "Do you not realize how you've been suffocating me? You never want me to leave the house. You have the audacity to accuse me of cheating, as if I am not always under you when I'm not at work. You spazz out on me over the simplest of things. You've changed, Shauka."

I frustratingly stuffed my hands into my pockets. "So, you won't come home because I got trust issues?"

"I won't come home because that's not my home. You keep lashing out on me, and your trust issues won't allow you to create one for me. And I get it. You were hurt. You lost Messiah, and you almost lost Jah. You need to heal from all of that pain because you're bleeding on me when I ain't the one who cut you."

My jaws tightened to keep the words from spilling out that agreed with her. I had been able to successfully run the crew without Messiah and Jah. That had come with ease, especially with the assistance of Najia and Nardo. However, I had been operating on auto pilot because so much had been missing. Nothing had been normal. Sariah had disappeared. It was as if she had never existed. I had threatened to kill her if she returned to the house that I had bought, so she never did. I'd sold it as soon as her mother moved her things out.

Though running the crew had come with ease, there was a constant reminder that my brothers were gone. Their absence had made it apparent that it could all happen again so easily. I thought I had successfully gotten rid of the scared little boy who had walked the streets alone, hungry, and cold. I had let him go, let go of his fear and reluctance. I had opened my heart to people. But that was all in vain because life could come at you any way it wanted, any time it wanted, and there was nothing to prepare you for the hardships that you were forced to endure. That little boy had come running back to play so easily. I often found myself lashing out on the people around me. Unfortunately, a lot of times, that had been Yaz. In the back of my mind, I wondered when she would get tired of being my punching bag. But she had always been so ride or die that I never imagined she would leave me.

"So, you're done with me?" I asked as I sat on the arm of her couch.

Yaz's eyes softened. "I could never be done with you. But I can't keep putting myself in the line of fire, especially now that we have Asa." She smiled as she watched him wobble about the area rug in front of the couch. "Take some time to heal from what you've been through. I'll be here when you're ready."

CHAPTER 18

FAYE SINGER

"Even though he fucked her, it was *so* long ago, Faye. If he only did it that one time back then, why let it ruin your relationship?"

"It's the principle, Chloe." It had been two days since I'd walked out of Jah's bedroom, and my face was still scouring. "Besides, the way he was talking sounds like he was done too."

Chloe sucked her teeth as she fluffed the pillows on the couch. "I doubt it."

"I'm serious," I said, the recollection causing my heart to ache. "He looked so over my bullshit."

"Then stop being such a bitch to him."

"I can't. I wish I would have never asked him."

If I could take it back, I would. Some truths weren't worth telling. Mia, of all people, had ruined my relationship, and I had allowed her to do it. She was off with her boyfriend and child, living happily ever after while I was miserable. But the fact that Jah had gone out of his way to hurt me in that way had planted hostility in me that I couldn't smother. I had tried to. He had gone through so much. I was so grateful that he was alive, too grateful to let something as small as Mia take him from me. But a constant reminder of his calculation was playing in a loop in my mind. I couldn't shake the awareness that he had been so mad over a lie that he'd deliberately hurt me.

Chloe watched me sadly as I created a bouquet of fake flowers on the grass wall we had just assembled in the living room.

"That looks pretty, friend," she said softly.

I stepped back, feeling the heaviness in my heart. "Yeah, it does."

"You think this one will make us as much money?"

I smiled confidently. "Hell yeah."

About a year ago, Chloe and I had decided to get into renting Airbnbs. The first one we got was a luxury condo in the south loop. We had put our money together to furnish and decorate it. Bookings came in so fast that we were able to get another and another and then another. Most of our Airbnb's were located near medical centers and college campuses. We got so much business from doctors, residents, students, and parents that were visiting. We were standing in our most recent one, a two-bedroom condo in Hyde Park that was sure to stay booked because of its location in the tourist neighborhood of the campus of the University of Chicago.

We were making so much money that I suggested to Chloe that she quit her remote job. However, she was so scared of struggling again that she kept it so she could stack her money.

I had come such a long way from the pitiful, married woman putting up with an old man beating her because I didn't have any other way to take care of myself. I was now fully independent and an entrepreneur. I was a boss. But I was still weakly dealing with a nigga who had insisted on hurting me. Only this time, I didn't see the purpose of continuing to make myself suffer.

SHIT.

I groaned when I noticed Jah's G-Wagon running in front of the building Chloe and I owned.

"Mmm humph. I know that's right, Jah! Get your motherfuckin' girl!" Chloe exclaimed as she parked.

I seethed at Chloe's grin. "Shut up, bitch," I grumbled.

I grimaced as Jah climbed out. When I first met him, I couldn't imagine a time that my eyes would fall on him and see nothing but perfection. Now, all I saw was the source of my frustration and pain.

With a deep sigh, I climbed out of Chloe's car. Chloe hopped out behind me excitedly, completely choosing the other side.

"Hey, bro!" she greeted him, all too hyped.

"What up, sis?"

They met on the sidewalk and hugged. Then Chloe put her key into the security gate and let herself in.

I couldn't read Jah's expression as he looked at me.

"Can we talk?" he asked.

I swallowed hard, answering, "Yeah."

It was a beautiful day outside. It was late May. The summer was coming. It was a comfortable and inviting seventy degrees. So, when Jah followed me into the security gate, I sat on the bottom concrete step.

Jah slowly sat next to me. "I don't know what to say."

Admittedly, I was caught off guard. I had expected him to beg for my forgiveness, for me to treat him in the worshipping way that I used to. But when I looked at him, his eyes were as tired as mine. He wasn't even looking at me. His weary countenance was anchored on the street ahead of us. He watched as cars sped down the four-lane one-way.

The silence between us was so still that the melodies of the streets were deafeningly clear.

"It feels like we're always here," I finally said. "I've been putting this all on Mia, but it's not her. It's the fact that I barely got the chance to heal from the first blow before you delivered the next one. It's so toxic. It feels like I went from one toxic relationship to the next one."

He angrily scoffed, shaking his head. "Ain't no fucking way you're comparing me to Doon."

His bite made my response lodge in my throat.

He chuckled wryly. "You're right, though. This *is* toxic, and neither one of us deserves it. I'm sorry for hurting you. I've tried for six months to show you that. None of it is enough, and I can't blame you. I want you to be happy. Clearly, that ain't with me. So..."

My eyes grew as he stood. He never looked at me. His eyes were still on the road.

"So, I'm gonna let you go be happy, sweetheart."

I sucked in hot air as he took a large step toward the gate. I was speechless when he grabbed the metal knob and opened it.

"Jah!" I called out, standing. "Are you serious?!"

When he looked back, his eyes were so sincere that I gasped a bit.

"You're obviously too mad to let go of this. And like you said, ain't no use in you leaving one unhappy situation to be in another one."

He was actually walking away, and that crushed me. Suddenly, none of it was worth it. I hopped off of the bottom step and took off after him. But he was already climbing into his truck. Fearing embarrassment, I stood at the gate, watching him drive away.

"WHAT THE FUCK?"

Sitting with my back against my headboard, I stared aimlessly at Chloe's dramatic display of complete dismay.

Chloe had the hurt and shock in her eyes that I was too stunned to exemplify.

"So, he just... he... he broke up with you?" she stuttered.

"Mm humph," I mumbled with tears in my eyes.

Chloe's arms began to flail wildly. "Bitch, I told you to let this go! Why are you giving Mia this much clout in your relationship? That bitch ain't thinking about you! So, why do—"

"I don't know, Chloe!" I spat, cringing in embarrassment. "I *don't know*! I just couldn't let it go! I was hurt. I felt so fucking betrayed."

"And now I bet you feel so *fucking single* while that bitch is flossing all over Facebook with her nigga and her baby!" Disgusted with me, Chloe shook her head. "You compared him to Doon?"

Recoiling, I held my face with my hands. "I know," I cried. "And I should have never said that."

Suddenly, Chloe shook her head with determination. "Fuck sitting in here and pouting. Go get your nigga back!"

A sad pout formed on my lips. "Not right now. Obviously, he needs a break from me."

Chloe gave me a stern glare. "*Break* your motherfucking neck over to that estate and get your nigga back."

TORY CLARK

"Man, Joe, it feels good as fuck out here."

I smiled into the phone as I watched Devin walk into the warm afternoon air.

"Oh, you're from Chicago," I replied at the realization.

He grinned. "Yeah, I am."

"That wasn't a question," I sassed with a smirk.

"Oh. How did you know?"

"Your accent, and you just said 'Joe.'"

He flushed, causing deep dimples to appear on his chocolate skin. "I didn't even realize that I said it. And we definitely have an accent. I didn't hear it until I started traveling all over the world, though."

"When did you leave Chicago?"

"I moved to Philly after I was drafted last year."

That made sense. Devin was a beautiful man. His athletic and financial status made him even more attractive. But he surprisingly didn't act like a bougie, narcissistic athlete. He was much more down to earth than I had assumed he would be. It had to be because he was still close to his home roots since it hadn't been that long since he'd left.

As I sat in my bed talking to Devin on FaceTime, I forced myself to shake off my nervousness. Talking to a man other than Messiah felt wrong. But I could not deny that Devin's conversation that afternoon was making me feel like a woman again. For over a year, I had only been a mother. I had been completely ignoring any intimate needs that were burning within. Devin was smoldering the flames of those desires with a mere conversation. I was relieved, and my curiosity sparked with each smile we shared.

I had to keep reminding myself that Messiah was okay with this. I hadn't found the courage to tell him that I had met Devin. I preferred to wait to see if there would actually be anything to tell. But Messiah had told me enough times that he would understand if I needed to date.

"So, when are we going out?" Devin asked as he got into his car.

"Who told you I wanted to go out with you?"

"Your eyes... your eyes told me, baby."

Shit.

I playfully rolled my slanted irises into the phone. However, goose bumps sprouted all over my chocolate coating. A blush was fighting to add to my expression. I held my cheeks tight to keep myself from smiling. The thought of being courted, dressing up to entice a man, a night without breast feeding and yelling at kids sounded like heaven. I needed that. My mom helped a lot with my kids. Karen had even picked up Faith a few times to spend time with her. But hanging with the girls was not the same as a night out in the company of a man, specifically a fine-ass man with money. I craved courtship and affection.

But I didn't understand his interest in me. He was a football player... a *professional* baller. Men with fewer credentials only offered drinks during Netflix and chill so they could fuck. And they were most definitely turned off by a woman with three kids.

Devin's bedroom eyes narrowed on me. "Why you lookin' like that?"

"There are so many women in Chicago you could pursue who don't have three kids, especially a six-month-old."

He playfully sucked his teeth. "Girl, I ain't worried about those kids."

I giggled, hating that he was actually making me smile. We maintained intense eye contact for a few seconds.

"I'll let you know," I finally told him.

"Ah'ight. I'll take that. But let me know soon. I leave town in a few days."

"Okay."

"I'll holla at you later."

"Okay. Bye."

"Bye, sweetheart."

As I hung up the phone, I began to smile and blush so hard that my cheeks were hurting.

"You should go."

I let out a startled gasp as my mother sauntered into my room in *my* Versace robe, eating a bag of microwave popcorn.

"Huh?" I asked, perplexed.

"You should go out with him."

I kissed my teeth as my mom sat at the foot of my bed. "Mama, why were you listening to my conversation?"

She shrugged as she tossed some popcorn in her mouth. "You were loud. I was in the nursery putting Faith down for a nap."

I chuckled, shaking my head. When Messiah had first gone to prison, my mom was a lot of help. However, it seemed as if her help was selfish. It wasn't for me. She really enjoyed the relationship she was building with me and the kids. But being with us also gave her something to keep her busy, which took her mind off of my stepfather's embarrassing disloyalty and betrayal. My mama was old school, so she didn't believe in divorce. Thus, she and my stepfather were still married on paper. But she kept her distance from him and the church where his mistresses attended.

Once Messiah bought me the new house, she became a permanent fixture in my home. She loved the lavishness of the house and had turned one of the guestrooms into her own suite. I wasn't mad at all since I practically had a live-in babysitter at this point.

"Messiah has told you many times that it's okay for you to date," my mom told me. "He won't be mad. He's an understanding man."

A prideful smile appeared. I was so happy that my mother had let go of her inhibitions. She didn't look at Messiah in the same light as she had looked at Kidd. She saw past the street shit and realized he loved me and my kids unconditionally. I still hadn't told her that he and his brothers had killed Kidd. She thought he had only taken the plea to save his brothers and crew from further investigation.

"You don't have to wait for Messiah out of guilt," my mother added. "You're stressing yourself out trying to hold him down when nobody has put those expectations on you, not even him. He loves you enough that he will understand. You are the only person keeping yourself so lonely."

NARDO DAVIS

Later that night, I was lying in bed catching up on the last season of Ghost when my shorty, Laila, walked through the door with this sneaky grin on her face. Instantly, my grin matched hers. If she wanted some dick, I would easily turn the TV off. I was so turned on by Laila. She was a rare, natural beauty. Her wavy hair fell down to her waist. The mixture of an Indian mother and a Black father gave her a smooth, tan complexion that was free of any imperfections. Her curves had been manufactured in the womb, not on a surgical table. Her tiny upper body and waist made my T-shirt she wore look oversized. But the massive curves of her hips and ass spread the hem to its limits. Instead of climbing into the bed, she simply stood at the foot of it, biting her lip nervously.

I raised my brow and put the episode on pause. "What's wrong with you?"

"I-I... uh..." She blushed as she stuttered. "I have something to show you."

"What?"

Sighing nervously, she took her hand from behind her back and revealed a stick that she was holding.

My brow rose higher. "What's that?"

Biting on her plump bottom lip, she inched around the bed to my side and slowly sat next to me as I sat with my back against the headboard. She lifted the stick, and I immediately recognized the blue tip. The words Clear Blue Easy lined the handle.

"I'm pregnant." Her tone was nervous yet excited. She watched me reluctantly, anxiously anticipating my response.

Slowly, a smile spread across my lips. Laila had been my girl for a year. She was picture-perfect. We had our issues, though. She was an educated college student who wanted me out of the game. But she was turned on by my bad-boy swag and money. She would prefer me to have a profession that her parents would be proud of, however. Since she had been raised in a traditional household, she was sort of a nag. She spoke about marriage more than I liked. But all of that paled in comparison to the way she threw down in the kitchen and in the bedroom and the submissive nature that her culture had taught her.

Her doe-shaped eyes widened even more in response to my smile. "You're happy?!"

I nodded, allowing my grin to grow until it touched my ears. "Yeah, I'm happy, baby."

She squealed and threw her arms around me. As we embraced, I felt her body relax.

"I was nervous," she confessed.

"Why?"

She pushed back against my chest, looking into my eyes. She was so bashful as she said, "We've only been together a year. I was scared that it was too soon."

I shrugged, still holding her around the waist. "Shit happens. But I'm not mad about it happening with you."

Her blushing continued as we released one another. I honestly felt good about having another kid. It felt like a chance to fix what was broken with my first child. I had been trying to establish a relationship with my son. I had gone down to Miami a few times. But he was so close to his stepfather that he wouldn't let me in. I didn't blame him. I was just hoping that as he got older, he would find room in his heart for me too.

"Are you happy?" I asked her.

She flashed a girlish grin at me. "I had no plans to have a baby right now. You know I want to go to grad school and—"

"And you still can."

"Yeah, I know, but I always wanted to have a baby after I was *married*."

"Then you should have jumped off the dick like I told you to when you were riding that motherfucka to death."

She giggled and covered her eyes like she wasn't the nasty motherfucker that was riding my dick like a professional cowgirl a few weeks ago.

"But we got the morning-after pill," she whined.

I shrugged with a chuckle. "Obviously, that shit didn't work."

Her pout deepened. "I guess not."

"You want to have an abortion?"

Her body stiffened. "Hell no."

"Nobody has to know."

"No," she insisted, placing a hand on my leg. "I want this baby. This is *our* baby. I'm happy. I just have to adjust to the fact that it will happen sooner than I had expected."

"Bet," I said with a nod. "Then we're having a baby."

Her cheeky grin met mine. "We're having a baby." Laila looked down at my shirt where it covered her flat stomach. "I guess I should tell my mom and dad." Laila's nervousness returned. She was graduating from undergrad in a few weeks. But she was still living with her parents, who were traditional. They wanted her to get an education and get married before having kids. But she was a rebel, so I trusted that she could hold her own.

"Why don't you wait a while," I suggested. "Enjoy the news before you tell them and have to hear their fussing."

"You're right." She climbed into bed and snuggled under me. She then grabbed the remote and pressed play.

I was no longer paying attention to Tariq and Kane. I was thinking about Laila having my baby. I was shocked that I honestly had no reservations. The only reluctance that I felt toward it was because of Najia.

Laila was beautiful. She was damn near perfect. But Najia had something over me. I was so in love with her. I was addicted to her, but she was addicted to her pain. Instead of pushing away the trauma that gave her crippling anxiety when it came to men, she pushed me away. I couldn't keep denying myself of the role I was supposed to play in a woman's life because Najia was scared of being loved.

She was broken, and she enjoyed the pieces.

MESSIAH DISCIPLE

I grinned as soon as Najia answered the FaceTime call. "What up, sis?"

She showed all thirty-two of her teeth. Every time I called her, she was so happy to hear from me. "Hey, brother."

By now, I had damn near every correctional officer in my unit wrapped around my finger. So, I was able to speak freely on my phone in my cell in broad daylight. I still had my security, Kofi, standing at the front of my cell in case the asshole guards were coming through.

"You look pretty." Najia was all made up as she drove through the city.

She blushed. "Thank you."

"Where you goin'? You and Nardo going on a date?"

She playfully frowned. "Whatever."

"Oh, I forgot. You still treating that nigga like he's a fuck boy," I taunted her.

"No, I'm not," she said and then sucked her teeth. "Anyway, what you want?"

"Your mom came to see me today." Karen had surprised me again that day. She had been surprisingly so supportive during my sentence.

She had only visited two more times. I was cool with that because this prison was no place for her. But she was really involved in Faith's life.

Najia groaned as she turned a corner. "*Your* mom."

I shook my head. Najia was being so fucking stubborn.

"I still feel some type of way that *she* can visit, but *I* can't."

"You see my face every day, sis."

"I want to hold you, brother," she said sadly. "I want to hug you."

Even that thought made me recoil with anxiety. "I can't handle that. Karen is my adoptive mother. We ain't blood. I can get a hug from her and not fall apart. I can watch her walk away without breaking down. But I couldn't take it if you ever came here."

"I know," she pouted.

"She still wants to talk to you, though. She misses you." I had been advocating for Karen for over a year. She missed Najia so much. But I was really pushing so hard because I knew Najia needed her too. She was too ornery to admit that she missed her mother. There was a disconnect in Najia's heart that only a mother's love could mend.

"I don't give a fuck," she snapped, seething. "I'm still not convinced that she's on some narc shit."

I scoffed. "Girl, that lady ain't setting us up. It's been two years. The detectives stopped investigating Miguel's disappearance a long time ago because of what *she told them*. She knows what happened to him and still hasn't said anything to the police. She's legit."

"I'm still not convinced."

"Why are you being so stubborn? You know you miss her. You and Karen were close. That's your mother. She needs you as much as you need her."

Frustrated, she groaned. "Can you please change the subject before I hang up on your ass?"

I scoffed at her stubbornness. "Fine. When you gonna stop being a bitch and tell Nardo how you feel about him?"

"Bye, nigga!" she spat.

My jaw dropped when she actually hung up. I was about to call her right back when one of my crew members, Tommy, approached my cell. Kofi looked back, silently asking permission to let him. I permitted with a sharp nod.

"What up, though?" Tommy spoke, gliding into the room.

"What up?" I returned.

Tommy grabbed the railing of the top bunk while putting his weight on the bed. "We gotta hit them white boys. Them mother-fuckas still ain't paid up."

"Do what you gotta do then."

"Bet. I was just keeping you abreast of the goings-on."

"Just don't kill nobody, my nigga," I told him sternly. "I ain't adding not another day to my sentence."

He responded with a sharp nod. "I got you, big dawg."

CHAPTER 19

JAH DISCIPLE

Queen was pissed that Faye and Yaz weren't at our weekly family dinner.

"Both of you are so damn stupid!"

Queen had been the only mother figure I'd had as a shorty, so when she spazzed out, I cringed as if Cynthia was standing over me, scouring in disapproval.

"The only one of you who got some sense when it comes to women is Messiah!"

I reared my head back in amazement with a deep chuckle. "Wow."

Queen hardly found anything funny, though. "Yeah, *that* should make you feel real fucking stupid!" she snapped, perched on the edge of her loveseat. "Both of you have really good women at your hands and feet, and you're fumbling the ball because of your past. Are you two gonna keep letting fear push away a good woman?! You wanna be sixty- or seventy years old, living with your brothers and fucking lotion?!"

Sitting on the arm of the couch, Buck chuckled, shaking his head at his wife while holding his forehead with his hand.

Shauka's entire face balled up in disgust. "Don't talk about my dick, Queen."

Ignoring him, she glared at me. "I thought you bought Faye an engagement ring."

"I did."

"Then why did you break up with her?" Queen asked.

"Because I need her to get it through her head that she and I are more important than some raggedy bitch I fucked damn near two years ago."

Queen sat back, shaking her head. "I doubt her bitterness had anything to do with that."

"How come?" I asked.

"She's tired, Jah. You went through a lot when you were sick, and so did we, especially her. She was right there, day in and day out. The pain she felt when you were in that hospital doesn't go away just because you're better now. Trauma, more specifically, near-death experiences, take a toll on a person, especially when you're emotionally attached to the person who's going through it."

"If she had told me all of this, I would have understood. But for six months, I've been walking on eggshells in my own house. She clearly isn't over it, and we can't move forward like this."

"She deserves some fucking grace," Queen gritted out. "That girl put her entire life on pause while you were in the hospital with machines breathing for you and while you were learning to walk all over again. She was right by your side!"

"And that's why I give her the world."

"But you can't afford to give her the smallest thing she needs."

I raised a brow. "And that is?"

"Patience!" she snapped.

"It's been six months, Queen," I reminded her. "I've been patient."

"And if it takes six more months, so fucking what?! You were wrong. You fucked that girl out of spite. What the hell did you think was going to happen if she ever found out?"

"I'm just giving her some time and space so she can see that she and I are more important than a mistake I made. I understand she's hurt. But the constant bickering and hostility is tainting our relationship. It's not worth it. Mia isn't worth it. Besides, if she's as tired as you say she is, then she really needs some space from me. She's been all about me for a year. Maybe she needs some time alone to regroup and focus on herself."

Buck slowly nodded his head. "He's right, Queen."

She shot daggers at him immediately, and he shut up.

"And *you*," she said to Shauka. "Don't no woman wanna raise her child in a fucking circus. She wants her own space. You can't make her live in a room in a house that you share with all your siblings. Grow the hell up."

Shauka shook his head sternly. "Last time I did that, I got played."

"You sound like a little-ass boy."

"He *is* a little-ass boy," Buck interjected. "He's twenty-two years old."

She cut her eyes at him again. "I'm not talkin' to you."

Buck raised his hands in surrender.

"Stop punishing her for what Sariah did," Queen told him. "You're constantly riding her, unloading on her, because of what another woman did. Get off her neck. Since when did you turn into the type of nigga that asks a woman about another man's dick?"

Shauka's eyes bucked. "She told you that?"

"*Did!*" she spat, making me chortle. "That girl has lived and breathed you for years," Queen went on. "That's your best friend. You finally have the woman you have been fantasizing over since you were a little boy, and you're going to push her away because of Sariah?! You gon' let Sariah make you lose Yaz? Does that make any fucking sense to you?" Stubbornly, Shauka just stared at her. "Both of you went through so much in the last year and a half. But guess what? The two women who adore you went through it with you. The aftermath of everything you experienced is falling on them. And that shit is a heavy burden to bear. Trust me, I know. I've been married to this motherfucka for damn near as long as I have been alive. Everything he suffers, I suffer too because I'm his, and he's mine. We would have never lasted as long as we have if he hadn't acknowledged that with compassion and patience and continue to do so regularly."

Buck nodded slowly while watching Shauka and me.

"I'm done fussing." Queen stood, still wearing a frustrated scowl. "Let me get in this kitchen before I burn this cornbread."

Without a word, she stormed off, leaving Shauka and me to stew in our own stupidity.

"She's right," Buck added with less aggression than his wife. "As men, we want our women to be compassionate and patient, but we gotta be the same for them, especially when we are the ones making it hard to be with us."

As Buck occupied Queen's vacant seat, I had no disagreements. But I had attempted to give Faye just that. I recognized that she had been the one with me at every rehab appointment. I realized that through it all, she'd still been there. But it was clear that she was unhappy. She needed space to figure out what she really wanted, and I loved her so much that I was willing to give it to her. Because of her devotion, I loved her unconditionally, so unconditionally that if she was happier without me, I would be happy for her.

TORY CLARK

After finishing my plate at the weekly family dinner, I crept off and met Devin at a bar. I didn't only feel like I was cheating on Messiah; I felt like I was cheating on the entire Disciple family and Faye and Yaz, who I had become friends with.

I was overly nervous as I walked. I felt my legs shaking, barely keeping my balance on the five-inch stiletto sandals I had paired with a simple tube top dress. It was very warm that night, so my chocolate skin was dewy with perspiration as I ran my hand over my arm anxiously.

When Devin saw me, he stood, showing his perfect white teeth. His towering frame caused a shadow that I stepped in happily. "You look nice," his seductive baritone complimented me. His hands on the small of my back made goosebumps race to the surface of my skin.

"Thank you."

I had reservations about meeting him all day up until the moment I walked up to him at the bar. But the instant his eyes swallowed me dominantly, I knew this was what I needed.

When he wrapped his arms around me, warm notes of flowers and tonka beans pulled a sensual moan from my lips that was buried into his chest. I was so embarrassed that a hug that lasted longer than what a correctional officer would allow made my clit beat against the seat of my thong.

I could have stayed in Devin's arms forever, imagining that Messiah was free and holding me like this again. However, he let me go to my disappointment.

He helped me onto the barstool next to his. Immediately, we fell into an easy, humorous conversation like the ones we'd had since we met a few days ago. He and I had a lot in common since we'd been raised in the same city and were only a few years apart in age.

"I don't know why you keep saying you got three kids like that's a big deal. Every chick I meet got a few kids. If she doesn't, I'mma think something is wrong with her pussy."

My mouth dropped as I cracked up.

"I'm kidding," he said, laughing. "But stop thinking that a man isn't going to want you because of your kids. A real nigga don't care about that, especially if he can afford to take care of them."

"Well, luckily, I don't need a man to take care of mine. They have a great provider."

Devin was aware of Messiah. But I had only told him that he was the father of my kids. I didn't divulge the specifics that we were in a relationship, but he was incarcerated. I didn't think it was necessary this early on because I didn't know Devin like that, and I had no idea how far we would go or *if* we would go anywhere at all. I still wasn't convinced that he was the typical athlete that was simply piling on names to his list of hoes. However, I hadn't been out in so long with a man that I had completely let go of any inhibitions. So, after a couple of hours of lots of laughing, dancing, and several drinks, I found myself in Devin's hotel room a few blocks away.

"*Mmm.*" I melted as he kissed my neck no sooner than we sat on the bed. His tongue felt like warm honey against my skin as it massaged the nape of my neck. I had missed intimacy for so long that a wet neck was making my pussy leak. I could feel the seat of my panties becoming drenched with my juices as his large frame softly laid me down on the bed.

Am I about to do this?

My heart was pounding to the point that I could hear each beat in my ears.

If I'm this nervous, should I do this?

I was having an intense debate with myself. Yet, one thing to me was clear: I had been holding down Messiah while mothering three kids and neglecting my own needs. If for no other reason than that, I deserved this.

NAJIA DISCIPLE

Although Jah was back running the crew with Shauka, they kept Nardo in the fold because of the work he had put in during Jah's absence. Therefore, he had been invited to the family dinners at Buck and Queen's as well. Every week, I looked forward to him coming because it was one of the moments when I knew that, after a few drinks, I would get some time with him. So, I wasn't surprised that he'd offered to walk me to my car when I announced that I was leaving.

"Are we linking later?" I asked. "I can get us a room at the Sheraton on 22nd."

Because he had a woman, I hadn't been to his house in a while, and he respected my brothers too much to fuck their sister in their house. So, we often hooked up in my rehab property or hotel rooms.

"That's actually what I wanted to talk to you about."

After approaching my car, I leaned my back against it, looking seductively into Nardo's mysterious, slanted eyes. He looked so alluring, dressed in all black from head to toe. The only color on his body was the sparkle of his diamonds and his tan skin.

"What's that?" I asked, engulfing him flirtatiously.

Our eyes locked for an intense few seconds. The tension between us routinely became explosive. There was an acute chemistry between Nardo and me that ignited when I opened my eyes on that boat, and he was standing over me. That chemistry had not faded.

I feared it never would.

Nardo broke our gaze by pulling his eyes away and taking a step backward. I watched his demeanor change from being enveloped by me to refusing to fall victim to our chemistry.

"I want to be the one to tell you," he spoke carefully. "I don't want you to hear it from nobody else."

My brow furrowed. "What?"

"Laila is pregnant."

Cement boulders fell into my throat like an avalanche. I saw the delight in his eyes when he said it. Gawd, I couldn't breathe!

He watched for my reaction, but I was too stubborn to allow it to show my disappointment or any other emotion. I swallowed hard and kept my head held high. "Okay. What does that have to do with us?"

He rolled his eyes and scoffed, shaking his head at my constant resistance. "We can't do this no more, Najia," he said with disgust in his words.

My heart began to skip beats that only *he* could produce.

"It's not fair to Laila. She's my woman, and soon she'll be the mother of my child. I only keep her away from my circle and my crew out of respect for you. I don't bring her to parties. I don't bring her to family dinners. It's not fair. So, we gotta stop creeping."

I could only look at the ground. I didn't want Nardo to see the fear and regret in my eyes. Yet, I slowly nodded.

"And that's cool with you because you don't want to be with me, *right?*"

The silence was conjuring my eyes on him. Reluctantly I looked up, and he was watching me very intently. I knew he was daring me to just say it, to finally be more scared of losing him than I was scared of having him.

Again, I nodded slowly. "Right."

Revolted, he snarled and turned his back to me. He stalked away, shaking his head. But the distance finally gave me a chance to breathe, to feel. Suddenly, heartache consumed me. I dug in my pocket for my key fob and unlocked the doors while I quickly rounded the hood. I jumped into my car and allowed the tears and sobs to make an appearance. Shockwaves of grief filled me, waking me up to my own demise.

CHAPTER 20

FAYE SINGER

A s I pulled into a parking space at the dealership, my text notification rang. When I saw Jah's name flash on the dash, I leapt toward my phone.

Jah: How you doin'?

Faye: I'm okay, I guess. You?

Jah: No complaints.

The strings of my heart twisted into knots. This was how it had been for the past few days between Jah and me. I appreciated him keeping in touch, but it was torture on my soul. I missed him, and his effort had done its job. I now realized that the sullenness that I had been spewing all over our relationship wasn't worth losing him. We had been attached by the hip for nearly a year. Now, it felt like I was missing a limb.

Faye: I miss you, Jah.

Jah: I miss you too.

His words were hopeful, which encouraged me to put my heart on the line.

Faye: Then let's fix this. I'm sorry. Can we talk in person?

I nervously gnawed on my bottom lip, waiting for his reply. It felt odd not to have laid eyes on him in so many days. If nothing else, I just needed to see him.

Jah: It's not just about Mia. You spent a lot of time in the past year taking care of me, worried about me, being there for me. I think you're tired. You need some time for you.

A heartbroken pout had been permanently placed on my expression since Jah had broken up with me. It only deepened as I read his last text over and over again. He was so calm about this breakup that I feared he was happier without me.

I decided to leave him on read and climbed out of my car. I dragged myself into the dealership, forcing back the looming thoughts of Jah so that I could focus on the managerial meeting I was about to walk in on. Julio had been running the dealership into a prosperous business. It had transitioned into a lot that sold newer, more luxury vehicles. The profits I had been earning as a co-owner were substantial enough that, combined with the money I was making from the Airbnbs, I was more financially comfortable than I had ever been in my life. I had even traded in Doon's car for a 2023 Audi truck. A few years ago, I would have never imagined myself driving a new vehicle and living in a modern condo in Bronzeville.

I was finally the woman I wanted to be. Everything was as it should be except for my love life. I could never get that right, and I feared that I never would.

❦

I HADN'T HEARD A SINGLE WORD SPOKEN IN THAT MEETING, NOR had I offered any input.

"Do we need to cover anything else?" Julio asked his secretary, Maritsa.

Maritsa scanned the agenda in front of her and then shook her head. "No, sir. We've covered everything."

Julio leaned back in his chair with a small smile. "Great. The meeting is adjourned. Thanks for coming in, Faye."

As I stood from the chair across from his desk, I told him, "No, problem, Julio. I appreciate you keeping me in the loop."

Julio's son, Angel, watched me curiously as I exited the office. I hadn't realized that he had followed me out until he softly tugged on my elbow.

"Hey," I heard him call out tenderly.

I stopped my exit and turned to face him.

"You good?" he asked, his alluring eyes squinting curiously.

I forced a smile. "Yeah."

"No, you're not. You were distracted the whole meeting."

I looked down at my Gucci sneakers, attempting to push past the relentless aching pounding in my chest.

"I'm on my way to lunch," Angel said. "Why don't you come with me?"

I forced my emotionally tired orbs back on him. "I'm good, Angel. But I appreciate it."

Angel's expression turned flirtatious. "C'mon. You look like you can use a drink."

Since his dad had hired him a few months ago, Angel had been flirting with me heavily every time I stepped into the dealership. He had just moved to Chicago from Atlanta after graduating college. Since he wasn't from the city, he knew nothing about the Disciples and had no fear of flirting with me.

"So, you're just going to tell your boss that you're about to get drunk on lunch and come back to work?" I taunted him with a smile.

He grinned with guilt. "I think she'll let me get away with it."

Exhaling heavily, I slightly rolled my eyes with a smile. I desperately needed something to get my mind off of Jah.

"You're paying?" I asked with a raised brow.

Angel's smile widened, blinding me with its glow. "Of course."

Finally, I relaxed and gave in. "Bet. Let's go."

I followed Angel to a Mexican restaurant a few blocks from the dealership. It was a small, mom-and-pop restaurant that had the most delicious tacos I had ever tasted and extremely strong margaritas.

"So, what made you move to Chicago from Atlanta?" I asked with a frown.

Angel chuckled. "Why you say it like that?"

"I hear Atlanta is way more poppin' than Chicago, and it's much warmer."

Angel shrugged as he pushed his empty plate away from him. "When I graduated, the job opportunities weren't coming in like I had thought they would. My father offered to put me on at the dealership in a managerial position since my degree is in business, so I accepted. I do hate the fucking cold, though. Shit!"

I laughed while Angel shivered as if the brutal winter was still lingering. His smile caught my attention. It lit up his naturally handsome face. He was mixed with Mexican and Black. So, his skin was tan, and he had wild, long, curly hair that reminded me of Shauka's. He was six feet of a very hard body. He spent a lot of time in the gym. Much of our conversation had been about his fitness journey. He had once been over three hundred pounds. He had lost the weight freshman year and had been in the gym ever since.

"I like Chicago, though." As he rested his elbows on the table and leaned in, his woody scent swallowed me.

Allowing my eyes to float over him, I noticed the tattoo on his bulging forearm. It was a display of Greek letters, hands forming a sign, and a crest. The hues of red were blindingly bright against his skin.

"What does that tattoo mean?" I inquired, still staring at it.

He looked down at it and smiled proudly. "I'm a Nupe."

"A what?"

He softly chuckled at my foolishness. "A Kappa."

I cringed with embarrassment. "*Oooh.*"

"You aren't familiar?"

"I've heard of them."

"You didn't go to college?'

My eyes lowered shamefully. "No, but I wish I had. I should have been on somebody's college campus instead of married at such a young age. I can't imagine how different my life would be today."

"I'm not sure about that. I went to an HBCU, which was a great experience. But all I did was party." He laughed with guilt. "I barely fucking graduated. I ain't gon' lie."

He went on, telling me about his experiences at Clark Atlanta. It was such a positive difference listening to a fine-ass man tell stories about his life on a college campus and pledging rather than hearing vague street stories minus certain details that would incriminate him in felonies.

Being with Angel made me realize how easy it was to be with a regular guy. There was a peace that I felt sitting across from him because he didn't run a crew, he wasn't broken down by the streets, and he didn't have trust issues. It was refreshing to spend time with a man who had an open heart because he was raised on love rather than survival.

I was starting to see how Jah breaking up with me could turn out to be a good thing.

TORY CLARK

My leg nervously bounced as the door opened and prisoners started to file in. I could feel the goosebumps appearing on the surface of my skin.

When Messiah spotted me, his smile was short-lived. He looked at me oddly, sitting at the table alone. I had left the kids at home that weekend. I needed some privacy with him.

"Hey," he spoke hesitantly as he approached.

I stood on wobbly legs.

As we embraced, he asked, "Where are the kids?"

"I left them at home."

He let me go, and we sat down. His eyes took me in, obviously detecting my nervous disposition.

"Why?"

"Because..." I said with a shaky breath. "I need to talk to you."

"What you gotta say that you couldn't have said over the phone all week? We talk every day, all day."

I let out a long, nervous breath. "I went out with someone, Messiah."

His head tilted, but he remained quiet.

"On a date," I emphasized.

His expression remained stoic, but he slowly sat back in the seat. "Okay," he simply responded.

"I'm sorry." My voice cracked, and tears raced to my eyes.

Messiah's reaction was immediately sympathetic. He sat up and gently grabbed my hand. "Don't be. You're a beautiful woman with needs. I didn't expect you to wait for me."

"I wanted to," I cried. As a tear fell, I quickly wiped it away. "I *want* to. I just... I needed the attention, the time—"

"I get it."

"But I didn't like it." As Messiah's brows curled, I added, "I enjoyed the date, but at the end of the night, I still wasn't satisfied because it wasn't you."

His sympathy deepened as his thumb made soothing circles in the palm of my hand.

"Did you fuck him?" he asked.

My body tensed. My heart started to pound as guilt bubbled over. "No."

The fact that Messiah looked relieved made my guilt multiply.

"We were about to, though," I forced myself to confess. "But—"

He recoiled, interrupting me, "I don't need to know the details, baby."

"I couldn't do it because it wasn't you," I assured him anyway.

Thinking of it had me quietly sobbing. It felt good being in Devin's arms, but it didn't feel right. Devin was fine and rich, but he wasn't Messiah. So, I soon stopped him after he started kissing me on my neck, and I hurried out of the hotel room. Embarrassed, I blocked Devin even though I knew he would most likely never talk to me again anyway.

"I love you," I cried as my yearning eyes stared into Messiah's. "I want to be your wife. I want to be yours even though you're in here."

"I love you too, baby girl."

Letting his hand go, I used both of mine to dry my face. I felt so relieved that he finally knew the truth.

"Who was he?" Messiah asked reluctantly.

I shrank, lowering my eyes. "Devin Adams."

Messiah's upper body lurched forward as his eyes widened. "The NFL player?!" he barked so loudly that the correctional officer on post narrowed his eyes at him in a warning.

I couldn't help but giggle at his dramatic response.

"Damn, baby!" he quietly exclaimed. "You baggin' NFL players?!"

I was laughing uncontrollably. "Shut up."

"My bitch so bad," he said, obscenely narrowing his eyes at me. "That's what you deserve, you know that? You're loyal, dedicated, and so fucking loving. You deserve a nigga like that who can show you the world and give you whatever that fuck you want in life."

"I have that," I said, taking his hand again. "I have that right here. I am so desperately and willingly in love with you, and I am honored to wait for you."

NAJIA DISCIPLE

"Have you taken your mother's call yet?"

I cringed, shaking my head. "No."

My therapist, Samantha Cruze, gave me ridiculing eyes. "*Najia...*"

"I know."

"It's important for your healing process that you talk to her," she pressed.

"*I know*," I returned.

"Are you hiding from her because you feel guilty?"

I frowned. "Guilty for what?"

"Because you didn't tell her what Miguel was doing."

I recoiled in shame. "When I think of reuniting with her, I do feel guilty. I imagine her wanting to understand why I never told her, why I hid it from her. We talked about that at Starbucks that day, but I know that wasn't enough for her. I know that she will be hurt that I didn't tell her and allowed her to lie with a man for years who was doing those things to her daughter. I can't face that."

Samantha's eyes sympathized with mine. "She will understand."

"It's not just that. I-I... it's..."

"Take your time," she softly said, trying to support me in voicing my thoughts.

I sighed as I attempted to wrap my head around my feelings toward Karen. "She was a great mother to me. But it's hard to be in her presence and not think of her husband and what he did to me."

"So, you want to leave her in the past with Miguel?"

"I would love to, but I do miss her. I need her."

Stubbornly, I wanted to act as if Karen no longer existed. However, the broken little girl, still suffering in my heart, wanted to be in her arms as she assured me that everything was going to be okay. My brothers were trying to support me, but their support was hard and masculine like them. A mother's love was like nothing else in the world. It knew no laws, no pity. It dared all things and crushed everything that stood in its path. That was why Karen made that drive to visit Messiah and sat amongst people she would never willingly be in the presence of.

I needed that, but my refusal to face her, to face the fact that I had let her lie with a monster, was so much stronger.

⚜

When Nardo told me about Laila's pregnancy and ended things between us, I sprinted back to Samantha's chair. That heartbreak oddly felt as crushing as my past trauma. I knew I needed professional help to deal with it because I refused to be back on a bridge, ready to take my own life again. I hoped that this time the therapy would be more helpful because my heart was open to change. I needed to get better so that whenever I came across another man like Nardo, I wouldn't lose him to the trauma of my past.

After therapy, I arrived at the estate to see Nardo's ride in the driveway. My heart began to pound nervously. I knew he had been sincere when he'd ended things, but admittedly, I hoped that our bond would weaken him and bring him back to me.

I felt a little better as I climbed out of my Hellcat. The session that day helped me realize that if Karen wanted to talk to me, my fears may not have been valid. I was starting to see that it was possible that we could rekindle our relationship at some point. We hadn't been able to dive into my issues with commitment just yet. But I knew that it was coming with time.

As I walked into the house, I heard lively chatter in the den. When I recognized Nardo's voice, the hairs on the back of my neck stood straight up. Longing drew me toward him. I hoped that laying eyes on me would convince him to keep us going, that he had come there to take me against my will. Yet, all hope vanished when I walked into the den and saw Nardo sitting on the couch with Laila next to him.

"H-hey, sis," Shauka stuttered as everyone noticed me.

Suddenly, uncomfortable tension entered the den. All laughter and lighthearted conversation ceased.

"Hey, brother." Someone cleared their throat. Looking behind me, I saw Jah. "Hey, Jah."

"What up, sis?" he responded as his eyes uncomfortably danced.

"How you doin', Najia?" Nardo saying my name still sounded so fucking sweet.

"I'm good," I forced.

"Oh, *you're* Najia!" Laila quipped with a smile. "It's nice to finally meet you."

The tension became so explosive that it was suffocating. "Hi," I forced. "Nice to meet you too." I made an about-face and quickly left the den.

All hope for me and Nardo evaporated at that moment. I had only seen her on his social media posts. He had never posted her personally, but she had tagged him in a few posts. He had never brought her around the crew out of respect for me, and now she was sitting in my fucking house.

He was truly done with me.

"Najia."

I was a few feet from my bedroom door when I heard Jah calling my name, but I kept walking toward my room. Before I could close the door, Jah's large stature blocked the doorway, stopping me.

"You okay?" The concern in his tone conjured tears that I was desperately trying to hold back.

"I'm fine," I lied.

"You sure?"

"I'm good." Yet, my voice cracked, giving my sadness away.

He pulled me toward him and wrapped his arms around me.

"Why you let him bring her in here?" I cried.

"Because that's his woman, Najia. You don't want to be his woman. So, let him go so he can do his thing. He can't keep keeping that girl away from us because of you."

Sucking my teeth, I tore out of his grasp and moped toward the bed.

"Najia—"

"You're right," I pressed, interrupting whatever logic he was about to spew. "You're right. I just need a minute."

Jah's uncertain glare stayed on me for a few seconds before he gave up and walked out.

It was only fair that I let Nardo go. I had refused every effort he'd made to claim me. I couldn't ruin his happily ever after because I was too scared of my own.

SHAUKA DISCIPLE

"Good night, lil' man." I pushed past the regret that was bubbling in my throat and smiled into the phone at my son.

"Da-da!"

"*Yeeeah*, man, I'm Daddy."

Asa was at the age that he would not sit still. Yaz was failing at keeping him in her arms as she held her phone up so that he would stay in the camera.

"Okay, Shauka," Yaz said with a sigh. "I gotta put this boy to bed."

Yaz was barely looking at me as she put Asa down on the floor.

"Ah'ight." I was so short and dry that she looked at me curiously. But since she knew what the bitter expression on my face meant, she blew out another heavy breath and said, "Good night, Shauka."

I hung up without saying another word.

Grief demanded to be dealt with. It walked instead of running. It was always with us. Sometimes, it packed itself away and exploded at a later date. Mine was currently riding me like a backpack that I couldn't take off.

Groaning, I rested back on the couch in the den. I took a sip of the cognac that I had been clutching in my hand before Yaz had called so that I could tell Asa good night. The fact that I'd had to tell him good night over the phone pushed me to gulp down the rest of the dark liquid in the glass. I felt like I was losing my mind. I hated that Yaz and Asa weren't in arm's reach. I despised that I had become so crippled that I couldn't breathe without having my family right up under me.

Sighing, my elbows went to my knees and my face into my free hand. I despised that I was like this. I had never been a man that was scared of anything. But suddenly, I was living with a constant fear of the worst happening at any moment.

"Shauka, are you okay?"

I kept my hand over my face, unable to answer Najia. The room felt like it was spinning. I couldn't breathe.

"Shauka, what's wrong?"

I felt her hand on mine. She slowly pulled it away, revealing the wildness in my eyes.

"I don't know," I admitted weakly. "I don't know what's wrong with me, sis."

She watched my irregular breathing fretfully. "You don't feel good?"

"I don't know what the fuck I'm feeling. I feel nervous, scared. And I can't breathe. My fucking chest hurts." With each word, I was feeling more and more out of control.

"It sounds like you're having a panic attack."

Unable to deal with the feeling of my emotions unraveling, I began to rock back and forth.

"Breathe in for at least five seconds and then hold it for three seconds," Najia coached me.

Desperate for relief, I followed her directions.

"Now, breathe out for five seconds. Make sure you're breathing in through your nose and either out through your nose or out through pursed lips like you're whistling."

As I followed her instructions, I actually started to feel better. My heartbeat started to regulate, and I felt like my breathing had begun to normalize.

"How do you know about this shit?" I asked her.

"I've had quite a few panic attacks."

I kept repeating the breathing exercises until I finally felt a little calmer.

"You should really consider going to therapy, Shauka."

"I don't need that shit as long as I got this," I said, holding up the cup of cognac.

Sucking her teeth, she took the glass from my hand. "And this shit doesn't help anxiety, bro." She placed the cup on the floor.

"So, you're saying I'm crazy?"

She watched me with chastising eyes. "Anxiety doesn't make you crazy, Shauka. It's a result of a lot of things like trauma, death, and stress—all of the things that you've been dealing with your whole life without seeking professional help."

"I haven't felt like this all of my life. But I have for a while. I feel like this when I lose it on Yaz."

Sympathy deepened in her eyes. "I'm sure that it started when everything happened with Jah, Messiah, and Sariah. It's a natural reaction to trauma. Even if you don't look into therapy, I can help you with some natural ways to remedy it."

"I hate this shit," I confessed. "I'm going to lose Yaz if I don't get my shit together."

"You are not going to lose her," Najia insisted. "She's still with you, just not exactly like you wanted. She is giving you the space you need to get help."

"I don't even know what this shit is, so how will I get help?"

"Well, you've acknowledged that you do have a problem, which was the first step."

CHAPTER 21

MESSIAH DISCIPLE

I skittishly stood next to the correctional officer in the empty room. I rolled my neck, hoping that it would calm my nerves. Yet, I still felt my nerves exploding wildly.

Karen placed a loving hand on my shoulder. "Calm down. It's going to be okay."

I nodded, unable to relax. Kofi noticed how frazzled I was and laughed, shaking his head tauntingly.

"Where are we going?" I grinned when I heard Tory's confused voice on the other side of the closed door.

The door to the room slowly opened. The correctional officer that had escorted Tory past visitation entered first. Then a wide-eyed Tory slowly inched into the room behind him. My baby looked beautiful in a flowing maxi dress that appeared to be painted onto her curves. The bottom of the dress reminded me of a mermaid's tail. The cream color made her brown skin look like a candy bar. She had the chocolate, and I had the nuts.

Tory relaxed when she saw me, but she was still reluctant as she took small steps toward me. "*Whaaat's* going on?" she asked slowly.

Then a devilish smile spread on her face. "Are we having a conjugal visit?!"

My dick hardened at the thought. I hated to have to shake my head. I would love to stick my dick so far into her that she'd burp my nut. But this was actually much better.

"I hope not," Karen said with a giggle.

"Nah." I grinned slyly while taking her hand. "We're getting married."

Tory's mouth opened wide like a cartoon character. Her eyes blinked so slowly that I feared she was going to faint.

Finally, she found her voice. "What?!" she squealed, jumping up and down. "Are you serious?!"

"Yes, baby," I said, closing the space between us. "You said you wanted to be all mine even while I'm here. I've wanted that, too, for a while now. So, I put in the request."

"Oh my God, baby!!" Her high cheek bones were forcing her eyes to nearly shut closed because she was smiling so hard. "No wonder you told me to leave the kids at home."

I licked my lips arrogantly, proud that I was making her smile. "Yeah."

Tory looked behind me at Karen. "That's why you told me to get all dressed up today!"

Karen was grinning so hard that her cheeks were crimson red. "Yep!"

The door to the room opened again, and the chaplain rushed in. "So sorry I'm late," she said with embarrassment. "Are we ready?"

Tory gazed dreamingly into my eyes as the chaplain rushed past us.

With her eyes still anchored on mine, she cupped my face and pressed her glossed lips against mine. "I love you so much, baby."

"I love you more."

We held an autumnal gaze that I wished could last forever because I had never seen my woman so happy. But the intensity of our intimacy was causing uncomfortable tension in the room.

"*Ooookay*, love birds," Karen sang awkwardly.

"Yes," the chaplain added, watching us admirably. "Let's get started."

NAJIA DISCIPLE

That night, a knock on my bedroom door took my attention away from the episode of Ghost that I had been watching.

"Yea?"

The door opened, and Shauka's head popped in. His eyes were wide as if he were scared, so I got nervous. "What's wrong?"

"Somebody's at the door for you."

My brow rose. "Who?"

"Come see."

Both of my brows then curled curiously as I slowly climbed out of bed. I slipped my feet into my furry house shoes and then cautiously left out of the room.

Yet, I froze in the doorway when I saw Karen standing nervously in the foyer.

My eyes quickly fled from hers, focusing on the floor.

"Najia..."

Tears sprang to my eyes the moment she called my name so softly that I instantly remembered how soothing a mother's love was.

I could see her Louis Vuitton loafer inching carefully toward me. Then I felt her dainty hands on my back. Her touch made my soul bleed an ocean of tears. The enormity of my sobbing echoed through the foyer.

"Gosh, I missed you," she said softly as she took me into her arms. "My baby girl. I love you so much."

I allowed her embrace to hold the ten-year-old girl that wanted to tell her that her husband had sneaked into my room the night before. I allowed her to comfort the teenager that suffered alone for years in her room, too afraid to hurt the only parent that cared enough to love her correctly.

She held me as I cried for as long as I needed. We stood there until my knees began to ache.

When I finally peeled my head off of her shoulders, I noticed that Shauka was right there, sitting on the bottom step.

Karen reached into her purse. She pulled out a handkerchief and patted my face dry. As she did, I held on to her wrist.

"We can talk." Karen's words were gentle as she watched me with watery eyes. "Or we can just catch up. Whatever you want to do."

"We can just catch up."

She nodded. "Okay. Well, Messiah sent me over. He wanted me to show you all the video of him and Tory getting married today. He said it was too long to send via text or email."

I smiled at Messiah's efforts. Then Karen took my hand. "Where can we sit?"

"In the den." My voice was still so needy and weak.

Karen smiled over at Shauka. "You're Shauka, right?"

Shauka stood, walked over to her, and stuck out his hand. "Yes, ma'am."

"Very nice to meet you."

"You too. Thank you for taking care of my brother and sister."

"It was my pleasure. They helped me way more than I helped them."

Shauka nodded coolly, but I could see the emotions in his orbs behind the curls in his face.

"Well, come on. Let's watch your brother get married." Karen took my hand, and I led her into the den while Shauka followed.

The tears started to flow again as I watched my once childish, slutty, wild, unhinged brother marry the love of his life. I envied the electric smile on Tory's face as she said her vows.

Thoughts of Nardo invaded the moment. I had never seen myself worthy of marriage, but it would dismantle my already frail heart if I ever had to see him say I do to any woman other than me. But I was proud of myself for being strong enough to walk away. Any harm that I would have spewed on him because of my trauma, I took with me. I saved him from it all. I was proud of that. Even though my heart was broken, I could hold my head high because I had saved Nardo from me.

JAH DISCIPLE

♫ *I just got the key, they let me in, no ID*
Doors openin' up for me and now I see
I've been blind for a while now
I've been blind for a while now (ayy, I've been blind, hey) ♫

As I sped through the city on my way to the trap house, my phone rang, cutting off Da Baby's lyrics. When Messiah's number flashed on the dash, I answered the FaceTime call, "*Yoooo*!"

"What up, my dude?" Messiah was grinning into the phone from ear to ear.

"What up, lil' nigga?"

"Shit. Chillin'."

I shook my head with a chuckle. Messiah had been chilling way too hard behind bars. He was in there, living like a king. His hustle hadn't stopped. But I was proud of the man he was becoming. Prison had matured him into a man that I was proud of. I knew my father was smiling down with pride from heaven.

Because of the sacrifice he made, there had been no further investigations into our crew.

"Just left the gym." Messiah curled his bicep into the camera.

"Damn, layoff arm day, bro."

He laughed cockily. "What's goin' on with you?"

"On my way to the spot. I saw your baby girl yesterday. She's getting so big."

"I know, right?" Messiah's face flushed red around his smile as he thought of Faith.

"Her lil' chocolate self looks just like her mama."

Messiah frowned, clicking his tongue. "Man, she looks like her daddy."

I shook my head, laughing at his naïveté. He always swore that Faith was the splitting image of him, but she looked like Tory had spit her out.

"So, is it done?"

"Yeah." Messiah grinned from ear to ear. "I'm a married man, my nigga."

A proud grin spread throughout my beard. I was so shocked when Messiah told me that he was making arrangements for him and Tory to marry. Yet, I was proud. That decision was only further proof that prison was maturing Messiah.

As I watched him smile boastfully while he spoke of his wife, I could feel emotions fighting to break free. At proud moments like this, I yearned for my parents to be alive to witness them.

"How does it feel to be a married man?"

"Shit, it feels good as fuck," he boasted with a smile. "You're next, right?"

I sighed. "Hopefully..."

"When are you going to get shit right with Faye?"

"Soon. I'm going to get up with her today before she forgets about a nigga."

His brow rose inquisitively. "Why you say that? You haven't been talking to her?"

"The last few days, her text messages have become few and less often." Thinking of it made my heart race with anxiety.

"I told yo' ass you should have never played these games with her," Messiah replied, shaking his head.

"I wasn't playing games, man. I just needed her to get her head right."

"Yeah, okay–"

My other line beeped. The dash showed that it was Koop.

"Aye, hold on. That's Koop."

"Gon' 'head. I hear the guards coming. I'll holla at you later."

"Ah'ight bet." I clicked over to Koop. "What up?"

"Aye, your girl at this spot with a dude."

I had heard him clearly, but I was too stuck to respond with anything but, "Huh?"

"Faye," Koop pressed. "My lil' yeah-yeah dragged me to that new spot in Hyde Park, Chemistry. I see Faye in here at the bar on a date with some Mexican-looking motherfucker. You need me to handle that?"

Fuming, I replied, "Nah, I got it."

"Bet."

After hanging up, I made a sudden U-turn in the middle of Cottage Grove and headed north, speeding wildly like a bat out of hell.

❦

After stopping at the estate, I sped to Chemistry, praying that Faye was still there. An hour later, I barged through the front door of the restaurant. The way my eyes skidded chaotically around the place caught the attention of the hostess.

"May I help you?" she asked nervously.

My eyes bounced around angrily as I looked for Faye. Soon, they landed on her. She had the nerve to be sitting at the bar smiling in the face of some Lorenzo Tejada-looking motherfucker. "Nope," I spit at the hostess.

I pushed past the patrons waiting to be seated. I felt all eyes on me as I charged toward the bar. Faye was so busy cheesing in the face of this lame that she didn't notice me until I was standing over her. She finally tore her eyes away from him and looked back. Her jaw dropped as she was caught off guard by my orbs shooting fire at her.

"Let's go." I grabbed her by the arm and snatched her off the barstool. Patrons and staff around us gasped as she barely caught her footing.

Her date jumped to his feet. "Aye—"

I was clinging to Faye's arm as she fought to free herself from my grasp. I glared at him over her head and threatened, "Nigga, this ain't it. Don't lose your life over what was never yours."

Faye recoiled with embarrassment. The Tony Montana look-alike opened his mouth like he wanted to say something but quickly learned his place. As I dragged Faye away, she scrambled for her purse that was hanging on the barstool. Eyes were still on us as I dragged her toward the exit.

I didn't let her go until we were outside.

"What the fuck, Jah?!" she shrieked, stomping her foot.

"You tell me what the fuck!" I barked.

Her eyes ballooned in shock at the way my bite had matched her energy.

"You're supposed to be at home realizing that you and I are more important than you giving a fuck about me fucking that raggedy bitch, but you out here on Love is Blind and shit!"

"Oh, so you were playing games?" she asked, folding her arms across her chest.

"I didn't know what else to do!" I barked, shrugging. "You had me scared to come to the crib, Faye! We ain't supposed to be living like that. I knew I had put you through a lot. Mia was nothing compared to what you had to go through when I was sick and in rehab. I thought the stress of everything had put you in a bad emotional state, so I gave you some space so you could think and heal, not date some pretty-boy, punk-ass nigga!"

"Well, he asked me out the other day, and I had a good time. So, when he asked me out today, I didn't see why I shouldn't accept his offer."

Realizing the confidence she had told me that shit with, I took a step back. "You like this nigga?"

"I don't know him like that to like him. I love *you*, but you broke up with me!"

I stuck my hand in my pocket. "I broke up with you so that when I gave you this, we'd be good." I pulled her engagement ring from my pocket and held it between us.

Her mouth fell wide open, and tears came to her eyes.

"I want you to be my wife. You're the only woman on this fucking planet who deserves it. You've had my heart since the moment I first laid eyes on you. And you earned my lifelong commitment by staying by me at the worst of times. Be my wife, baby." I took her hand and brought her into my shadow. She stared at the ring with shock pooling in her eyes as I asked, "Will you marry me?"

SHAUKA DISCIPLE

"Fuck, baby. This pussy so good."

Yaz's moans were muffled because her face was in the pillow. She was face down, ass up in my bed. My hands were gripping her waist as she threw her ass back on my dick. I would have thought that Yaz's sugary center was getting better with time. But I knew that it was her stinginess with it as of late that had it feeling like a new model. I had grown used to having her at my beck and call. In the past, if she wasn't at work, she had been under me. But now that she was tired of my attitude, she had been rationing out the pussy.

"Shit, baby." The pussy was crippling me. I was a fiend for it.

I started driving my dick so deep into her cove that she lifted her head from the pillow and looked back at me with curiosity.

Looking into her eyes caused my nut to rush toward my tip and burst inside of her. "*Aaaaargh*! Fuck!"

The power in the nut made me fold over, landing on top of her. She fell onto her stomach, and I rolled over to keep my weight from smothering her. I lay on my back, heaving, unable to catch my breath as she rolled over and out of the bed.

"Where are you going?"

She looked at me with telling eyes as she picked her sundress up from the floor. "Home."

I sucked my teeth like a frustrated boy. "Yaz."

"Don't start, Shauka," she warned as she stepped into the dress and pulled it up over her voluptuous curves.

I sat up on the edge of the bed. "Why are you doing this?"

"You need to work on yourself."

"What that got to do with you spending the night? You gon' keep leaving out of here and going home like we teenagers?"

"I can't get comfortable here with you again. You haven't changed that fast."

My shoulders sank. "I feel like I'm losing you."

Finally, she gave me sympathy. She slowly pulled her spaghetti straps over her shoulders and inched toward me. "You'll never lose me."

As she sat down next to me, I told her, "I'm sorry."

"Shauka, it's not even about you being sorry—"

"I'll buy us a house."

Yaz's lips pressed into a tight line. "I don't want it out of desperation. I want it because *you* want it and because you trust me enough to become a family with you and Asa."

"I trust you," I tried to insist.

"But do you trust yourself with me? Have you let go of the recollections that Sariah put in your head to be with me without worrying if I'm doing you like she did?"

I loved her too much to lie, so I just lowered my head.

Sighing, she said, "Exactly, baby."

She attempted to stand, but I stopped her with a hand on her thigh. She reluctantly sat back down as I turned my body toward hers.

"I have anxiety, Yaz," I admitted, causing her brow to deepen. "I had a panic attack last week. I hadn't fully understood when Najia suggested that I was having a panic attack. But since then, she's been sharing different links to websites that broke down what anxiety is.

After learning what panic attacks are, I realize that the emotional explosions have actually been panic attacks. And I remember experiencing them a few times when I was younger. I just didn't know what it was."

Yaz's body slumped as my confession sunk in.

"What if it never gets better?" I asked, letting her hear my fear.

She laid a comforting hand on my leg. "It will."

"It doesn't feel like it ever will."

Yaz's shoulders sadly sank.

"Sariah's deception, Jah's near-death experience, the fear I had when I was wondering where Jah's and my next meal would come from. I thought we had made it out of all of the bad shit. But everything that has happened has made it clear to me that I can suffer losing my loved ones again at any moment. That realization has me suffering from stress and anxiety that I've been punishing you with. But it was out of the fear that you or my son could leave out of that door and never come back. I could never survive that."

Yaz's mouth opened and closed, but she couldn't find the right words, so she rested her head on my shoulder.

"I'll get better," I assured her before I kissed the top of her head.

"And I'll be ready for you when you do."

TWO YEARS LATER...

CHAPTER 22

SHAUKA DISCIPLE

"How is it that you're older than I am, but you still haven't learned how to tie a tie?"

Jah clicked his tongue. "Because when do I have to wear one, motherfucka—"

"We in a church," I interrupted, narrowing my eyes at him.

Jah shrugged a shoulder. "The Lord knows my heart."

Nardo chuckled as he sat behind us on top of a desk, clutching a glass of brown liquor. Frey, Codey, and Chris were seated on the couch, drinking as well. We were already dressed and ready to take our positions at the altar. Jah was the last to perfect his finishing touches.

Jah continued to flinch and squirm as I tied the Windsor knot around his neck.

"Bro, stand still," I fussed. "What you all jittery for?"

He frowned, fighting to remain still. "I got PTSD from weddings."

Rearing my head back, I looked at him offensively. "Really, my nigga?"

He shrugged while nervously tugging at the sleeves of his suit jacket. "All I'm saying is this wedding better not end like the last one I was at." He narrowed telling eyes on me.

Sucking my teeth, I shot back, "Fuck you, bro."

He, Nardo, Frey, Codey, Chris, and Koop laughed way too hard as I finished tying the knot. Even the photographer chuckled as he continued to take off-guard photos of us.

Jah turned his back to me and admired himself in the three-way mirror standing in front of us. "*Ooooo!*" he sang lowly with narrowed eyes. "A nigga look like *money*."

Jah indeed looked like a dapper, grown-ass man in the tailored, skinny-fit, three-piece suit. His dark skin made the tan wool pop even more.

While gawking at his reflection in the mirror, he adjusted the Sedona-colored tie I had just perfected.

"Don't fuck it up, bro," I warned.

He frowned deeply, looking at me through the mirror. "Don't worry about me. Worry about making sure you gon' actually say 'I do' this time."

My groomsmen shared another hearty chuckle as I shook my head. Thankfully, I was able to laugh as well.

"Oh, I'm gonna make it to say 'I do' *and* to fucking my wife on the beach this time. Ain't no doubt about it. Yaz a real one."

Though many of them were still laughing, they nodded in agreement.

"She is, bro," Jah said as he stepped away from the mirror. "Sis definitely is a real one. It's about time you made her an honest woman." He grabbed my shoulder and squeezed it in admiration, the way that a father would. Looking at him, I couldn't help but feel our father's presence. He had always looked like our father. But the more Jah aged, it was as if he was morphing into a dark-skinned Frank.

I let out a relaxing sigh as I replaced Jah's spot in front of the three-way mirror. I could feel the difference in my confidence this time. On my previous wedding day, when I was to marry Sariah, I was operating on autopilot. I knew I was marrying the wrong woman. I was just doing what I knew a man was supposed to. Now, I was just as giddy as any bride would be. I was finally marrying the love of my life.

Jah's ringtone started to blare over the conversations in the large dressing room.

"Yo', this is Messiah!" he announced before he answered, "What up, kid?!"

"*Yoooo*!" Messiah shouted through the FaceTime call. "What's going on? Y'all ready?"

Hearing Messiah's voice brought about the only reluctance I felt pertaining to this day. I hated that my brother couldn't be present, standing with me on this special day. I would have waited four more years to get married just so he could be there. However, Messiah insisted that I put Yaz first.

"Give Shauka the phone," I heard him tell Jah.

Chris handed me a glass of brown liquid that I knew he had poured from the four-thousand-dollar bottle of Rémy Martin Louis XIII he'd brought with him. I took the phone from Jah.

"What up, bro?"

"What's up, kid?" I replied as my feelings started to erupt. Messiah had more than emotionally matured behind bars. The camera was so close to his face that I could see how his incarceration had aged him. He had a full beard. His baby face was now chiseled. His eyes were less jovial. They were now more stern and on-guard.

Messiah saw the look on my face and gave me a taunting smirk. "I know you ain't crying already. You ain't seen her walk down the aisle yet."

The guys started to make jeering noises toward me as I lowered my head.

"You supposed to be here," I told Messiah, letting my feelings flow. "But I appreciate you for not being here. You made a sacrifice for this family and crew that we'll forever be indebted to you for."

Jah and the crew agreed as Messiah smoothly grinned. "Aye, don't start. Save your tears for Yaz. I'm there in spirit."

I swallowed hard, fighting back the tears threatening to spill over the edges of my eyelids. I sniffed and took a gulf of the cognac.

"Yaz bet' clown today," Messiah joked.

Jah bellowed in laughter. "I just told him that shit."

"I'mma kill her ass if she does," Messiah said.

We all cracked up.

"I'll holla at y'all in a few," Messiah said. "I'll call y'all back after the ceremony. Tory's mom is gon' have me on during the ceremony, so I'm not gon' miss it."

I nodded. "Bet."

Messiah grinned proudly. "Congratulations, bro."

"Thanks. I love you."

"Love you too. And don't worry. Yaz loves the fuck out of you. She is going to beat you to that altar."

I nodded. "No doubt."

As I hung up, there wasn't a question in my mind that Yaz was going to make it down that aisle to me because she and I had put in the work.

Once I learned that I was suffering from anxiety, I went to work to fix it. Najia had given me her therapist's information. But, after the first three sessions, I realized that therapy wasn't for me. Instead, I made an appointment with a primary care physician who told me that it was perfectly okay that I wasn't comfortable with therapy and that there were many reasons why therapy might not be a good fit for me at the time. But he did prescribe me Zoloft and suggested that I look into natural supplements to help with the panic attacks. Najia and I did some research and found that Ashwagandha naturally helped reduce stress and anxiety. I also found that Indica did as well. So, I started incorporating both supplements into my daily routine along with Zoloft.

After a few weeks, the symptoms started to reduce. Now that I knew what anxiety and panic attacks were, I was able to pinpoint where the uneasiness and anger were stemming from. I was able to control it to the point that Yaz got comfortable fully opening back up to me again. Soon after, I moved into her condo. But within six months, I had found us a beautiful estate of our own only a few miles from the Disciple estate.

Yaz and I had built a deep connection. Trust, mutual respect, and understanding were a given because we had mastered that as best friends for nearly a decade. Our love was a slow burn. We had supported each other through the good and bad times with ease. We related with ease. But we needed to know each other intimately. So, though I would have married her two years ago, we took that time to teach each other romantically.

Now, we were about to say "I do" in one of the most beautiful churches in Chicago. Jah was, once again, my best man. I had decided to have our original, day-one crew as my groomsmen. We had all put in work to expand our crew into a global empire, and they were my brothers at this point.

"Ah'ight, y'all," Nardo said, checking the time on his phone. "We need to head to the sanctuary."

With a deep breath, I drank the last of the cognac with one big gulp. The anxiety wanted to explode into a rapid heartbeat, and crazed worry that this ceremony would end like the last one. But I fought and reminded myself that Yaz was different.

As we all abandoned our drinks and got ready to leave the room, there was a knock on the door. I figured that it was the wedding coordinator.

"We're coming," I said as we approached the opening door.

But we all froze when it opened. My brain went blank, and my eyes forgot to blink. Every part of my body went on pause while my thoughts tried to catch up.

"*Yoooo*!!" Nardo erupted as he jumped up and down so excitedly that his tall frame nearly pushed his head to the ceiling.

"What the fuck?!" Chris barked.

Frey, unable to speak, simply ran wildly around the room, screaming.

Yet, Jah and I just stood completely still. Unable to speak, breathe, or blink.

I could hardly see from the repeated flashes of the photographer's camera, but I knew it was Messiah standing before us, grinning from ear to ear. He glided toward us, wearing the same suit that adorned the rest of our bodies. The only movement I felt was the tear sliding from my eye, down my cheek, and into my beard.

Still smiling, he wrapped one arm around my neck and then brought Jah in with the other.

"What the fuck is going on?" Jah asked with his voice cracking.

Yet, I still couldn't find words. I just stared astonished behind Messiah as he embraced me. Tory, Buck, Queen, and Karen were standing near the doorway they had just followed Messiah through, tears streaming down their faces.

Jah pushed back, looking awestruck at Messiah. "W-what... how... I—"

"I applied for early release based on good behavior," Messiah told us, still grinning. "I was granted a probation hearing and was released this morning."

"I knew about the probation hearing, so I went to your tailor and had him make Messiah a suit in case he was approved for early release," Tory explained. "I picked him up this morning."

"Why do you think my face was so close to the phone when we were talking a few minutes ago?" Messiah asked. "I didn't want y'all to see that I was in the car."

Looking at my tears, Messiah smirked. "Bro, I told you to save those for Yaz."

Finally, I was able to smile and threw my arms around him again. "Yo', I can't believe this shit!"

This was what surreal felt like.

This was bliss.

NAJIA DISCIPLE

♫ *Something 'bout your hands on my body*
Feels better than any man I ever had
Somethin' 'bout the way you just get me
I try and I, don't 'cause I, can't forget ♫

I could hear one of the Disciple Record artists, Celine, belting out a beautiful rendition of ICU as me and the rest of the bridal party gathered in the lobby.

"What is taking the guys so long?" Yaz's eyes were wide with concern as she looked around the lobby. "They should have been in the sanctuary by now."

"Don't start to panic," I told her, standing next to her, holding her train. "I'm sure they are just late. They were probably up late last night drinking."

"Yeah, don't trip. I'm sure everything is okay," Faye offered in agreement as she rubbed her round belly. She was nine months pregnant and ready to pop at any moment.

I still saw deep worry in Yaz's eyes. "And where the hell is Tory?"

That had me stumped as well. She was supposed to have met us at the church two hours ago so we could all get dressed together, but she'd never made it. Her mother had brought Faith to the church already dressed with her flower girl basket along with Hope and Honor.

"She said she got on the red eye this morning," I answered. "Maybe her flight was delayed."

Pouting, Yaz smacked her lips. "She should have gotten her drunk ass up and got on the jet with us."

The bridal party had gone way too hard the night before at Yaz's bachelorette party. We had flown out to Houston yesterday morning and partied all day. At the last club, Tory disappeared. She had sent us all a text that she had gotten a room to lie down for a few hours because she was too drunk and would meet us at the private jet hangar. But she had overslept.

"This cannot be happening right now," Yaz whimpered, signaling tears.

"Don't cry, Mommy," Asa said as he stood next to her in his tan suit, holding his ring bearer pillow in one hand. In the other, he was holding the handle of a wagon that had been painted the same shade of orange as our dresses and the men's suit accessories. Inside it sat his eight-month-old brother, Amir, dressed in an identical suit, sitting atop a bed of flowers that were shades of the wedding colors. A sign that said, "Here comes my mommy, the bride," was attached to the front of the wagon.

Asa's comforting, tiny voice had done the opposite and made Yaz's tears flow even more.

"Unt uh," Angela said. She carefully slid toward Yaz on her six-inch heels while holding the train of her gown. "Do not start crying already and mess up that beat-ass face."

We all looked at Chloe curiously as she reached into her bountiful cleavage. When she pulled out a handkerchief, we all started cracking up.

"What?" she laughed. "Thankfully, I'm prepared, unlike you bitches."

"I know you got one for me since you have so much room in there," I joked.

We all laughed again. Even Yaz as Chloe dabbed at the corners of her eyes.

Chloe and Faye were now very successful Airbnb owners. They had properties in all the major cities as well as Jamaica and Mexico. Chloe had used her money to perfect her once mundane appearance. She had gotten her body down in the Dominican Republic. She was built just like a Dominican doll. She had perfect triple-D breasts, an invisible waist, and a huge booty. Then she'd flown to Turkey to get veneers. She had even gotten lip fillers. Her Malaysian tresses fell forty inches. Luckily, she didn't look overdone. It was just obvious that she'd had cosmetic work done. She looked like every street nigga's fantasy. So, Chris had cuffed her a few months ago.

Suddenly, we heard thunderous footsteps rushing down the nearby stairway. Then they were accompanied by robust laughter that we all recognized. Yaz sighed with relief as our eyes went toward the steps.

First, the photographer appeared, descending the stairs backward as he took photographs. The videographer followed. Nardo, Jah, Shauka, Chris, Codey, and Frey came jogging down the last few steps and into the lobby. They were followed by Karen, Queen, Buck, and Tory.

My eyes jumped out of their sockets in surprise when I saw the next person. He looked different. His stance was wider and stronger. His walk was proud and secure. I still doubted my own eyes because he wasn't supposed to be here.

"*Aaaaaaaaah!*" I screamed so loud that my throat burned. I dropped my bouquet and dashed toward Messiah, pushing past everyone in my way.

"Oh my God!" I heard Yaz exclaim, which was accompanied by more screams of shock and happiness.

Messiah had barely made it down the last step before I threw myself into his arms. I began to wail with happiness as he put his arms around me. My heart pounded outside of my chest and against his as he held me close. I could feel my palms sweating as they held him close for the first time in too many years. My breaths were coming in short and shallow gasps as I tried to wrap my head around him finally being in my presence instead of on the other end of a phone.

"I love you, sis," he said before I felt his lips pressed lovingly against my cheek.

Sobbing, I held him even tighter, refusing to let him go. "I love you too, brother."

⚜

It had taken us all twenty minutes to dry our faces and fix our makeup. Yaz and Shauka were so excited that Messiah was home that neither cared about him seeing her before she walked down the aisle.

Previously, I was the maid of honor, who was going to march in alone. But Messiah marched in with me. As we did, gasps and exclamations of pure joy erupted from the attendees, who were pleasantly surprised to see Messiah free from prison and at his brother's wedding.

Much of the ceremony was breezing by in a blur because I was so elated. I wasn't able to focus on any other emotion until Shauka began to recite his vows.

"I used to think of you as my best friend, but now I know that's not enough," he started. "Every time I look at you, I feel warmth in my chest that I can't explain. I want to hold you close, kiss you deeply, and spend the rest of my life making you happy."

Immediately, tears reappeared as I looked behind him into Nardo's eyes. I had never been able to get over my feelings for him. They were just as strong as they'd always been. I had never dated another man because I knew that no one could fill his shoes.

"We've been through so much together over the years, and I always imagined we'd end up here," Shauka went on, making my ability to withstand intolerable. "As we stand here today about to become husband and wife, I know that there's no one else I'd rather be with. You know me better than anyone else in the world, and I trust you with my heart completely."

I blinked back tears as Nardo allowed our gazes to connect and lock. He and Laila were engaged. She had become a fixture in our family and crew. But there was still chemistry between us that we felt every time we were near each other. However, I could never say the words that mirrored Shauka's. I had played with his heart enough. I was whole. I was ready. But he was taken, and I was no longer willing to be his side chick. We both deserved more than that.

"Being with you has shown me a whole new level of emotion. You make me feel alive in a way I never have before."

There wasn't a dry eye in the bridal party as Shauka recited his vows. We were all dabbing at our eyes. Sniffles surrounded us as we watched Shauka pour his heart out. The saltiness of my tears was introduced to my lips as they slid between them. Yet, I kept my eyes on Nardo, wishing that it was him and me standing in front of that priest, professing our love for one another.

"I can't wait to spend the rest of my life exploring this incredible connection we share as best friends, lovers, parents, and partners."

MESSIAH DISCIPLE

"Okay! I need the wedding party to meet me in front of the church in twenty minutes for photos!" The photographer's voice rose above the many conversations buzzing throughout the lobby. Many of the wedding guests were filing into the lobby to speak and take pictures with the bride, groom, and wedding party. Many of them wanted to take pictures with me because my release was a surprise to everyone except Tory, Karen, Buck, and Queen.

My reputation and influence did not stop with the correctional officers and inmates. Many of the prison officials knew my father and Buck because many of them were reformed street niggas from the same hood that they used to run. So, when I applied for an early release, it was quickly moved up the chain of command, and I was easily granted a parole hearing. I had refrained from telling anyone about the hearing because I didn't want my family to get their hopes up. But once I was granted parole, I quickly informed Tory, Buck, Queen, and Karen, who all had a hand in helping me surprise my family on the day of my release, which happened to be Shauka's wedding day. Tory had left Yaz's bachelorette party early and hopped a flight back to Chicago. She needed to get home in time to prepare to drive to the prison to pick me up that morning and get back in time for the wedding.

Before surprising my brothers, Tory had gotten the kids from her mother and brought them outside so that we could have a private family reunion. The way that Honor and Hope clung to me made me feel like a proud father. I had missed three years of their lives physically, but emotionally I had never missed a beat. In my heart, they were very much my children, as Faith was.

"Aye, Tory, come here. "

She looked at me questionably as I took her hand. "What do you want?"

Her reluctance was warranted because I had had my dick in her every chance I got. The first time was when I pulled the car over on the expressway after she picked me up. I pulled her out of the car and bent her over on the passenger's side. I gave her the punishing strokes that I had been dreaming about for three years. Then I got it again as I got dressed at a truck stop.

"Messiah," she said in a warning tone as I pulled her into a hallway. "What are you doing? We are going to miss the bridal party photos. "

I waved contemptuously. "Fuck those photos. I'm trying to get in this pussy."

"No," she pressed, pulling back. "We are in a church."

She giggled as I turned every doorknob that we passed. Finally, one of the doors opened, and I dragged her into what appeared to be an office.

She gasped when I closed the door. "Boy, this is the pastor's study!"

"Girl, this dick don't care, and neither do I. Turn around, pull that dress up, and bend over."

She continued to look around nervously. "You can bend over or sit on the desk. Those are the only two choices you have because I'm about to get in *my* pussy."

She knew I wasn't playing games. Cringing, she slowly pulled the long, orange dress up around her waist. That bountiful ass appeared underneath, making my dick rock up even more. She placed both palms on top of the desk and bent over so far that her cheek was pressed against the wood.

"Oh, God," she suddenly groaned softly. "Is this a picture of the pastor and his family?" I chuckled at her squeaky whining as she slammed the picture down.

Anchoring my hands on her waist, I slid inside of my wife. I had been fantasizing about doing this since the moment we were married. I had waited for the moment that I was inside of her, but once I said "I do", I knew this pussy would feel different.

As I gazed upon my wife submitting to me, I felt my heart begin to race. I had been dreaming of this moment for so long, and now that it was finally here, I could hardly contain my excitement. I could feel the pre-cum racing to the tip of my head. She was more beautiful than ever, with a radiance that seemed to glow from within.

As I stroked that pussy, I felt a surge of desire wash over me. I wanted to show her just how much I loved her in the power and depth of each stroke. As our bodies merged together, I felt a rush of heat and pleasure that was overwhelming. I wanted to savor every stroke, to make this feeling last forever.

I pulled out of her and turned her around so that her back was on the desk. I then lifted her body and scooted her up so that she was comfortable. She looked around nervously, but I kissed her deeply to help her relax.

"I love you, Mrs. Disciple," I spoke into our kiss.

She whimpered.

I then slipped into her and broke our kiss. I put my mouth against her ear and whispered sweet nothings in her ear, telling her how much I loved her, how I'd missed her, and how I wanted to be with her forever. The passion between us built and built until I was on the brink of exploding with pleasure.

I didn't want to cum yet, so I pulled out and disappeared under the dress. My lips began exploring every inch of her center as she moaned and withered with delight.

"Oh, God," Tory cooed. "I'm getting my pussy eaten in a church. God is going to get me."

Chuckling, I stood to bust this nut before people came looking for us. Looking down at her, I assured her, "Baby, you are my wife. The Bible says, 'Let marriage be held in honor among all, and let the marriage bed be undefiled, for God will judge the sexually immoral and adulterous.' *That ain't us, girl.*"

CHAPTER 23

NAJIA DISCIPLE

I was still obsessed with wallowing in my feelings for Nardo at the reception. My smile was weak as I watched Jah dance with Renee and Ariel. My therapist had told me that it was okay to let myself feel the emotions, so when they bubbled up some days, I did. Yet, as I sat at the bridal party's table, Shauka's vows were on replay. He and Yaz were what I fantasized for Nardo and me. He had been my best friend at a time when I felt loneliest. So, I sat nursing the yearning with liquor from the open bar as many of the artists from Disciple Records performed as everyone partied and took pictures.

The reception was even more packed than the wedding had been because Yaz had opened it to everyone. So, many of the crew's distributors from around the world had come to celebrate Shauka and Yaz's union.

"Where are you going?" Angela asked as I pushed back from the table suddenly.

"I need to go to the restroom." Drinking so much had finally pushed me to break the seal.

She nodded as she stuffed her mouth with a forkful of roast beef. I laughed, realizing she was on her second plate. She had gained about thirty pounds during her pregnancy. But Jah loved every ounce of it.

Faye had accepted Jah's proposal that day outside of the restaurant. And they got married soon after. But they had settled for a small wedding because Faye didn't have any family to invite to a large one.

Along my way to the bathroom, I was stopped by friends and associates who wanted to take pictures and compliment me on my dress. By the time I darted into the bathroom, I rushed to pull the long gown up before I ruined it.

As I sat there, I took advantage of the silence. Things had been so hectic since Messiah showed up that I hadn't had a moment to breathe. I took out my phone and saw many Instagram notifications. Opening them, I saw that one of the Chicago blogs had posted about Shauka's wedding with the caption, "Well, it seems as if Shauka finally picked the right one."

I shook my head, not understanding how my brother dealt with the constant invasion of privacy. Luckily, the blogs found little interest in the Disciple brothers' introverted little sister.

Finally, I stopped scrolling and decided to venture back into the festivities. As I washed my hands, the door opened.

"Aye, this is occupied!" I warned, pushing it closed.

"Sorry, it wasn't locked."

Hearing Nardo's voice, I froze. I stared at myself in the mirror, fighting to keep the wave of emotions from making me dizzy. Taking a deep breath, I dried my hands and opened the door. As always, as we locked eyes, the tension covered us like a cloud.

"My bad," he said.

"It's okay." My breath was trembling. Every time I got around him, my nerves suffered from uncontrollable fidgeting.

"You okay?" he pried, tilting his head to the side as he looked me over. "It's crazy that Messiah is here, isn't here?"

"Oh my God." I grinned from ear to ear. "I can't believe he surprised us like that. It made this day even more special."

He nodded slowly. "Yeah, it is." He looked behind me into the bathroom.

I gushed with embarrassment. "Oh, I'm so sorry."

We laughed at the same time nervously as I stepped to the side.

I used to think of you as my best friend, but now I know that's not enough.

Shauka's voice rang in my ears, intensifying my longing. As Nardo attempted to close the door, I stuck my hand out, pressing it against it.

He peeked around it, obviously puzzled.

My heart hammered against my chest as my lips parted. "I love you."

He blinked animatedly.

"I'm in love with you." The relief of finally saying those words made me feel like I was about to faint. My knees got weak. "I can't stop thinking about you. You're the reason behind everything I do. I'm successful because I want to impress you. I go to therapy to get well for you. I get dolled up, hoping that if I run into you, you'll notice. *I love you*, Nardo."

He parted his lips, but reluctance entered his eyes, keeping him from saying a word in response.

I saw that he didn't have anything to say, but the relief felt so good that I continued to vomit every emotion I'd felt for the last three years. "And I know that I kept pushing you away. But I got the help that I desperately needed. I know how to manage my issues now. I know not to let my trauma win. And I hate that I'm here now all whole but still broken because I don't have you."

"Why are you telling me this?" he questioned with annoyance.

Suddenly, I was embarrassed, but I swallowed it. "I just saw my brother marry his best friend while mine is about to marry someone else. So, I had to say something, tell you my true feelings."

"Najia, I'm engaged," he said frustratingly.

"I know." I watched him longingly and pleadingly as he watched me with irritation all over his face.

"Why tell me this shit now?" His brows furrowed angrily. Sucking his teeth, he stepped out of the bathroom and around me. "This is some bullshit."

The bite in his voice made me flinch.

"Why put this on me now? That's so selfish," he snapped as he walked away. "You wanna pour your heart out because you want what Shauka and Yaz have? You pushed me away multiple times when I was trying to give it to you. I wanted to give you *everything*, but you pushed me into the arms of someone else who was ready to receive me. Now, you want me to do what? Leave her and my kid because *now* you're ready?"

Sheepishly, my eyes lowered to the floor.

"It's too late for us," he said, shredding my heart into pieces. "But I'm happy you're whole now."

As he began to stalk away, I inhaled sharply, finally able to breathe in the rejection.

Feeling the oncoming tears, I rushed back into the bathroom. Slamming the door, I dug into my purse. Once I found my phone, I dialed my therapist with trembling fingers. I had been consistent with my sessions. Thus, I had built the type of rapport with my therapist that allowed me to call her when needed. And she gladly answered when she could.

Tears streamed down my face as I anxiously anticipated her answer with bated breath.

"Hi, Najia."

I breathed a sigh of relief, clinging to my phone. "Hi, Samantha," I cried. "I need to talk."

FAYE DISCIPLE

"I made it home," I said with a heavy, relieved sigh as I closed the door of the estate.

"Okay, girl. Holla at me tomorrow." I could hardly hear Chloe, so I assumed she had stepped back into the reception.

"Okay, bye." I hung up as I leaned against the wall near the front door. I then kicked off my heels. It was a wonder how I had managed to keep them on all day.

As I inched toward the staircase, I could feel the swelling in my ankles, feet, and toes. Yet, I was unsure whether it was because I had been in heels all day or if it was because I was due to give birth in a few days.

The quietness in the estate wasn't odd anymore. Shauka and Yaz had moved out. Najia had as well. Greg and Hattie were still on staff, however. The only time there was ruckus in the house was when all of the siblings and their kids were over, which was weekly. Though everyone had their own residences now, the bond between the Disciple siblings was still hermetic.

Climbing the stairs, I anticipated throwing myself into bed. I was tired, and I feared that I would wake up in the morning still wearing my bridesmaid's dress. The first two trimesters of my pregnancy had been a breeze. But many women had told me that it was because this was my first pregnancy at a young age. Now, however, I was feeling all of the last-trimester symptoms. I had left the reception early because I could no longer open my eyes while the party was just getting started for everyone else.

As I walked into the bedroom, my phone started to blast Jah's ringtone.

"Hello?"

"You made it home?"

"Yeah. I told Chloe to tell you."

"Oh, I had to dip out of the reception real quick."

"Why?"

"I needed to handle some business. One of our distributors needed to cop before leaving town."

"Oh, okay."

"After that, I'm coming right home to you, baby."

I blushed. "You don't have to. You can go back to the reception. I'll be knocked out. I know you wanted to hang with Messiah."

"I'll be surprised if he'll even still be there. He's been trying to get Tory home all night."

I giggled. "They kept disappearing. I just know they were fucking."

"Of course they were."

"I still can't believe he surprised us like that."

"That shit was amazing."

"I jumped up and down so hard that I thought my water would break."

"Now, you've given my baby girl shaken-baby syndrome in the womb."

"Whatever." As I continued to laugh, a yawn sneaked. I sat at the foot of the bed with a relieved groan.

"You okay?"

"Yeah. Just finally sitting down."

"Oh, okay. I'm pulling up to the spot now. Let me handle this. I'll call you back."

"Don't. I'll be sleep. I'll see you when you get home."

"Okay, baby. Love you."

"Love you too."

My eyes were closed when I hung up. Yet, my lips were curved upward into a small smile. I had only been Mrs. Faye Disciple for two years, but it still felt surreal and made me blush when I realized that I was Jah Disciple's wife.

I had accepted his proposal that day outside of Chemistry. Though dating Angel for that short time had shown me how much easier it was to be with a regular guy, the yearning for my street nigga had super-seded that realization. I would rather have a few bad days with Jah than the good ones with a man who didn't own my heart.

We were married three months later. Neither of us wanted to wait much longer. We knew that we loved each other unconditionally, and his hospitalization had made it painfully clear how short life could be.

Our wedding was small and intimate. Since I didn't have family, I was anxious about having a big wedding. So, Jah and I had gotten married privately in a beautiful restaurant that Jah had rented out for the day. The crew and the Disciple family and staff were in attendance. Chloe had been my maid of honor.

We didn't plan on having kids soon. We wanted to enjoy one another first. We had honeymooned in Bali. We took trips all over the world. We had partied in Thailand. We had dined in Paris. We had hung out with the locals in Kingston too. But all of that travel and bliss had gotten me pregnant a year and three months into our honeymoon phase.

After learning about Mia, I would have never thought I would be nine months pregnant with a thirty-thousand-dollar ring on my left hand. But Jah had spent the last two years showing me that he would never hurt me like that again. He wasn't perfect, but neither was I. But we were more than perfect together for each other.

"Oh!"

A sudden surge of liquid jolted me out of my drift to sleep. I sat up, dazed and confused, blinking my way back into reality.

"What the fuck?" I began to claw at the long dress, trying to gather it around my waist to see. "Shit!"

I reached around the bed, finding my phone. With a shaky hand, I called Jah.

But he didn't answer.

So, I called again and got no answer.

"Fuck!" Panicking, I climbed out of bed and started to strip out of my dress. I kept dialing Jah as I changed into a T-shirt dress.

"*Arrgh*!" I growled when I got Jah's voicemail for the fifth time.

"Answer the fucking phone!" I spat to his voicemail. "My water just broke!"

◈

"You have to push, Faye."

"No," I sobbed.

"Faye, they are going to give you a C-section if you don't push," Chloe insisted.

"No," I whimpered again.

Chloe's flashed a concerned look to the nurse standing next to the bed, rubbing my head. Tearfully, I rocked back and forth, unable to cope.

"Where is Jah?" My voice was trembling with fear.

By the time I'd finished getting dressed, I began to have contractions. Jah still hadn't answered. Since Hattie and Greg were still at the reception, I'd had to drive myself to the hospital. Along the way, I called Chloe, and she immediately left the reception. She barged into the emergency room just as they started wheeling me up to labor and delivery.

"I've been calling him, boo," Chloe said in a soothing tone. "Shauka and Messiah are calling him too."

"Then why isn't he answering?" I sobbed. "Oh God..." Another contraction was coming.

"You have to push, Faye," the nurse insisted.

While groaning to endure the pain, I shook my head vigorously.

"Faye, please," Chloe begged.

As the contraction subsided, I could feel a bead of sweat drip down my brow.

The nurse tore her concerned orbs from mine and looked at Chloe. "We may need to call the OB and prepare for a C-section before the baby goes into distress."

Gasping, Chloe stabbed daggers at me. "Faye! Did you hear her?! You have to push! Stop acting like this!"

"No," I cried.

I was a wreck. Every dreadful possibility had invaded my thoughts. I had witnessed doctors trying to bring Jah back to life. I had sat next to him, wondering if he would take his next breath. Because of that, I felt the very possible occurrence of his death every time he didn't answer the phone or simply coughed.

"The fetus' heart rate is dropping," the OB tech announced, causing the nurse and Chloe to unravel into a frenzy.

"Faye, you have to push!" Chloe spat.

"Call the OB!" the nurse told the OB Tech. "Get her down here now!"

Suddenly, the door tore open so violently that it slammed against the wall behind it. A wide-eyed Jah barged through the doorway, wearing a guilty expression with a hint of relief.

"Where the fuck have you been?!" Chloe spat as I sighed with such relief that I collapsed onto the bed in uncontrollable sobs.

"I'm sorry, baby." Jah rushed toward me. His large frame urged Chloe out of his way so that he could take her spot next to me.

"You scared me," I wept.

"I know. I'm sorry," he said, gently holding my hand. "I got pulled over in a traffic stop, and those asshole cops searched my car for an hour."

"You couldn't answer the fucking phone?!"

"It was in the car. They wouldn't let me get to it."

"Okay, okay!" the nurse interjected, smiling at me. "You ready to push now."

The fear was still ravishing me, leaving me unable to focus. Tears continued to flow from my eyes.

"Baby, I'm here," Jah assured me as he leaned in closer to me and wrapped his arm around my shoulders. "I'm sorry for scaring you, but I'm not going anywhere. You hear me?"

Sobbing, I nodded.

"Now, c'mon," he encouraged me and kissed my forehead. "Let's have this baby."

MESSIAH DISCIPLE

Finally, I lay on a comfortable mattress with plush pillows, satin sheets, and a fluffy comforter.

"Oh my God," Tory laughed.

I pushed the covers from over my face, peeking at her. "What?"

Tory was standing on her side of the bed, looking down on me, wearing a bra, boy shorts, and hazy eyes. "I'm laughing at you wrapped in those covers like a burrito."

"This shit feels good. I've been anticipating this moment as much as I have been waiting to get inside of you."

Tory's eyes fell sympathetic as she climbed into bed. Sucking her teeth, she attempted to make room for herself.

"How the hell am I supposed to have room with all these kids in the bed?" she fussed with a deep frown on her face.

I smiled lovingly at Faith, Hope, and Honor as they lay chaotically in our king-sized bed. Honor's head was at the foot, so his feet were on my stomach. Hope's head was next to mine. Faith was lying sideways on Tory's side of the bed.

Faye carefully lifted Faith and placed her closer to Hope. "Why did you tell them they could sleep with us?" she fussed. "This is not how I imagined our first night in bed would be after you were released."

I rolled over on my side to look into her eyes. "Me either. But I want all of you near me. It's been way too long."

Reuniting with everyone that day had been a fantasy. Yet, finally being at home with my wife and kids was surreal. It was a level of bliss that was scary. I didn't feel worthy of such happiness.

Suddenly, Tory fell into a dreamlike state as she stared at me.

"What's on your mind?" I pried.

Her smile was weak from the long two days we had just endured. "You."

"I'm not fucking you in front of the kids."

She playfully rolled her eyes. "I wasn't thinking about that, nasty ass."

"What are you thinking about then?"

"The sacrifice you made for this family. I love you so much, and I will forever show you my appreciation." She sniffed as her eyes began to glaze over. "You've grown so much. You're far from the immature, hot boy I met, Messiah. And I'm so glad you pursued me."

Fighting my own emotions, my jaw clenched. I clung to a stoic façade. I had cried so much in prison that I refused to shed a tear at the moment, even if they were happy tears.

"I appreciate you giving me a chance, Mrs. Disciple."

I wished for the ability to kiss her, but tiny heads and feet blocked our path. So, I simply reached over our kids for her hand and held it.

"I appreciate you for chasing me." Her words were groggy as her eyes fluttered closed.

It had been a long day, but I didn't feel sleep coming. I was too excited to be with my family again. So, I simply lay there, watching them breathe and sleep. Pride swelled my chest as warmth spread through my body and filled me with a sense of contentment.

I had thought that the sacrifice I had made had been for my family and crew. But ultimately, it had been for me. I was finally the man that

I needed to be. I had spent so long running from responsibility, avoiding commitment, and chasing after fleeting pleasures. But, now, I saw the value in those very things.

It wasn't an easy journey to get to this point. I had made a lot of mistakes, hurt a lot of people, and disappointed myself more times than I could count. But I had learned from my mistakes and had grown stronger because of them. I had faced my fears and demons and had come out on the other side a better man.

Now, I was the kind of man my family and friends could be proud of. I had finally become the man I had always wanted to be, a man that Frank would be glad to call his son.

Every mistake, every year I had spent in prison, had all been worth it.

CHAPTER 24

NAJIA DISCIPLE

After emerging from the bathroom, I decided to stay away from Nardo and forget my feelings for him. He had been right. I had waited until the most inopportune time to finally confess my love for him. Samantha had helped me realize that Nardo was most likely a vessel to push me to heal so that I would be ready for my true soul mate. Keeping that in mind, I was able to party at the reception without another breakdown. Shauka and Yaz had insisted on partying until they were scheduled to board the private jet at four in the morning. So, I wasn't climbing into bed until then.

Oddly, as I finally laid my head on my pillow, my phone rang.

Peering at it as it lay on the nightstand, I saw that it was Karen.

"Mom?" I answered. "What are you doing up?"

"I woke up and saw that you never told me if you made it home."

"I'm sorry. Yes, I'm home."

"It's okay, sweetie. Go back to sleep."

"You sound wide awake."

"Well, you know I wake up at about five every morning."

"True. Well, I'm going to sleep. Thanks again."

"For what, sweetie?"

"For helping Messiah surprise us. That was..." A tired smile spread to my weary eyes. "I have no words."

"Oh, it's no problem. I wouldn't have had it any other way. You know that."

"I know," I said, yawning as well.

"Get some sleep," Karen replied. "Let's do dinner tomorrow."

"Okay."

"Good night."

After hanging up, solemnity soon returned. Samantha had been able to talk me out of my complete breakdown. Yet, the sting of Nardo's rejection was still in my heart.

As I drifted off to sleep, my text message notifications began to chime. Groaning, I opened my eyes and took my phone from the pillow next to me. After unlocking it, I smiled as pictures from Karen flooded our text message thread.

Najia: Ma, it's four in the morning. You can send these tomorrow.

As soon as I sent the message, I saw the typing indicators pop up. So, I waited.

Mom: ☺You're right. Good night. I love you.

Najia: Good night. Love you too.

After two years, my heart still filled with joy when I thought of how far Karen and I had come. As the months went by, we slowly returned to the mother-daughter bond that we'd had before chaos erupted in our lives. With the help of my therapist, Karen and I were able to talk about Miguel's abuse. Karen was able to ask every question she needed an answer to in a joint session. Soon, I was able to open up to her in ways I never thought possible. I had told her about the struggles I'd had, and Karen had listened with compassion and understanding that took my breath away. In turn, she shared her own struggles and setbacks concerning Miguel's abuse, and the two of us found common ground in our shared experiences.

Just as I drifted off to sleep, my doorbell rang. My brows furrowed with confusion. Yet, I figured that it was one of those early next-day deliveries from Amazon, so I continued to lay there feeling sleep devour me.

My doorbell rang again.

"What the fuck?" I blurted irritably as I grabbed my phone. I then went to my Ring app to look at the camera.

I sprang up when I saw Nardo pacing my porch with his hands in the pockets of the suit he'd worn to the wedding. Gasping, I ran to the door on trembling legs. I hadn't bothered to grab my robe. I flew down the stairs in my bra and panties. I darted to the front door on my bare feet. Yet, after tearing open the door, my body went completely still. The blood froze in my veins.

Nardo didn't say a word. He invited himself in, stepping over the threshold and taking me into his arms. Once he closed the door with his foot, he took my mouth with his, kidnapping mine into a breathy and needy kiss.

He pressed back against the wall and brought his heavy chest flush against mine. His hands ventured all over my body, every curve, writing poetry all over it as his tongue tasted the words. Then he squatted before me, pulling my panties down with him. He lifted one leg on his shoulder. The delicate dance that his tongue performed with my throbbing button was divine. The back of my head pressed into the wall behind me as I stared up at the high ceiling, wondering what the hell this all meant.

AN HOUR LATER, WE HAD REACHED THE PINNACLE OF ECSTASY together. Our bodies were satiated with pleasure after we'd come together in a burst of passion. As we lay there, spent and satisfied, I knew that no matter what this time truly meant, I would cherish this moment forever, and I would always love him with all of my heart.

I was, panting, fighting the urge to ask him the typical question on the tip of my tongue. Feeling his eyes on me, I forced myself to face the biggest obstacle in my life.

As I turned my head, our eyes locked on one another's.

"So, are you going to let me love you now?"

"Yes," rushed out of my throat desperately.

His expression was so stern as he asked, "You sure?"

"*Yes*. I'm ready," I promised. "I've done the work. I love you too much. I would have only said it if I was ready."

Finally, his stoic expression formed into a sincere, trusting smile. He reached over, placing a hand on my stomach.

"What about Laila?" I didn't want to ask. I wanted to stay in this moment.

"We broke up."

"What?!" I exclaimed, sitting straight up.

Nardo watched my shock oddly. "You didn't notice that she wasn't at the wedding?"

"Honestly, no," I said, shaking my head with a bewildered glare dancing in my eyes. "It was so much going on with Messiah. And then once you responded the way you did outside of the bathroom, I wasn't trying to pay any attention to you. When did you all break up?"

"A few days ago."

"Why?"

"She could feel that I was in love with you."

"So, why did you react that way earlier?"

"I was mad at you when she broke up with me because she was right. I have always been in love with you. But you didn't want me. So, I didn't have her, *and* I didn't have you. And even though you were saying everything I had wanted to hear, I didn't trust it."

Deep remorse and sympathy caused my eyes to lower. I lay back down, but on my side, bringing us nose to nose. "You can trust me. I promise to make up for the time I made us lose. But I needed this time to heal to become a better woman for you so that we won't lose more time than necessary because now that I am here, you aren't getting rid of me."

Nardo grinned, causing a light in his eyes that made the sun jealous. Then he grabbed the back of my head. As our tongues clashed, I fell into complete bliss, thankful for the journey that had brought me into this man's arms.

Trauma flows through us like a river. It will wear us down and create new channels. Yet, the new person that it creates can arise as more beautiful than ever in due time.

SHAUKA DISCIPLE

That next afternoon, Yaz and I were on the white sandy beaches of the Maldives. The hectic chaos of the wedding festivities was finally over, and we were able to relax in a luxurious private mansion on the beach in the Caribbean tropics. Behind us was the elegant stretch of the swimming pool on the flawless wooden terrace that served as the focal point of the mansion. The property was large enough to host a family, but it was perfect for the luxurious, upscale honeymoon that Yaz had wanted and deserved.

"What are you grinning at?" Yaz blushed as she glided toward me in a red bikini that stood no chance against her munificent curves.

"My wife, *shiiid*." Yaz looked good as hell after giving birth to two kids. She had gained fifteen pounds after having Amir. She hated that most of it was in her stomach. She wanted to get a tummy tuck. I supported her, but as a grown-ass man, I found the evidence of her having my children such a fucking turn-on.

Sighing, Yaz sat in the beach chair next to me, pushing wild coils out of her face. I watched her stare off into space, losing herself in whatever thoughts had rendered her speechless.

"What's on your mind?"

"I just... I..." She breathed deeply, finally giving me her beautiful eyes and breaking into a sincere smile. "I just can't believe we're here."

I nodded slowly in agreement.

"I wish that we would have been mature enough to confess our feelings for one another sooner. It would have saved us a lot of hurt."

"I don't wish that."

Yaz's brows curled. "You don't?"

"Nah." I shook my head confidently. "I don't wish that we had happened sooner. Love happens when it's supposed to."

Her heart melted. An admirable pout painted her glossed lips as I grabbed her hand.

"I love the bond that we built," I told her. "I appreciate that we were best friends first. This shit is fun. I don't know whether I want to bend you over or dap you up."

She broke out in giggles.

Watching her milky skin turn red, I was reminded again that this was my wife. Finally, I had the woman of my dreams. I felt so blessed to have her despite all that I had done to lose her. "You see a light in me that not many people see," I said, causing her smile to fade into a proud and loving gaze. "No matter how dark my soul got, you saw me for what I could be. You were a gift that I had never expected to receive. Thank you for being my wife *and* my best friend. I love you, not just for who you are, but for who you've helped me become."

Tears slid down her face.

I grabbed her hand, squeezing it slightly. "What's wrong?"

"I just feel so blessed, considering where we came from," she sobbed. She attempted to wipe her tears away with the back of her other hand, but more flooded out of her eyes to replace them. "Who knew that a snaggle-tooth homeless girl who was being used and mistreated by so many people would end up so loved?"

I squeezed her hand gently as she cried tears of happiness and gratitude. Yet, I was the most grateful one between us. I had imagined that the person who knew me best, who had been my rock through thick and thin, would also become my wife. But now that my dream had actually come to fruition, it had left me feeling indebted to God. Yaz had been my confidant, my partner in crime, and my sounding board for so many years, and now she was the mother of my children and my partner for life. I appreciated her more than words could express. She brought out the best in me without trying, and I couldn't imagine facing life's challenges without her by my side for the rest of my days.

JAH DISCIPLE

A week later, my family and I were gathered around the table for family dinner. Over the years, we had begun to switch the location between different houses since everyone had started their own families. That night, dinner was at my estate since Faye was still healing from birth, and our daughter was only a week old.

"Oh my God, she is so precious." Queen cooed into my daughter's face as she rocked her back and forth on the couch. "Look at this lil' chocolate thing!"

"Yeah, she came out black as hell," I boasted proudly.

Princess was too young to have real features, but she had come into this world with dark skin. Princess Cynthia Disciple had been born seven pounds, eleven ounces, and with her heart in my hands. I had heard my brothers express the feeling of having children, but I never fully understood until I heard my daughter's first cry. Immediately, the protector in me multiplied. I wanted to protect her from everything, even the hurt that I could bring on her. I had been responsible for my siblings for most of my life, but being a father was a new level of responsibility that I wanted to be great at.

"C'mon, you guys!" Najia exclaimed from the entryway of the den. "The food is ready."

My siblings and their spouses, Buck, Queen, and Hattie, and all of the Disciple grandkids eagerly stood. The aroma of Greg's feast had been assaulting our noses for over an hour.

"Queen, you can give me the baby," Faye said as she slowly scooted out of the den.

Queen sucked her teeth. "Girl, please." She waved her hand dismissively.

Faye shook her head with a chuckle as I lingered behind to help her into the kitchen. "You know you aren't getting her back until they leave, right?"

"I barely get to hold her now. Hattie is a baby hog."

"I heard you!" Hattie's voice darted from in front of us.

Faye guiltily sucked her lips in as I laughed.

Once seated at the table, everyone dug into the soul food feast Greg had prepared. Conversations erupted around the table as I looked on proudly. I was still in disbelief that Messiah was finally back at the table with us. I looked on in amazement as Faith sat on his lap, eating off his plate. Messiah was just as obsessed with his kids as he had been with his siblings. His devotion to Tory and his kids reminded me of my father. Shauka sat holding Amir, who was so attached to his father that Yaz was jealous. The other bigger kids sat at a smaller table alongside us. Shauka had yet to wipe away the grin he'd had at his wedding. It was cheesy, but I was appreciative that he had gotten the help that he'd needed to finally gain the woman who had owned his heart all of this time.

Watching Najia finally relaxed in Nardo's presence made my heart smile. I was so relieved that she was finally open to receiving the love and devotion she so easily gave others.

I felt like a proud father as I watched them all talk about recaps of Yaz and Shauka's wedding and recaps of their honeymoon.

"I have something to tell you all," Yaz said.

We all watched her playful, guilty smirk apprehensively.

Her eyes lowered sheepishly. "I'm pregnant again."

"Gawd damn!" Najia blurted.

"Amir is only eight months!" Queen added as if we didn't know.

Buck sat shaking his head slowly. "Can't trust this nigga to pull out food from the oven."

Hearing that, we all cracked up.

"We're done after this one," she insisted.

"Yeah, I'm getting a vasectomy," Shauka added.

"Aw, hell nah!" Messiah blurted. "You gonna let some doctors cut your balls off?!"

"That's not *at all* what a vasectomy is, my nigga," I told him.

Messiah angled his head. "Bro, I know. I was obviously being facetious."

"This motherfucka knows all the big words now that he's out of prison," Najia taunted with a laugh that everyone joined in on.

"Well, since we're all making announcements, this is a good time for me to make mine as well," I said, getting everyone's attention.

Faye stared at me with wide eyes as she sat next to me.

Smiling at her, I grabbed her hand. Looking into her eyes, I told her, "I'm getting out of the game."

I looked around the table at my brothers and Nardo for a reaction. When I had decided to retire when Princess was born, I wasn't sure if they would understand. But they all gave me understanding eyes and pride.

"I need to give my wife some relief. I don't want her to worry about me anymore. Plus, I'm getting older. I've been doing this since before I was old enough to drive. I'm tired. It's time for me to relax, especially since I'm done raising y'all."

My siblings sucked their teeth while Buck gave me a proud smile and nod.

Faye squeezed my hand, getting my attention. The relieved tears in her eyes validated my decision.

Looking at Messiah, Shauka, and Nardo, I told them, "The crew is yours."

Nodding, they respectfully raised their glasses to me, and I did the same reciprocally.

"I'm grateful for the opportunity to be your brother and to have played a part in shaping the people you've become." I cleared my throat, feeling my words start to crack. "I love you all, and I know our parents are looking down on us with pride."

Najia's smiled weakly as her eyes glazed over. Shauka and Messiah's expressions were masculine and stoic. Yet, I saw the emotions in their eyes. Queen and Hattie's tears were silent whimpers as a lone tear fell from Buck's eye.

"Okay, enough of that emotional shit!" Messiah said, shivering as if he were disgusted.

The day that my parents died, I knew that it wouldn't be easy for us. I never imagined that I would be raising my siblings, but I wouldn't have had it any other way. Seeing them all grow into such incredible men and Najia into a smart and beautiful woman, despite the challenges we've faced, filled me with pride and joy. I knew our parents were smiling down proudly on us from heaven, joyful over the family we had built and the love and devotion we shared.

I was so proud of the people we had become.

THE END

To receive a text message announcing the release of the finale, using your phone, text the keyword "Jessica" to 872-282-0790.

For the readers that love books written by Black authors with Black characters, these totes are for you. We can enjoy so much more than just books. Here are some stylish totes to carry your books in!

The Buy Now, Pay Later option, Klarna, is available. You can start enjoying what you've ordered right away while using Klarna's pay later option. Simply choose KLARNA in the PAYMENT section of the CHECKOUT screen.
Purchase here: http:// www.LitByJess.com/shop

CHICAGO URBAN BOOK EXPO

The 8th Annual Chicago Urban Book weekend is approaching! Make sure you get your tickets: www.ChicagoUrbanBookExpo.com

OTHER BOOKS BY JESSICA N. WATKINS:

PROPERTY OF A SAVAGE (STANDALONE)

WHEN MY SOUL MET A THUG (STANDALONE)

SAY MY FUCKING NAME (STANDALONE)

RIDESHARE LOVE (STANDALONE)

A RICH MAN'S WIFE (COMPLETE SERIES)

A Rich Man's Wife

A Rich Man's Wife 2

EVERY LOVE STORY IS BEAUTIFUL, BUT OURS IS HOOD SERIES
(COMPLETE SERIES)

Every Love Story Is Beautiful, But Ours Is Hood

Every Love Story Is Beautiful, But Ours Is Hood 2

Every Love Story Is Beautiful, But Ours Is Hood 3

WHEN THE SIDE NIGGA CATCH FEELINGS SERIES (COMPLETE
SERIES)

When The Side Nigga Catch Feelings

When the Side Nigga Catch Feelings 2

IN TRUE THUG FASHION (COMPLETE SERIES)

In True Thug Fashion 1

In True Thug Fashion 2

In True Thug Fashion 3

SECRETS OF A SIDE BITCH SERIES (COMPLETE SERIES)

Secrets of a Side Bitch

Secrets of a Side Bitch 2

Secrets of a Side Bitch 3

Secrets of a Side Bitch – The Simone Story

Secrets of a Side Bitch 4

A SOUTHSIDE LOVE STORY (COMPLETE SERIES)
A SOUTH SIDE LOVE STORY 1

A South Side Love Story 2
A South Side Love Story 3
A South Side Love Story 4

CAPONE AND CAPRI SERIES (COMPLETE SERIES)
Capone and Capri
Capone and Capri 2

A THUG'S LOVE SERIES (COMPLETE SERIES)
A Thug's Love
A Thug's Love 2
A Thug's Love 3
A Thug's Love 4
A Thug's Love 5

NIGGAS AIN'T SHIT (COMPLETE SERIES)
Niggas Ain't Shit
Niggas Ain't Shit 2

THE CAUSE AND CURE IS YOU SERIES (PARANORMAL COMPLETE SERIES)
The Cause and Cure Is You
The Cause and Cure Is You 2

HOUSE IN VIRGINIA (COMPLETE SERIES)
House In Virginia 1
House in Virginia 2

SNOW (COMPLETE SERIES)
SNOW 1
SNOW 2